the Story of Us

felicity everett

arrow books

Published by Arrow Books in 2011

2 4 6 8 10 9 7 5 3 1

First published in Great Britain in 2011 by
Arrow Books
The Random House Group Limited
20 Vauxhall Bridge Road, London, SW1V 2SA

www.rbooks.co.uk

Addresses for companies within The Random House Group Limited can be
found at: www.randomhouse.co.uk/offices.htm

The Random House Group Limited Reg. No. 954009

A CIP catalogue record for this book
is available from the British Library

ISBN 978-0-099-55369-4

The Random House Group Limited supports The Forest Stewardship Council
(FSC), the leading international forest certification organisation. All our
titles that are printed on Greenpeace approved FSC certified paper
carry the FSC logo. Our paper procurement policy
can be found at www.rbooks.co.uk/environment

Mixed Sources

Product group from well-managed
forests and other controlled sources

www.fsc.org Cert no. TT-COC-2139
© 1996 Forest Stewardship Council

FSC

Typeset in Sabon by Palimpsest Book Production Ltd,
Falkirk, Stirlingshire
Printed and bound in Great Britain by
CPI Cox & Wyman, Reading RG1 8EX

For Adam

1982
Stella

Stella took a deep breath and rang the bell. There was, after all, nothing to be frightened of. Soon she would be coming and going from this address without a second thought. These girls, these *women*, would be her house-mates, probably her friends. There was to be no interview; the room was hers. Bridget had fixed it up already, so there was really no need for her stomach to churn or her finger to slip moistly off the doorbell. The door opened and she found herself looking at the back of someone's head.

'. . . his fucking tutorial in any case and that's what I told him . . .' the girl was saying over her shoulder. She turned cheerfully towards her visitor. 'Hello, you must be . . . Oh God, Bridget just told me and I've forgotten in the five seconds it took me to walk from the kitchen to the front door.'

'Stella.'

'Stella, Stella, Stella.' The girl beat her fists repeatedly on her temples as if that were the only possible way to commit to memory such a bland and forgettable name.

'OK. Got it. Come in. We're in the kitchen,' she added, clacking her way back down the hall in her stilettos. Stella struggled behind her, dragging a suitcase in one hand and a rucksack in the other. It didn't seem to occur to the girl to help, nor to introduce herself. Not that there was any need for the latter. Vinnie was a legend. Stella had first seen her in the Common Room of the School of Cultural and Community Studies, about three weeks into the first year. She had been perched on the edge of a low-slung chair, her slender legs entwined like black bootlaces, her minuscule rah-rah skirt and peroxide bird's-nest hair apparently only enhancing her reputation as an intellectual giant. Stella had loitered by the vending machine, trying to catch the gist of what Vinnie was saying about Sylvia Plath's Electra complex. Further research had put a name to the face, and wherever Stella went on campus after that, her eyes were drawn to Vinnie and her entourage. There always seemed to be an entourage: men with rockabilly haircuts and drainpipe jeans; women dressed like Vinnie in downbeat trendy clothes and Egyptian-style eyeliner. People like that would be dropping round to Albacore Street on a regular basis, Stella realised. She would have to smarten up her act.

'. . . I mean, apart from anything else,' Vinnie was saying as she led Stella through to the kitchen, 'they knew when they offered me a place that my degree was always going to come second to directing.'

Stella, stranded in the doorway, took a covert look at the other two housemates, as yet unknown to her, who were sitting at the kitchen table drinking tea. One had the old-fashioned bloom and waist-length hair of a pre-Raphaelite beauty and was wearing a pair of oversized denim dungarees, which only emphasised her waif-like frame. (This, Stella concluded, must be Nell, the home-schooled hippy Bridget had told her about.) The other one was big-boned and imposing with a wedge haircut and strong handsome features, which to Stella's mind were not greatly enhanced by make-up that appeared to have been applied with the aid of a set square. This must be Maxine from Bolton. And then there was Bridget, who was even now meeting Stella's gaze with an apologetic eye-roll. How at ease her friend seemed around these awe-inspiring women. Was it possible that she too would, at some point, cut across them carelessly in conversation, lay a casual hand on one of theirs to make a point, send them up fondly for their little vanities? It scarcely seemed possible.

'Anyway, enough of the fascist tendencies of the English Department,' finished Vinnie. 'Allow me to introduce our new housemate.' She turned with a flourish to Stella. 'Everyone, this is . . .' She paused, bit her bottom lip and made her eyes round with mock contrition. 'Fuck. Sorry. I've forgotten again.'

'God, Vinnie, you're hopeless,' Bridget groaned. 'Don't mind Vinnie, Stell, her head's full of sawdust. No room left for odd items of extraneous information, like *the name of her new housemate*.'

'Not sawdust, Bridget,' Vinnie protested, '*theatre*.' She turned confidentially to Stella, who had sunk unobtrusively on to the nearest chair: 'I'm directing *The Caucasian Chalk Circle* in a matter of weeks and none of the cast knows a single fucking word of the script yet. Not that that's any excuse for forgetting your name, but when the reviewers shoot my production down in flames and I'm drummed off my English course for non-attendance, I hope you'll forgive my momentary lapse.'

'Of course,' Stella said gravely.

'You see, Brid, I'm forgiven,' Vinnie crowed. 'I love her already. I *love* you.'

'Thanks,' said Stella uncertainly. Vinnie laughed, a throaty smoker's laugh, her vermilion mouth cracking her white china-doll face in two. Stella's stomach squirmed with pleasure and embarrassment. She couldn't believe she lived on the same planet as this woman, let alone in the same house.

For the first time, she allowed herself to feel a glimmer of optimism about the year ahead. Was it possible she might heal herself here? She leaned towards her rucksack and took out the bottle of Hirondelle that she had bought from the off-licence on the corner. It had seemed a reckless purchase at the time for someone whose bank balance still had to absorb the payment of a hefty non-returnable deposit on a flat that she would never now inhabit; but seeing the gratitude of her housemates, she couldn't feel any regret.

'Ooh, wine, lovely!' said Vinnie.

'It's going in the fridge till dinner,' said Bridget firmly. 'I'm not having you guzzling it all now.' And then to Stella:

'I've made a veggie pasta bake. Do you want to do the tour while it's heating up?'

'OK,' said Stella.

'Well, kitchen, obviously,' said Bridget, waving her hand complacently around the huge airy room. 'It's very well equipped. There's a garlic press and a Magimix. He left all his herbs and spices. Oh, and there's a really good Italian coffee percolator and a chicken brick.'

'He?' Stella said.

Trevor Cunliffe,' Maxine supplied, 'Dean of English and American Studies. He's gone on sabbatical for a year. Told the letting agency to find him some nice quiet female tenants. I suppose he thought we'd be less likely to wreck the joint. I wouldn't mind, but he's the course convenor for Women's Studies – bloody hypocrite!'

'Doesn't surprise me,' said Bridget flatly. 'All men are sexist, but the right-on ones are the worst of the lot. I knew this mature student last year, used to go round wearing a badge saying "the future is female". Reckoned it helped him pull.'

'*Mike*'s not sexist,' said Nell defensively.

Bridget picked up Stella's rucksack and walked into the hall, motioning for Stella to follow. Stella did so, reluctantly, wishing she could stay and hear more about Mike, but as the kitchen door closed behind her, she could only pick up Maxine's tone of flat-vowelled scepticism and Vinnie's throaty laugh.

'Is Mike Nell's boyfriend?' she asked Bridget as they bumped the bags up the stripped-pine staircase.

'In her dreams,' Bridget replied. 'He's her philosophy tutor. Mike O'Meara? CCS? Married. Kids. Ancient. Don't know what she sees in him, but she's definitely got it bad. I don't give much for his chances.'

'Flippin' heck,' murmured Stella, regretting it as soon as she said it. Why wouldn't the F word trip off her tongue, the way it did with Vinnie and the others? She would try harder in future.

'Bathroom.' Bridget flung open a door on the landing to reveal a light square room with a modern avocado suite, lacquered cork flooring and a spider plant cascading shoots down into the bath. Over the loo, drawing-pinned to the pine-clad walls, was a spoof *Gone with the Wind* poster, in which Ronald Reagan and Margaret Thatcher posed in front of a mushroom cloud, recast as Rhett and Scarlett. 'She promised to follow him to the end of the earth. He promised to organise it!' said the strap line.

'Good poster,' Stella said approvingly, though she would secretly have preferred not to be reminded of the precariousness of her existence every time she got caught short. She had been morbidly preoccupied with such thoughts since her love life had unravelled. It only took a fighter plane to zoom over the seafront or an unfamiliar siren to sound for her to flinch in anticipation of a blinding flash which would make her eyeballs melt – though common sense told her that Brighton would not be the epicentre. At this distance from London, she reasoned, she would be more likely to suffer an agonising death from radiation sickness. In the early days of her separation from Matt, there had been a grim comfort in the thought, so she took her increasing unease at the prospect of a lingering death to be a good sign.

'The trick is to get in before Vinnie,' said Bridget, 'otherwise all the hot water's gone.' After only ten minutes' acquaintance, there was no need to ask why Vinnie should get away with such selfishness. It had been obvious from the moment she'd clapped eyes on her that Vinnie was a special case and universally regarded as such, without malice or envy.

'Wait till you see her room,' said Bridget, reading her thoughts. They went further along the landing and Bridget opened the door to the master bedroom. It was a tip; clothes, books and make-up everywhere. But it had a commanding view over the garden, a roomy double bed, and, beneath the chaos, a shag-pile carpet and a beanbag chair. Vinnie had disregarded Trevor Cunliffe's Blu-Tack ban and stuck film and theatre posters all over the expensive Sanderson wallpaper.

'That's her mum, in that one,' said Bridget, pointing to a poster promoting a National Theatre production of Shaw's *Saint Joan*.

'Barbara Napier? You're kidding!'

'Nope.' Bridget looked grimly proud. Stella wished she could unknow this piece of information. How could she ever treat Vinnie like a normal human being now?

'The other rooms are nice too,' said Bridget, and they were. Nell's was half the size of Vinnie's, but she had hung a tie-dye bedspread over one wall and strewn the floor with cushions. Above her bed was a poster showing a seagull soaring in a cloudless sky, accompanied by the legend 'They can because they think they can'. There was a lingering herbal smell, which might have been cannabis, or joss sticks, Stella wasn't sure. Maxine's room was smaller still, and, like Vinnie's, it had clothing covering every surface – mad stuff, to Stella's fastidious eye: giant houndstooth checks; T-shirts in Day-Glo colours; a turquoise jacket with vast padded shoulders; flamboyant, mannish hats. In one corner was a makeshift bookshelf, constructed from planks and house bricks, an idea Stella determined to copy. This was crammed with books on political science and sociology and seemed as sober and organised as the rest of the room was anarchic. On the wall were a Snoopy calendar and a large studio portrait of two rather ugly-looking babies.

They backed out of the poky space and hoiked the bags up a flight of attic stairs to an airy room with picturesque dormer windows to front and rear and quaintly sloping ceilings. An over-sized paper lampshade took up a ridiculous amount of ceiling space and a narrow pine wardrobe had been squeezed against the only wall which would accommodate it. A rattan screen in one corner turned out to conceal a small hand basin. Two single beds stood either side of a small pine chest, which served as a bedside table for both. Despite the constraints of layout and storage space, the room was spotless. It was the kind of bedroom Stella would love to have shared with a sister, if only she had had one, and seeing it, she felt almost tearful with gratitude.

'It's really good of you,' she said, dumping her case

beside the narrower of the two beds. 'You could have had all this to yourself.'

Bridget shrugged. 'I don't mind,' she said, 'as long as you don't snore.'

'Well, if you want to . . . you know, entertain up here, I can always sleep downstairs on the couch. There is a couch?'

'Yes – and the same goes for you. We can work out a code, like . . . if I leave my slipper outside the door, it means *I've* copped off, and if you do . . . oh God, sorry, Stell.'

Stella pinched the bridge of her nose to stave off tears. 'It's all right,' she said, 'I just . . . can't even think about seeing anyone else at the . . .'

'Of course you can't, come here.' Bridget held out her arms and Stella submitted to an awkward hug. 'You're better off without him.'

Stella pulled away and nodded brusquely. 'Right. I'd better get myself unpacked.' She leaned down and busied herself with the clasps on her suitcase.

'If there aren't enough hangers, you can double up some of my things,' Bridget said, opening the door. 'I'd better go and check on dinner. Should be ready in about ten minutes.' She paused for a moment and looked at Stella pityingly. 'Sure you're . . .?'

Stella nodded fiercely. She waited until Bridget's footsteps had died away and then took another long look around their little dormitory; its Milly-Molly-Mandy quaintness seemed to be evaporating with the remaining daylight.

She wandered over to the window and looked out. The whole of Brighton lay below her, its pastel-coloured houses turning mauve in the gathering dusk. In the far distance she could just pick out the silhouette of the derelict West Pier jutting, spindly and uncertain, into the oily blankness of the sea. She stood by the window, chin resting on her hands, until she couldn't feel her fingers any more.

'Ste-lla.' A voice she didn't recognise was bellowing her name from downstairs. She started, then hurried over and opened the door.

'Hello?' she called tentatively. 'Hell-o-o-o?' she repeated, and then cringed when she realised she was yodelling like her mother did over the back fence.

'You'd better get down here if you want some dinner. This lot don't hold back!' Now she recognised Maxine's voice, friendly, bossy, inclusive. Evidently her presence was required.

'Coming!' Stella clattered down the attic stairs towards the sound of laughter and conversation, and the aroma of slightly burnt pasta.

Bridget

Bridget put her Styrofoam coffee cup next to her new ring-bound folder on the table and sat down. She looked around at the other students. There was a girl in a black polo neck, hair sleekly bobbed, bright red lipstick; a grave looking Nigerian man in a University of Sussex sweatshirt; a chisel-faced guy with Joe 90 glasses; and, next to him, an artfully dishevelled young man, wearing a checked brushed-cotton shirt, a battered leather jacket and a light sprinkling of stubble. He caught Bridget looking at him and curled the corner of his lip in what may have been a smile. Bridget looked away and blushed. Before she could size up the remaining four students, the tutor came in.

'Hi, everyone, I'm Gerald Lefevre. We won't go into who you are just yet, but it would help me if you would introduce yourselves before making a contribution to the session, as I am sure you will all be most eager to do.'

He collapsed his gangling frame into the plastic chair that the students had left respectfully vacant at the head of the table and beamed at them. He was ginger, noted

Bridget with disappointment, even down to his nostril hair. And what was that accent? Canadian? Scottish? Distinctly odd, anyway, and not what she had been expecting for a film studies tutor called Gerald Lefevre. But what *had* she been expecting? Yves Montand? Jean-Paul Belmondo? She mentally crossed him off her list of fantasy suitors. Probably just as well, anyway; she didn't want to turn into a marriage-wrecker like Nell. Though it was hard to imagine Gerald Lefevre having a marriage to wreck.

'So I trust we have all taken advantage of the library's lavishly appointed new viewing suite and are by now familiar with the seminal works of the British New Wave?' There was an awkward silence. '*Ex*cellent. Who's going to be brave and lead off for the first seminar? Let's see . . . ?' He glanced around the table. 'How about you . . . ?'

Bridget shrugged miserably. 'OK.'

'What's your name?'

'Bridget Rowland.'

'So, *Bridget*. Which two films have you chosen to compare and contrast?'

'*A Taste of Honey* and *A Kind of Loving*.'

'Good. And what is your thesis?'

'Well, er . . . my thesis . . . I say thesis, it's sort of in note form, but I can, you know, extemporise if you like . . .'

'Extemporise away.'

Bridget stared at the first page of her notes. Her spidery italic script danced impenetrably on the page: 'historical perspective', 'angry young men', 'post-war upheaval'. Drivel, all of it. If only she hadn't stayed up till two debating the existence of the G-spot with her housemates last night. She was aware of her audience becoming restive. Pouncing in desperation on a likely-looking phrase halfway down the page, she launched in.

'You might say that *A Kind of Loving* is a typical example of the celebration of masculine sexuality that characterised the British New Wave.'

Lefevre took a greedy bite of the Eccles cake he had brought in for his elevenses and motioned with a revolving finger for Bridget to keep talking.

'Whereas *A Taste of Honey*,' she went on haltingly, 'subscribes to the same aesthetic of working-class realism, but manages to . . . er . . . subvert the masculine paradigm.' She looked up doubtfully. Gerald Lefevre's finger continued to revolve. Bridget's notes had taken her as far as they could, so she started to ad lib, hesitantly at first, but with increasing confidence, attacking *A Kind of Loving* in particular and the British New Wave in general for its misogyny and inverted snobbery. 'In fact,' she heard herself assert in what by now had become a querulous warble, 'I would go so far as to say that the theme of the scheming woman luring an unsuspecting young working-class bloke into bourgeois respectability is so common in these films as to be a cinematic cliché.'

'That's unfair! The real theme of these films is capital and labour.' Bridget looked up in surprise. It was the dishevelled young man in the leather jacket. His voice was soft and urgent, with a slight northern flatness to it.

'Name, please?' put in Lefevre.

'Steve. Steve Pinder. Yeah, I just think you're missing the point, Bridget, with all due respect. These filmmakers were of their time and place. Their views of women weren't unusual for the times they were living in and they're not what the films are really about. They're about individuals – men *and* women – being ground underfoot by the capitalist machine.'

'I don't agree,' said Bridget, jutting her chin defensively. 'The women are actually seen as agents of that reactionary bourgeois society, doing the bosses' work for them, bringing the men to heel.'

'Or dupes of it, surely? Aren't the women victims too?'

'Oh, sure, because they're the ones that end up holding the baby. But are we invited to care about that? When our hearts could bleed for Arthur Seaton in *Saturday Night, Sunday Morning*, because he can't go out and get drunk every night, or Vic because he's got to stay on the estate, married to Ingrid, instead of finding self-fulfilment?'

'What about *A Taste of Honey*?' Steve interjected with a triumphant look in his eye. 'There's nothing misogynist about that. It's a sympathetic depiction of a young girl getting pregnant—'

'*Made* by a woman,' interrupted Bridget.

But Steve Pinder was shaking his head, a smug smile on his face. Bridget could see now that his bohemian stubble had been cultivated to cover faint acne scarring. 'Tony Richardson made *A Taste of Honey*,' he said, tipping his chair on to its two back legs and lacing his hands behind his head as if to say QED.

14

'Shelagh Delaney.' Bridget turned to Lefevre in disbelief, like a footballer appealing a bad decision.

'Well, technically, Steve's right,' Lefevre said, 'Richardson produced, directed and co-wrote . . .'

Steve smirked.

'. . . but Delaney co-wrote the screenplay with Richardson and it was acknowledged to be faithful in intention to Delaney's stage play, so I think your broader point stands, Bridget.'

'Ha!' Bridget couldn't help herself. She met Steve Pinder's flinty gaze across the melamine tabletop. There was a slightly stunned silence.

'But I'd like us to take a less adversarial approach to our discussion, if possible. There's no right or wrong here. Opinion is what matters; opinion supported by evidence . . .' Lefevre encompassed Steve and Bridget in a slightly reproachful glance. And from then on he skilfully broadened out the debate.

Bridget didn't say another word. Steve Pinder did though. He kept dropping pretentious little nuggets here and there: 'André Bazin', 'the auteur theory', 'Cahiers du cinéma'. What a show-off. He was the most opinionated, pretentious, irritating little superannuated sixth-former she had ever had the misfortune to meet, she decided. She knew the type: grammar school existentialist, probably listened to Barclay James Harvest and smoked Camel. She shuddered inwardly. Poser.

She was first out of the door when the session wound up and pleased that she had arranged to meet Stella and

Maxine in Engam Common Room, because it gave her a reason to hurry away from the gaggle of students following her down the corridor. She was sure they were laughing at her. They were gaining ground as she approached the double doors out of Arts B. She quickened her pace so as to avoid the dilemma of whether to let the doors swing back rudely in their faces, or hold them open and risk having to engage. In the end she let the door go, changed her mind, grazed her knuckles trying to retrieve it and found herself muttering a grudging apology to none other than Steve Pinder.

'Hey, glad I caught you,' he said. 'That was really interesting what you were saying about women and stuff. I don't suppose you've thought about joining Film Soc? We could do with some more birds . . .'

Bridget's mouth fell open.

'I'm kidding. But seriously, you seem like you know your celluloid, so how about it? We're on our way to Falmer Bar now to draw up a list of films for the term.'

Bridget shrugged. They had reached the stairwell. Up one flight, Stella and Maxine would most likely have a cheese roll and a coffee waiting for her in the Common Room. Then again, she had promised herself that this term she would be more adventurous – branch out . . .

'Might as well,' she said, and, with a guilty glance upwards, fell in step beside him as he descended the stairs.

'What can I get you?' Steve asked when they got to the bar.

'I'll have a Pernod please,' she said, colouring slightly. 'Here, let me give you the money . . .'

'You're all right,' he said nonchalantly. 'You go and sit down.' He jerked his head towards a corner of the bar where three people from her seminar were chatting with a couple of equally trendy and intimidating newcomers. His tone irritated her – he seemed amused, condescending almost, his lip curled in a permanent smirk. He wasn't what you'd call good-looking: about five eight; head a bit too big for his body; square jaw with its fungal layer of stubble, vaguely reminiscent of Desperate Dan. His eyes were nice though: chilly arctic blue. Dangerous.

She squeezed on to the tatty banquette and struck up a stilted conversation with the red-lipstick girl, whose name was Tamsin and who kept darting possessive glances in Steve's direction. Bridget felt an unsisterly smugness rise up in her as Steve walked over with their drinks. She wasn't yet prepared to admit that she fancied him herself, but she liked the idea that someone else did.

'Shove up,' he said, putting the drinks down on the table. Both girls shuffled the few centimetres that were available to them, but there was no leeway. Steve swung himself down on to the seat, next to Bridget, and the length of his denim-clad thigh pushed hotly against hers. As much as she tried to distract herself by fixing her gaze on the legend 'Descartes = wank' scratched on to the tabletop in red Biro, she couldn't deny a shudder of visceral pleasure.

'Smoke?' Steve asked, and there were the Camels, casually fished out of the torn pocket of his leather jacket. Bridget shook her head – this was all she needed. If there was one thing guaranteed to put paid to Steve's nascent romantic interest in her, it would be the sight of her having an asthma attack. As if she instinctively knew, Tamsin put a cigarette between her immaculate lips and inclined her elfin face coolly towards Steve's Zippo lighter. Soon a fug of smoke hung over the table. Bridget took a slug of Pernod and braced herself for the tell-tale tightness in her chest. Steve and Tamsin had by now become embroiled in a debate over whether to kick off the term with Godard or Buñuel and were talking animatedly across her. Sinking back into the seat, Bridget braced herself against the first rasping cough, but the effort of suppressing it made her body convulse against Steve's thigh as if she were in the throes of orgasm. It was at this point that someone turned up the jukebox and put on 'If I Said You Had a Beautiful Body Would You Hold It Against Me?'. Bridget groaned inwardly, but she needn't have worried. Tamsin had Steve so firmly in her intellectual clutches by now that he was oblivious. By the time the song ended, Bridget's eyes were streaming and her face was bright red. The words 'What do you reckon Bridget?' died on Steve's lips as he at last turned towards her. She stood up abruptly, accidentally sloshing his pint into the ashtray, croaked something about having to meet someone, and stumbled towards the door.

She was striding, two at a time, up the shallow steps that led back to Arts B, taking in great lungfuls of clean air, when she heard her name being called.

'Bridget? Hey, Bridget! Wait a minute. I need to talk to you.'

She kept walking.

A hand tugged at the strap of her canvas shoulder bag. 'Whoa. Where're you running off to?'

'Told you,' she panted, 'I was s'posed to meet my friends after the seminar. I forgot.'

'Only you looked a bit . . . upset.'

'Upset? No, not at all.'

'Good, well, look, are you still interested in Film Soc or not?'

'Dunno,' she muttered. 'It seems like you've pretty much got it under control.'

'What do you think of Fassbinder?' He squinted up at her, shielding his eyes against the low sun.

Was this a test? she wondered suspiciously. 'He's all right.'

'Only they're showing *The Marriage of Maria Braun* in Brighton. D'you fancy it?'

'Doesn't Tamsin like Fassbinder?'

'I'm not asking Tamsin. I'm asking you.'

She examined her fingernails. 'All right then.'

'Great. I'll meet you at the New Continental, top of West Street, eight fifteen,' he said, turning to walk back down the steps. 'Don't be late,' he called over his shoulder.

She shrugged nonchalantly without turning round, pleased that he couldn't see the grin on her face.

*

Bridget looked at her watch for what seemed like the hundredth time. It was eight twenty-four. Another bus disgorged its passengers without Steve among their number, and Bridget wondered at what point pride required her to give up hope. She couldn't have felt more conspicuous if she had been wearing a placard saying 'Stood up'. Perhaps this was part of Steve's plan. Perhaps he and Tamsin were watching her from a safe distance, sniggering. The cinema was a fleapit. Only half a dozen people had gone in the whole time she'd been standing there and the last bespectacled cineaste had disappeared through its doors five minutes ago.

Unsure whether she was going on a date or a strictly platonic meeting of minds, she had dressed down for the occasion in ski pants, fringed boots and an oversized jumper. A slash of red lipstick, Vinnie-style, a single earring dangling from her left lobe and a black beret set at an angle over her hennaed crop, and she felt every inch the film student. Now she stood, shuffling from foot to foot in the frosty darkness, telling herself that it would probably be better if he didn't come. She might fancy him, but she didn't like him. He was the sort of bloke who'd always have her running to catch up.

'Hi.' He sloped up to her, looking vaguely sardonic. No apology, no appearance of haste or urgency. Her stomach lurched at the sight of him. 'Shall we go in?'

They both bought their own tickets and made their way into the dimly lit auditorium. It smelled musty and Bridget was glad it was too dark to see the upholstery on the old-fashioned tip-up seats. They sat in the second row from the back. Only six or seven other seats were occupied. Suddenly, and without ceremony or the interpolation of Pearl and Dean, the screen flickered to life and the film began.

She tried hard to concentrate, knowing that a detailed critique would be required of her later, but she was acutely aware of Steve's presence beside her; the creak of his leather jacket; the scuffling as he kicked off his shoes and slung one leg languorously over the seat in front; his elbow nudging hers on the single arm that separated their seats. Twenty minutes in and all she could think of was whether or not this was a date. She wanted it to be, she now realised, stealing a sidelong glance at him. But Steve just stared intently at the screen, apparently oblivious. She let her finger accidentally graze his; no response. She crossed and uncrossed her legs and shifted her body suggestively towards him. The plot lumbered impenetrably on. Someone went to prison; Maria became a nightclub hostess; she took a lover; red roses and machinery seemed to figure symbolically in some way.

At last, Steve looked across at her and smiled his wonky smile. Bridget melted. He leaned in and kissed her once on the lips. Her stomach turned inside out. They both stared at the screen again. His hand reached across in the darkness and took hers. She caught her breath, but before she could relax into the tentative romance of the situation, he had thrust it inside the waistband of his jeans and clasped it around the clammy helmet of his erect penis.

Her eyes widened in shock, but she didn't dare move. Besides, as she became accustomed to the situation, she found she didn't want to. The only trouble was, she had no idea of the protocol. She gave his dick a tentative squeeze, to which he responded with a muted groan, but after that, she didn't know what to do for the best. Clearly she wasn't expected to deliver a full hand job, here in the cinema; then again, she felt that it would reflect badly on her if he went off the boil. She compromised by delivering a sort of affectionate tweak every time she detected him starting to wilt, a state of affairs which could have continued satisfactorily if Maria Braun hadn't accidentally left the gas unlit in her shiny new post-war kitchen and her lover hadn't rung the doorbell, creating a small electrical spark and blowing the pair of them to kingdom come.

'Jesus Christ!' Steve gasped, doubling up.

'Sorry! Oh God. I'm sorry. It made me jump! Steve . . . are you all right?'

'I'll live,' he muttered angrily.

The credits were rolling now. He stood up, oblivious to the angry tutting of other members of the audience, who were intent on sitting spellbound until the third assistant boom operator had been name-checked, and hobbled towards the double doors. Bridget hurried after him.

'Serves us right, I suppose,' she laughed nervously, but he just stalked out on to the street and strode off down the hill, his head down, his face contorted, whether with pain or anger she couldn't have said.

'Steve, I'm really sorry,' she called, jogging to catch up with him. He stopped, but didn't look at her. 'It was an accident. Please . . . you're not being very . . .'

He looked up. 'I'm not, am I?' he said sarcastically. 'It's just that, generally speaking, a man likes a bit of warning before someone tries to rip his cock off.'

Bridget bit her lip in contrition. They had reached her bus stop by now and a 108 was already lumbering up out of the darkness. She could let it go, but at this time of night there might not be another.

'Well, this is me . . .' she said, reluctantly joining the queue of people waiting to board. He shrugged non-committally. Was this it? Were they really going to part without so much as a kiss, after . . . everything? She shuffled forward, willing him to say her name or put a hand on her sleeve to detain her. Will I see you again? she wanted to say. But she knew the answer. She'd humiliated him and made fools of them both. Reaching for the chrome rail, she raised one foot to the platform. Sod it.

'Steve?' She turned to him. 'Are you so badly injured that you can't, you know?' Ignoring the driver's impatient eye-roll, Steve turned briefly away from the brightly lit bus and stole a peek down the front of his jeans. 'Down, but not out,' he replied and leaped aboard, just before the doors hissed shut.

Vinnie

'OK. Thanks, everyone. Next rehearsal, tomorrow night, eight thirty.'

The last actor traipsed out of the rehearsal room and Vinnie collapsed into a chair.

'Fag.' She held out her hand to Pete, her assistant director, and he quickly supplied one and lit it for her. After a long and needy drag, she exhaled the smoke with a deep sigh.

'It's shit, isn't it?'

'It's going to be fine, Vin, don't be so hard on yourself. There's plenty of time to pull it together.'

'If Amanda can be persuaded to act as if she's performing at the Gardner Arts Centre and not the fucking Acropolis . . .' said Vinnie.

'I wouldn't worry. People will just think it's an alienation technique,' Pete said.

'Hmmm, that might convince your average punter,' said Vinnie, 'but my parents are coming down for this, and believe me, they know their Brecht.' She chewed her already ragged thumbnail. Pete's face lit up.

'I s'pose they've been in it, have they? Your parents?'

'*Chalk Circle*? Yeah, Daddy directed Mummy as Grusha in Berlin when I was nine.'

'Wow!' breathed Pete.

Vinnie shrugged. 'All I remember is being the only kid in the school nativity play without my folks in the audience.'

'You poor thing.'

'Oh, it had its up side. You should have seen the pile of Christmas presents I got that year. There's a lot to be said for parental guilt.'

'Do you fancy a quick one in Falmer Bar?' Pete asked, slinging his bag over his shoulder and scraping back his chair.

'Oh, sweetie, I can't. My housemates are cooking a meal.'

'That sounds . . . domestic.'

'I know; it's amazing actually. We all take turns. It's very nurturing.'

'You live with all those women, don't you?'

'*All* those women?' She laughed. 'There're only four of us – oh no, five now, actually. Do you find that threatening?'

'No, of course not.' Pete hesitated. 'Well, maybe a bit. I've seen you around on campus. You're all . . . I mean, they're all . . . you know . . .' His voice trailed off.

Vinnie grinned. 'What?'

'Quite fit,' he muttered sheepishly.

'Thanks. I'm sure they won't object to being lumped together as sex objects.'

He winced. 'I'm only saying.'

'It's all right. You're quite "fit" yourself.'

Pete had been scuffing along the corridor, rather shame-faced. Now he stopped and looked up bashfully. 'Oh, right. Are you sure you don't fancy a drink? You'll be waiting ages for the bus.'

'Not me, darling, I always hitch,' said Vinnie, kissing him absent-mindedly on both cheeks. 'See you tomorrow, yah?'

Vinnie sauntered across the dual carriageway, playing chicken with the speeding cars and prompting a mournful honk from a passing truck. She positioned herself at the front of the bus lay-by and stuck out her thumb. It was rare for the bus to arrive before she had secured a lift. Eight or nine cars whizzed by. Just as she was wondering whether she was losing her touch, one signalled, slowed and coasted to the other end of the lay-by to wait for her. It was an Austin Allegro. She sighed. Why was it always a sad old fuck in a jalopy? Now she'd definitely be late for dinner.

She climbed in and gave him a beaming smile. 'Thanks so much.'

'Seatbelt,' he said tersely. The command came with a definite whiff of halitosis.

She glanced across at him. He was old – forty at least – and wearing what she supposed was a car coat. He had receding hair and an unkempt beard. Obediently, she plugged in. She waited for him to ask her where she was going, but he just glowered through the wind-screen without acknowledging her. Two could play at that game. She folded her arms, sank her chin into the cocoon of her long woollen scarf and kept quiet. By the time they'd reached Moulsecoomb, the silence had become oppressive.

'Mind if I smoke?' she asked, rummaging in her bag.

'I certainly do,' he replied. 'You might have a death wish, but, I can assure you, I don't.'

'All right, keep your hair on,' she muttered. 'It's only a Silk Cut.'

'I was referring to your cavalier approach to personal safety. Have you any idea how dangerous it is to be out at night dressed like that?'

'Like what?' she said.

He glanced disapprovingly at her black fishnet tights and the car rumbled briefly over the cat's-eyes.

'Oh, for God's sake. This is nineteen eighty-two, not the Middle Ages.'

'Men haven't changed that much. What you ladies have got to realise is that most of them are Neanderthals. It's the biological imperative.'

'I'm sorry?' This guy was unbelievable.

'Men, *most* men,' he corrected himself, 'have ungovernable sexual urges. Going around dressed like that' – he threw her a contemptuous glance – 'is dangerous enough, but hitch-hiking, at night, on your own . . .' He shook his head and laughed mirthlessly. 'Do you *want* to end up dead in a ditch?'

Vinnie laughed scornfully. 'Sorry, but you don't look like you've got it in you.'

'I'm not talking about me.' He darted her a furious glance. 'I'm talking about all those perverts out there. Haven't you heard of the Yorkshire Ripper?'

'I thought they caught him,' Vinnie said.

'Maybe, but he's just the tip of the iceberg.'

'Jesus.' Vinnie rolled her eyes.

'Do you know what he did to his victims?'

This was starting to feel a bit creepy. Vinnie glanced over at the back seat, but there were no accoutrements of mass murder, only a Tupperware lunch box and a copy of the *New Scientist*.

'Don't worry,' he said with relish, 'I'm not going to tell you. You'd never get it out of your head.'

He was really getting on her nerves now, coming on like some caped crusader when he was obviously gagging for it. She wanted to goad him. Bring out his true colours. She shifted in her seat, allowing her skirt to ride up a little higher. They had stopped at a red light.

'You know what? You're probably right. Girls like that have it coming . . .' she said, turning towards him with a dazzling smile and crossing her legs suggestively. He glanced over. The look on his face changed: chin jutting, eyes blank; the way men's eyes went when their pricks were doing the thinking. He returned his gaze to the traffic lights, foot poised over the accelerator, fists clenching and unclenching on the leather-clad steering wheel. Vinnie's heart beat fast. At least this way something would happen.

The lights changed to green, his foot hit the floor and the car kangarooed forward and then stalled. He muttered to himself in frustration, twisting the key repeatedly in the ignition. The engine spluttered and coughed and eventually flooded. Adrenalin surged through Vinnie's body. Not tonight, then. If fate was determined to intervene, she wasn't going to press a point.

'Nice knowing you,' she said, flinging off her seatbelt and diving out of the passenger door. The red light came round again and cars behind started to sound their horns.

'Fucking bitch! Fucking cunt!' she could see him mouthing as he beat the steering wheel with both hands.

Vinnie's legs felt like columns of jelly, but she forced herself to stroll nonchalantly across the road in front of his car.

Once she had turned the corner into Hollingdean Road, she stopped and pressed the heel of her palm into her forehead. She lit a cigarette and breathed the smoke out. Then she laughed.

Halfway to Albacore Street, the laughter had long faded from her lips, her shoes were giving her blisters and there was a chill wind whipping around her exposed thighs. She was starving, she realised. It was nice to know that supper would be waiting for her when she got back. Her pace quickened as she finally reached the home straight. She chucked her fag end into the neighbour's front garden and ran up the steps to her own front door.

'Sorry, forgot my key.' Nell stood back to let her pass. 'Mmmm. Supper smells divine.'

'You're lucky there's any left,' said Nell drily, 'you're an hour late.'

But by the time Vinnie had regaled them with the story of how she had hitched a lift home from a serial killer and only escaped because his car broke down, she had them eating out of her hand. They only half believed her, she could tell, and yet it *had* happened. Weird stuff was always happening to her. But it was the story they cared about, true or not, and Vinnie was a teller of tales. She loved that she could do this: charm and cajole her way back into people's good books; dazzle them into forgiving her, however badly she'd treated them. And yet every time it worked, she despised them, and herself, a little more. She had hoped that Albacore Street would reform her; that these forthright, powerful women would do her the courtesy of treating her as an equal. But it wasn't looking good. She was reeling them in already – she couldn't stop.

Now, for instance, Stella, the new one, the Brummie, was hiding her doggy-eyed devotion behind a democratic chippiness.

'You ought to report him,' she said. 'Next time it could be one of us. It could be *anyone*.' She met Vinnie's eye and blushed.

'What could I say? He didn't attack me. I just sensed I was in the presence of evil.' Vinnie pushed away her empty bowl and reached for her cigarettes. 'That was yummy, Nell. Thanks ever so.'

'The police aren't interested in violence against women anyway,' said Maxine. 'Look at the Ripper. They thought his victims deserved it because they were prostitutes.'

'That's what *he* said.' Vinnie bounced up and down excitedly. 'He said *I* was asking for it because of how I'm dressed.'

'Typical!' Stella muttered.

'The myth of the male libido.' Nell nodded sagely. 'It's a module in Women's Studies.'

'Fantastic!' said Max. 'You choose Women's Studies to get a break from the bastards and you *still* end up talking cock!'

They all laughed.

'That's what you get for letting a man design the course.' Vinnie shrugged.

'Well, I think you're being unfair,' put in Nell. 'There are plenty of blokes who know how to keep it in their trousers.'

'Aah, Nelly, methinks you might like it better if one particular man didn't.' Vinnie put a friendly arm around her.

'For that,' said Nell, pushing it away in mock affront, 'you can wash up.'

'I did a *mountain* of washing-up this morning,' protested Vinnie. 'There wasn't a clean bowl in the house.'

'You washed up one bowl and one spoon. I saw you,' said Maxine, shaking her head in amusement. 'Then you used the last of Nell's milk on your cereal – and you never even finished it!'

'It was off, that's why,' said Vinnie, casting Nell a baleful glance as if she were the one at fault.

'It wasn't off, it was soya milk,' Nell retorted, 'and it's bloody expensive. If people don't stop nicking each other's stuff, we'll have to have our own shelves like in the first year.'

'God, that is so fucking petit bourgeois,' said Vinnie. 'I thought you were supposed to be a communist.'

'Just 'cause I grew up in a comm*une*, that doesn't make me a commun*ist*,' Nell said. A debate ensued about whether, technically, it did or not. While it raged on, Stella quietly got on with the washing-up.

'Anyway,' Vinnie said, bringing the discussion full circle, 'I think you'll find if you check the rota that it's Bridget's turn and she's not even here.'

Right on cue, they heard the sound of a key turning in the lock of the front door.

'Bridget, is that you?' called Maxine, her tone reproachful. There was a silence, then the sound of giggling and whispering.

'I knew it. She's only copped off!' announced Maxine, half indignant, half intrigued.

Bridget poked her head around the kitchen door. 'I know, I know . . . I missed your meal, Nell. I'm really sorry. I forgot there was a Film Soc meeting.'

'It was your idea to have communal meals,' glowered Nell.

'And you're not even *in* Film Soc,' pointed out Maxine.

'I am now,' smirked Bridget, 'my first one. It was exhausting. I might just go straight up if nobody minds.'

Max narrowed her eyes suspiciously. 'Who's that behind you?'

'No one,' said Bridget. Her companion goosed her,

causing her to twitch violently and suppress a giggle. 'No one you know,' she corrected herself, backing out briefly to remonstrate with him. There was a brief scuffle and then Steve Pinder put his head round the door.

'Evening,' he said.

'Hello,' said Maxine coolly.

'Sorry I hijacked your flatmate. Bridget and me were just boning up on some essential Fassbinder.' There was a snort from Bridget in the hall. 'Anyway, we're off now to . . . er . . . take some notes. Good to meet you.' He smirked and withdrew. Nell, Maxine, Stella and Vinnie looked at each other as the sound of footsteps receded up the stairs, punctuated by occasional bursts of dirty laughter.

'You see that's just typical,' said Maxine. 'Calls herself a feminist, but when it comes to a choice between spending time with her women friends and copping off with some spotty Herbert from the film society, there's no contest.'

'We've all been there though, haven't we?' said Vinnie. The others shrugged innocently and Vinnie gawped. 'Oh come *on*! Hands up anyone who hasn't blown out a mate 'cause they got a better offer? *Honestly.*'

Stella and Maxine raised their hands.

Nell and Vinnie exchanged a conspiratorial look and burst out laughing.

'Just you and me then, sister,' said Nell.

Vinnie watched from the wings as Celia delivered the last line of the play with a dying fall. There was a confused pause, which threatened to stretch into an awkward silence.

Pete shot her a look of panic and Vinnie crossed the fingers of both hands, but just as they were starting to squirm, Alun Geddes leaped out of his front-row seat and began to applaud loudly, quickly followed by Barbara Napier. The rest of the audience followed suit and soon a respectful ripple of applause had swelled, if not to a standing ovation, at least to what even the critic from the *Evening Argus* could only describe as a warm reception. The cast held hands in a circle, as Vinnie had told them to, and rotated slowly on the stage, each blinking into and out of the spotlight in turn, none taking more or less credit than his neighbour; the culmination of a directing style that Vinnie felt echoed the egalitarian message of the play. It had been a gamble – sometimes her attempts at Brechtian alienation had resulted in moments of unintended farce. On reflection, she could probably have done without the unicyclist and the fire-eater, but they could always be cut from the rest of the run. No doubt the presence of Mummy and Daddy had imbued the occasion with a little bit of showbiz glamour, and encouraged what might otherwise have been a rather stolid audience to up its game, but they'd pulled it off and Vinnie dared hope that she deserved most of the credit.

The cast were beckoning her onstage now. She shook her head modestly, but they insisted. There was no way she was going out there on her own. She tugged Pete's sleeve, but he was mulish in his resistance. You would almost have thought he didn't *want* his moment of glory. And in the end he timed it so catastrophically that the audience was already putting on their coats and shuffling towards the aisles as the company took their encores.

The stage lights dimmed and an elated Vinnie started to congratulate each cast member in turn.

'Fantastic! You really pulled out all the stops.'

'Amanda, you were *amazing*!'

'God, I am so proud of *all* of you.'

The atmosphere seemed to be one of relief, which she could understand – she felt hugely relieved too; but there was a strange reticence as well. Why would no one quite look her in the eye? And why were they so quick to shrug off her compliments? She even caught Clem and Gareth heading out to the foyer in full grease paint.

'You *can't* not come to the party,' she wailed. 'My folks are coming and all my flatmates. I want to show you off.'

It was only the news that Alun Geddes had laid on a keg of Directors and a case of champagne that changed their minds. But when the cast trooped into the green room afterwards, it seemed that news of the free booze had already got round. And not just among the theatrical community. As well as the usual Drama Soc groupies, there were at least a dozen hard-core politicos: the men, unshaven, in donkey jackets, jeans and Doc Martens; the women in identical garb, except for the substitution of leggings for jeans, their hair either cropped to show off their multiply pierced ears or gelled into extravagant coxcombs of green or pink. Vinnie didn't know whether to be indignant that the plebs had gatecrashed the after-show party, or pleased that her radical staging had demanded the attention of the hard left. She was still trying to make up her mind when Daddy beckoned her over to where he and Mummy were holding court beside the nibbles.

'Here she is: the brains behind the operation. Lavinia, darling, over here. Very well done. We're immensely proud of you. Aren't we, Barb?' He crushed Vinnie's rat's nest of hair briefly against his corduroy lapel. She breathed the faint smell of cigar smoke and Paco Rabanne and had to swallow hard to prevent her eyes welling up. But no sooner had his approval been briefly bestowed than he was back in conversation with a bunch of intense young people who wanted to know all about his glory days at the Royal Court. Mummy gave her an ostentatious double air kiss and told her what a clever little munchkin she was, but was soon comparing her daughter's interpretation of the play with her father's seminal Berlin revival of 1969.

'You have to remember,' she said, her filigree earrings dancing as she talked, 'that this was only a year after *les évènements de soixante-huit*. We were all frightfully anti-establishment and everything was up for grabs. Believe it or not, that production damn near caused a riot . . . '

Vinnie found herself clutching a glass of champagne on the outskirts of the group. She looked around for someone to talk to, but her housemates hadn't arrived yet and all the Drama Soc groupies had fallen under the spell of one or other of her parents. Even down-to-earth Pete was standing at Barbara Napier's elbow, rocking back and forth on his brothel creepers, nursing his pint and gazing at her in puppyish adoration. Pity. She had a soft spot for Pete, and he'd seemed to have one for her; but now she knew that it was just her theatrical connections he was interested in she would never be able to trust him. She'd still shag him, of course, but that would be as far as it went.

Looking away, Vinnie's eye alighted on a face that looked vaguely familiar. She gave him a doubtful half-smile and it wasn't until he and his friend were on his way over to her that she realised they had tried to sell her a copy of *Socialist Worker* outside the library last week.

'Congratulations,' he said, 'that was great! I'm Nick, by the way. And this is Dan.'

'Hi, great show.'

'Oh, thanks . . . Nick, Dan.' Vinnie found herself warming to them; to Nick in particular. He was tall and slightly consumptive-looking, with high cheekbones and chiselled features. His eyes were an arresting shade of green and his grown-out dyed-blond crop made him look like a mangy whippet.

'Brecht's the fucking business, isn't he?'

'Oh yeah, definitely,' agreed Vinnie.

'I thought you got the alienation spot on. A lot of people substitute irony, which isn't the same thing, for my money.'

'Right,' Vinnie agreed.

'You could maybe have hammered home the dialectics a bit more,' put in Dan, whose air of intellectual arrogance seemed at odds with his wimpish persona. In his parka and National Health glasses, he seemed an unlikely side-kick for the much trendier Nick.

'You think?' Vinnie said, without even looking at him.

'Oh no, I couldn't disagree more,' said Nick. 'I thought she got it spot on.'

'But if you read Adorno—' Dan started to say.

'I tell you what,' Nick interrupted, to Vinnie's intense relief, 'it was two thousand per cent better than the last Drama Soc production I saw.'

'What was that?'

'*Hamlet.*'

'Right.' Vinnie grinned. 'Fucking Shakespeare.' All three shook their heads in amused despair.

'Ever thought of putting your money where your mouth is, politics-wise?' Dan asked after a slight pause.

'You mean . . . getting involved in the students' union or something?' Vinnie wrinkled her nose.

'The students' union!' Dan scoffed, incredulous. 'That's got fuck-all to do with politics.'

Vinnie looked to Nick for elucidation.

'They're just careerists,' he explained gently. 'They're not interested in working people.'

'No?' said Vinnie.

'No,' said Dan firmly.

'They just want cosy little jobs in government,' said Nick. '*Any* government.'

'Oh, I know,' Vinnie remembered excitedly. 'Like "whoever/you vote for/the government/gets in?"' She imitated the monotone chant that she had heard at last year's CND demo.

'No, that's the fucking anarchists,' Dan spat venomously. 'They're worse than the careerists. Couldn't organise a fucking piss-up in a brewery.'

Vinnie recoiled, taken aback by his vitriol.

Nick smiled encouragingly. 'You're getting there,' he said, 'but the anarchists haven't got a *programme*. They're all pie in the sky. What *we're* about is organised grass-roots action. Now the Tories have got in, we've got a proper enemy again. This is the perfect opportunity to mobilise the working class.'

'Is it?' Vinnie was confused. She could have sworn the left had just taken a massive hiding. The unions were on the run; Thatcher had a mandate to dismantle the welfare state. Even Daddy had voted Liberal because he said the Labour Party didn't stand a cat in hell's chance. And although Sussex University was still a bastion of left-wing thought, there was a general air of defeat about the place. She had never before met anyone on the left who seemed so thrilled to have a rabid right-wing government. There was something rather intriguing about this Alice in Wonderland take on things.

Vinnie would have liked to know more, but at this point she was mobbed by her housemates.

'Vinnie, that was fantastic!'

'You're brilliant. That was honestly worthy of the West End.'

'Not fit to touch the hem of your garment, love!' said

Maxine, clinking her half of Directors matily with Vinnie's champagne flute.

It was lovely to wallow in this warm bath of approval, but at the end of the day, Vinnie reminded herself, none of them knew the first thing about theatre. Nick and Dan were the only ones to have paid her the compliment of engaging with her production (and only Nick seemed to have fully grasped her ground-breaking directorial style) yet now she could see them, out of the corner of her eye, making for the door.

'Mwah mwah. Thanks. Listen,' said Vinnie, disentangling herself from Nell's boozy embrace, 'let me introduce you to my new friends. Nick?' she called. 'Not going already, are you?'

He and his sidekick looked warily at the gang of super-confident females around Vinnie. 'Thing is, Dan's got an essay to finish by tomorrow,' he said, looking reluctant to be dragged away. He rummaged in his army-surplus knapsack and pulled out a copy of *Socialist Worker*. He scribbled something above the masthead in red Biro and then thrust it into Vinnie's hands. 'Really enjoyed our chat,' he said. 'Maybe see you again?'

Vinnie took it and glanced at the message. 'Barley Mow. Thurs 8pm', it said.

By the time she looked up again they had gone.

Maxine

As the train rattled further and further south, Maxine looked at her reflection in the rain-spattered window and thought she saw her old self dissolving. It was a good feeling. The rise and fall of telegraph wires on the periphery of her vision; the relentless rhythm of cutting and siding and station and tunnel lulled her into a reverie. Her visit home, which had seemed like a jail sentence when she had been on her way up to Bolton three days ago, was now sifting down into a jumble of faintly uncomfortable memories. She had survived. Snippets of it came back to her as her head lolled against the grimy upholstery of the seat.

'Course our Paula doesn't know she's born,' her mother had said. 'She thinks she's got it tough with the twins, but she gets that much help with 'em. Half of Bolton thinks they're *mine*, I'm out that often wit' pushchair. And Graham's very good, considering . . .'

'Considering what? That he's their dad?' Maxine had asked.

'Considering he's working double shifts at Warburtons,' her mother had reproached her. 'It's all very well the women's libbers saying men should do more, but *you* try getting up to skriking babies in the night when you've . . .' Her mother had caught sight of the stricken look on Maxine's face and trailed off, shamefaced. 'Anyway, your sister seems to think it's a fashion show,' she'd concluded mysteriously before turning her attention back to *Nationwide* on the telly.

The next day they had gone to Paula's for their tea. That her sister, just two years older, already had a home, a husband, a vinyl sofa and Swiss cheese plants might have made Max feel inadequate, but it just depressed her. Not that Paula's council house, with its faint aroma of fabric softener and chip fat, didn't have a certain allure – it was comfier by far than the hessian and stripped floors of Albacore Street, but neither place quite felt like home to Maxine. And then there were the twins. It was only the second time that Maxine had seen them. The first time they had been side by side in their incubators in hospital and she could legitimately focus most of her attention on her sister; but this time she would be under scrutiny – there was no avoiding it. In the end she had been leafing through *Cosmopolitan* when Paula had brought them down from their sleep and handed one of them into Maxine's arms with all the confidence of an antique dealer entrusting a Ming vase to someone with Parkinson's. Maxine had felt her mother's eyes batten on her, and noticed an awkward hiatus in the torrent of prattle that she had kept up ever since crossing the threshold. Willing herself to calm down, Maxine had felt the dead weight of his hot, towelling-clad body stiffen instinctively against her alien shoulder before the wailing began.

'Eh, it's only your Auntie Maxine, you little beggar, what's the to-do?' her mother had murmured. 'Jiggle him a bit, Maxine, he'll soon settle.' Maxine had duly jiggled, but with little confidence in her ability to quieten him. Breathing the milky farmyard scent of his hot head, she'd felt a wrench of pain and turned away from her mother's anxious gaze to hide her face. No wonder he bucked and shied away from her – babies were like dogs, they knew whom they could trust and whom not.

'There, there, our Daniel,' his grandma had murmured again, and at the sound of her familiar voice, the baby had arched his back and fluttered his hands, ready to fly into the safe haven of her arms. Maxine had passed him awkwardly back.

'He's a terror is our Danny. D'you want to give Steven a try?' Paula had asked and Maxine had been touched by her sister's willingness to sacrifice both babies' comfort, for however brief a period, in order to bolster her own fragile ego.

'You're all right,' she'd said with only a slight tremor in her voice. 'They'll come round to me in their own time . . .' She had smiled bravely. 'Probably when they're about fifteen and they want to have a good moan about you and Graham.'

Maxine pushed her head against the cold pane of the

train window and shut her eyes tight. A tear squeezed out anyway.

Seeing her discomfort, her mother had chivvied her and her sister out for a drink, not realising that the nearest pub, the Halliwell, was hardly likely to lift Maxine's mood. The Halliwell had been Paula's hangout. Max had preferred the trendier Quaffers – a bus ride away, where, as a precocious fifth former, one Cherry B would lead to another and before you knew it you'd be snogging some spotty oik from the lower sixth who thought he was God's gift because he wore mascara and his mum had bought him some PVC kecks off the market. How she wished she'd stuck with the spotty oiks instead of taking Paula's advice and seeking out the older blokes with money and cars who drank in the Halliwell; the ones that were supposed to know better, with their octopus hands and their barrel chests and their beery insistence that could tip over into coercion. Not that she was worried she'd bump into *him*. He'd long since moved away. But just the sight of the red swirl-pattern carpet in the public bar and the trill and clatter of the fruit machines was enough to make her stomach churn. And the barmaid, when she served them, gave Max the briefest nod of recognition, as might pass between soldiers of the same regiment who had witnessed the horrors of war.

'You're soon back,' their mother had said barely forty minutes later.

'Our Maxine wasn't in the mood,' Paula explained, and a look passed between them.

With the babies back in their matching bouncy chairs, the three women had perched at Paula's breakfast bar and eaten chop and chips.

'So how's International Relations, Max?' her mother had asked.

'It's business as usual: war, famine, pestilence.'

'No, I meant how are you getting on with it. I suppose you're a bit outnumbered, are you? Being a girl?'

'Yes, Mum, that's why I chose International Relations, to catch myself a husband.'

'Don't be like that. I just wondered if there was anybody special, that's all.'

'Ronald Reagan, Pol Pot, Lech Walesa . . .'

'Touchy!' Paula had muttered as she cleared the plates. Maxine felt guilty. She knew her mother was just trying to show an interest, stay close. It wasn't her fault her favourite daughter was travelling away from her like a space probe into a distant solar system, never to return.

'Actually I have met someone,' she'd said casually. 'We're going out when I get back.'

Her mother had made a 'well I never' face, and then carried on eating her Arctic Roll. Nothing would induce her to pry further after Maxine's initial rebuff and Max felt amused but also a little guilty, watching her wrestle her curiosity into submission.

The train passed into a tunnel and, catching her reflection in the carriage window, her smile faded. The truth was, she was beginning to get cold feet. She considered her mother's likely reaction if she had told her who that

45

someone was. As the dour red brick of Crewe gave way to the canals and car parks and goods yards of the Midlands and then to the Tudorbethan sprawl of Northamptonshire, she felt a new self emerging: bold, impenitent, frivolous; paradoxically, more northern. She prepared, once she got back to Brighton, to be the warm-hearted, flat-vowelled, speak-as-I-find girl whom she had left behind when she went home for the weekend. The girl that had few secrets and fewer inhibitions; who entertained her housemates with tales of her outrageous past; but who no one seemed to notice had been celibate for a year or more. It had been a smokescreen, all of it. But tonight the smoke was set to clear. She allowed herself to think of Jo and smiled: those earnest brown eyes; the long-fingered expressive hands, nicotine stained from their lengthy deliberations in the library coffee bar; the wide mobile mouth, whose utterances she could scarcely focus on for wanting to kiss it.

She wished they hadn't agreed to meet so early. The train had been delayed at Gatwick and there was no time now to go home first and make herself beautiful. She smiled at the thought. What were the chances? She had never been beautiful; still less pretty, like Paula. But she had nice eyes and she knew how to make the best of herself. Make-up helped, and a really good haircut. She could do with a 'do' now, actually. Her chiselled auburn wedge looked best when it was rigorously maintained, like a topiaried hedge. She didn't like her outline to get blurred. Her statuesque physique benefited from geometric shapes: long, boxy jackets, pencil skirts, triangular hair, sleek pointy shoes. Yet here she was in drainpipes, Doc Martens and Nana's old astrakhan coat, carrying a bag full of clean washing – as far from glamorous as it was possible to get. She glanced at her watch. She had perhaps seven minutes' leeway if she was not to be late. And with her heart thudding the way it was already, late could so easily turn into never, if she let it. She nipped down to the ladies' loo at Brighton station and gave herself a quick makeover, then slung her tote bag over one shoulder and headed down the hill towards the seafront. There was a November squall blowing in off the sea, and, even from the top of North Street, salt stung her face. She felt exhilarated, as though the shame of the past were being flayed from her body, leaving it renewed and invigorated, ready for a new beginning. She started to run.

It was hard to believe anyone would have braved the weather at all that Sunday night, let alone chosen a pub under the arches of the promenade, where the sound of crashing waves drowned out the shrill of the Space Invaders machines and the blare of the jukebox. But when Maxine entered the Fortune of War it was almost full. She quickly scanned the tables for someone sitting on their own, but everywhere there were huddles and cliques, talking and laughing. She glanced at her watch, thought about leaving, but decided to brazen it out. She went up to the bar and, thinking she'd need some Dutch courage, ordered a pint of Foster's instead of her usual half. The barmaid delivered it with a conspiratorial wink, which only added to

Max's consternation. She was about to pay when she felt a tap on her back.

'While you're there . . .?' An empty glass was waggled under her nose; laughing brown eyes beguiled her from an elfin face; silver salamanders dangled from two delectable lobes. Max's heart turned over.

Nell

'Oh my God, it's like something out of *The Waltons*!' exclaimed Nell, climbing out of her classmate's beaten-up Triumph Herald and surveying the house. It was a large stone cottage, a mile or so outside Lewes, with winter jasmine clambering over its wooden fretwork and muddy bikes and roller skates cluttering a large veranda. There was a CND poster in one window and a discreet Neighbourhood Watch sticker in another.

'Nice house,' said one of her companions. 'No wonder Faculty aren't opposing the budget cuts. If I had a cushy number like this I wouldn't want to get on the wrong side of the Vice-Chancellor either.'

'Oh, I know for a fact that Mike voted *against* the cuts,' said Nell quickly.

'*Mike*, eh?' teased one of the girls. 'And you're privy to *Mike*'s voting habits, are you?'

'Well, yeah, actually,' shrugged Nell. 'I gave him a bit of a grilling about it the other day in the Common Room.'

The other two exchanged a knowing glance, but Nell

just smiled to herself. Nobody knew what she saw in Mike. Not her flatmates, not her fellow Philosophy students. Sure, he was nearly twice her age and he had what you'd call an academic's physique – thin, pale, slightly stooped. His hair was receding at the temples, but he wore it in a ponytail, which gave him a youthful air. She loved the way he still dressed like an undergraduate (or the way he thought undergraduates still dressed, having failed to notice that time and trends had moved on). He wore jeans of an outmoded colour and cut, shoes like Cornish pasties and an ethnic-inspired waistcoat. But being a bit of a hippy chick herself, she found the whole Summer of Love aesthetic quite appealing. Her own tiered skirt, granddad vest and desert boots fitted in well in this bohemian setting. As she walked into the large hallway, her eyes darted here and there, taking in an African wall hanging, a heap of old *Encounter* magazines propping open the living-room door and a bentwood coat stand piled with bobbly, hand-crafted garments. It was a home from home, as she'd known it would be. The only surprise was that the music coming from the back room was Sade, rather than Dylan or Joni Mitchell. Must be his wife's influence.

'Come on through,' he said, leading the way towards the kitchen. 'Glad you could make it. Hope you won't find us old fogeys too dull. There should be one or two postgraduates dropping by . . .'

'Great place, Professor O'Meara,' said one of Nell's companions.

'Mike, please,' he said, laughing awkwardly.

'Hi . . . Mike,' said Nell. She leaned up to kiss him on the cheek, and he, under cover of being taken aback, turned his face at the wrong moment, enabling her to brush her lips fleetingly against his.

'Oops, sorry,' he said, managing a blush to cover his tracks. Sometimes she wondered if he'd done this before. Then again, how could he have? He wasn't the type – that was what had made him such a challenge. By now she was standing in a large farmhouse-style kitchen with one or two other early birds. Its grubby slate floor, dark green Aga and battered pine table, crammed with bottles of wine and a dubious-looking lentil-based buffet, were all more or less what she had been expecting, but she had forgotten about the kids. A cork noticeboard on the wall overflowed with photos of them, their freckled faces peering gap-toothed through tent flaps; bobbing in rubber rings; feeding chickens (of course there would be chickens). Their names adorned felt-penned scrawls of houses and dinosaurs. On the window ledge, crammed in beside a jug of sprouting mung beans, were wobbly clay pots decorated in primary colours. This was hands-on motherhood if ever she'd seen it. Poor kids, she thought, it was going to be a big upheaval for them. Still, they'd get over it. She had.

'I don't suppose you'll need any encouragement to help yourselves,' said Mike jovially. 'Excuse me while I just . . .' And he was gone. Probably couldn't cope with her proximity. She'd put on the merest dab of musky perfume and deliberately left her armpits unwashed. It was the sort of earthy sexiness she instinctively knew would appeal to him and, judging by the flap he'd got into in the hall, it seemed to be having the desired effect. She promised herself she would catch him on his own before the afternoon was over.

For now, she was being buttonholed by Marcus, the owner of the Triumph Herald, who had mistakenly assumed that her enthusiastic response to his offer of a lift must mean that she reciprocated his sexual interest in her.

'Food's bloody good,' he said, humus oozing from the corners of his lips. 'I wouldn't have got those chips if I'd known he was going to lay on a spread.'

She nodded vaguely and helped herself to an olive. Personally, she'd had enough whole food to last a lifetime. People always assumed she must be a vegan because of her background, but the truth was she adored red meat.

'I'm not stopping long, by the way,' Marcus said. 'Just going to fill my boots and do a bit of arse-licking, then I'm heading off. There's a proper party in Hove later, if you fancy coming?'

'Oh, this is proper enough for me,' said Nell. 'I'm going to stick around.'

'Well, good luck getting back,' he said sourly. 'We're miles from the station and it'll be a Sunday service.'

She shrugged and he wandered off.

Nell leaned against the pine dresser, happy just to be here, in Mike's home, drinking in the atmosphere. She noticed a woman dispensing wine on the other side of the room. Could it be? Surely not. She was wearing a Laura Ashley dress, orthopaedic sandals and a Purdey cut. Not at all what Nell had been expecting. She had pictured Mike's wife as a virago: formidable, bra-less, charismatic. This woman had pretty eyes, but they weren't helped by the sky-blue eye shadow she had inexpertly applied, and she didn't look nearly intelligent enough for Mike. She could hardly see this one discussing Althusser's theories of Marxist empiricism over supper. She felt relieved, but also a little disappointed. It didn't change her feelings for *him* one iota – nothing could diminish them – but she didn't want people to misunderstand. On the surface his leaving could look like a cliché: lecherous professor and sexpot student; but that would be a travesty. She wanted the world to know that theirs was a meeting of minds. She was so deep in her reverie that she didn't notice her hostess approaching with a tray of pitta bread and greying guacamole.

'Oh dear, you haven't got a drink yet. You must just dive in, you know. It's all on the table. Would you like some guacamole?'

'Thanks,' said Nell. She took a slice of pitta bread and dipped it reluctantly into the gloopy mess. 'I love your house,' she said. 'It's really homely.'

The woman smiled ruefully. 'You mean messy.'

'Not at all. God, compared to our place . . .'

'Ah student digs, those were the days.'

'Oh, I didn't mean my place in Brighton. I'm talking about where I grew up. We had a smallholding in Devon; practically a commune actually.'

'Sounds idyllic.'

53

'I couldn't wait to get away.'

'Really?'

'Yeah, there was never any peace. Kids everywhere, waifs and strays, animals . . .'

'So you find student life more relaxing?'

'Well, not relaxing exactly. Stimulating. Focused. It's my vocation.'

'That's nice.'

'What about you?'

'Me?'

'Are you happy?' Nell hadn't meant to sound impertinent; the question had just slipped out. Mike's wife looked faintly amused.

'As much as anyone is, I suppose. I'm not sure happiness is something one can realistically aspire to.' This was music to Nell's ears.

'It must be fulfilling, though, raising the next generation. My mother used to say there's no more important job.'

'I'm sure she's right, but I'm afraid I'm out at work most of the time.'

'Oh. Gosh.' Nell blushed. 'What do you do?'

'I teach.'

'Oh lovely, infants or juniors?'

Mike's wife suppressed a smile. 'At the unversity. I'm Sub-Dean of CCS. My name's Lesley, by the way.'

Shit. Nell had heard of Lesley Vicars, but she had assumed she was a he.

'So who looks after . . . ? I'm sorry, I'm asking too many questions, aren't I?'

'Hector and Hermione? The au pair has them after school. Now if you'll excuse me, I think that was the door-bell.'

Nell felt a pang of anxiety as she watched Lesley Vicars cross the room. Not such a push-over after all. You didn't get to be Sub-Dean of CCS without a touch of cold steel to your nature. Then again, looked at another way, it might put Nell at an advantage. It was plain to see that Lesley Vicars had taken her eye off the ball, marriage-wise. You couldn't juggle a career, a family and a relationship without something coming adrift and, if Nell got her way, that something was going to be Mike. She had already aroused his interest, that much was obvious – he was a man, wasn't he? Now all she had to do was show him that she wasn't just some flibbertigibbet student who wanted to fuck her way to a first, she was a serious proposition, a soul mate. But she'd have to find him first.

There was no sign of him in either living room, so Nell decided to try her luck upstairs. She could always claim to be looking for the bathroom if anyone caught her. As luck would have it, the first door she pushed open turned out to be the master bedroom. She slipped inside, closed the door behind her and leaned briefly against it, stopped in her tracks by the intimate smell of used bedclothes and long-established coupledom. She walked over to the bed and pulled back the duvet, intoxicated and appalled by her own daring. To her relief, the bottom sheet was unstained. She leaned over and sniffed the pillow. This was his side all right. She rested her head on it for a moment. Then

55

she stood up, with a sigh, and leafed through the books on his bedside table. There was a biography of Disraeli, a copy of *Rites of Passage* by William Golding and at the top of the pile a well-thumbed Len Deighton thriller. She smiled indulgently.

Over the bed was another wall hanging, a beautiful tapestry reproduction of one of the more athletic poses from the Karma Sutra. She pursed her lips, turned and walked over to the mantelpiece where there was a clutter of family photographs, including one of Mike and Lesley in what looked to be their twenties, she leaning her head girlishly on his shoulder (no sign yet of the ball-breaking career woman she was to become); he gazing down at her adoringly. Nell turned it face down on the marble surface. Tucked into the corner of the overmantel was a small black-and-white photo of a little boy peering from behind a tree. He was wearing an old-style school cap and his eyes shone with an indomitable curiosity, which she recognised at once. She plucked the curling photo from its resting place and slipped it into her bag. She was about to rummage through the pile of essays that were lying on top of the desk in the corner, to see if hers was among them, when the sound of a toilet flushing nearby brought back to her the precariousness of her adventure. She was sneaking out of the room when she almost bumped into a small child hurtling along the landing. He stopped for a moment and looked at her. It was like seeing a ghost – the same beady-eyed intelligence; the same flaxen hair. Luckily he was so intent on getting wherever he was going that it didn't seem to occur to him to wonder what a strange woman had been doing in his parents' room and he ran on around the corner. Intrigued, Nell followed him, like Alice after the White Rabbit. There were two doors. She picked the one that was ajar, knocked tentatively and went in.

'Hector?' The room was empty. She looked around at the cheerful chaos surrounding her. Bunk beds stood in one corner, a large toy cupboard in another. A hammock full of stuffed animals was slung across the middle and beneath it the carpet was barely visible beneath a clutter of toys, most of them primary-coloured Scandinavian ones of proven educational value. On the wall, two hand-painted posters celebrated the birth dates of Hector and Hermione, one decorated with a toy train, the other with a rainbow. They were twins, Nell realised. No wonder Lesley had been so keen to get back to work. Her eye fell on an open-plan blond-wood doll's house standing on a low chest in front of the window. She had had a similar one as a child, on which she had imposed the rigorous order that had been so conspicuously absent from her day-to-day life. She couldn't resist going over and setting it to rights. She was so absorbed in arranging all the little pots and pans on the miniature dresser that she didn't notice the door opening.

'Oh, hello.' He looked taken aback.

'Mike!' Nell stood up, blushing with confusion and pleasure.

He frowned. 'I was looking for my son . . .'

57

'Hector? He was around earlier. They both were. We were playing with the doll's house. Then they got bored and went off to play hide-and-seek, but I couldn't tear myself away. I had one just like this when I was little, you see . . .'

'You like kids, do you?' He seemed wary.

'I like *your* kids. I was saying to your wife earlier – she was telling me, you know, how crazy it all is, with work and the au pair and everything, and I said to her, any time you want a babysitter, you only have to ask.'

'That's a generous offer. Perhaps not awfully practical though. You live in Brighton, don't you?'

'Oh, I can always stay over,' she said airily. 'Or if you didn't mind running me back . . .' She stood up and pretended to scrabble in her bag for a pen and paper. 'Here's my number.' She went over to where he was propped against the door-jamb and thrust it into his hand. 'I really mean it,' she said, smiling up at him. 'Any time.' Then she ducked coquettishly under his arm and made her way downstairs.

Stella

It was Stella's turn to cook and she had been determined to impress, but on reflection it had been a mistake to put tinned tuna in a paella; the basmati rice didn't seem quite right either. The bottom layer had welded itself to the pan and could only be shifted with a fish slice. Somehow she had contrived to make a dish that was both sloppy and undercooked; predominantly tasteless yet with pockets of incongruous piquancy. The looks on the faces of her house-mates spoke volumes. Maxine's mouth churned like a cement mixer without ever getting around to actually swallowing. Nell pushed the food around her plate politely, and claimed to be feeling a bit bloated. Bridget divided it into sections, as if it were a three-headed hydra that must be dispatched one head at a time. Vinnie ate a couple of forkfuls, then said, 'Look, I'm sorry, Stella, but this is completely foul.'

There was a nervous pause; all eyes turned on the chef, who was in the act of washing down her own mouthful with a swig of red wine. It burst back out, via mouth and both nostrils, pebbledashing her plate an unsavoury pink.

'You're right,' she agreed when she had stopped laughing. They were on their second bottle of wine by now, so it wasn't difficult to see the funny side.

'I'd have thought you'd be a good cook,' said Nell after Stella had mopped up her regurgitated dinner with a piece of kitchen towel, 'you're so organised and practical.'

'I *am* a good cook,' protested Stella. 'I just wanted to try something a bit different.'

A look passed around the table that said, in this, if nothing else, she had succeeded.

'Yeah, I'll vouch for her,' said Bridget. 'She's never cooked anything *this* bad before. Mind you, that fish pie you made last summer in France . . .' She trailed off.

'What?' Vinnie lit a cigarette. 'Did someone die or something? Why's it gone all quiet?'

'Oh no, it's nothing,' said Bridget hurriedly, 'change the subject.'

'No, come on. What about the fish pie?'

'Well . . .' Bridget darted a wary glance at Stella. 'We bought salt cod from the supermarket by mistake. You're supposed to soak it overnight, but—'

'It wasn't the food,' Stella broke in quietly, 'it was the holiday. You know the boy I was supposed to move in with? That was when it all kind of . . . fell apart.'

'Oh, poor darling. Men are such shits,' said Vinnie dismissively. It would have been easy to leave the matter there. And until tonight, Stella would have been keen to do just that. But maybe enough time had elapsed now, or perhaps the underlying affection with which her atrocious meal had been derided made her feel a sense of belonging. At any rate, she found she actually *wanted* to talk about it.

'No, no, he wasn't a shit. He was . . . lovely, actually,' she said. 'It just sort of . . . petered out.'

'Well, that's a very generous take on it, Stella,' said Bridget, waving away Vinnie's smoke with mild annoyance. 'He actually copped off with some French girl right under her nose—'

'Yes, but it wasn't right, even before that,' interrupted Stella. 'I could tell as soon as we got there.'

'Yeah, the sod wouldn't come and pick us up on his moped,' Bridget chimed in. 'Said we should get a cab. After we'd hitched all the way from bloody Roscoff.'

'Looking back on it, that was the writing on the wall,' said Stella thoughtfully, 'but I was so pleased to see him. And the last time we'd been together, he was all over me.' She half smiled at the memory. 'God, it was amazing. I couldn't believe it when I got off with him. I mean, *me* and Matt Dennison.' She shook her head in disbelief.

'Oh, *I* know him,' put in Vinnie. 'Isn't he that pretty History of Art student with the personality byp—'

Nell jabbed Vinnie with her elbow.

'And the thing is, he's not a bit big-headed about it either.' Stella didn't seem to have heard. 'You know, there I was, sitting in East Slope Bar, chatting away to *Matt Dennison*, just drooling over those Slavic cheekbones, those eyelashes, the way his hair curled over his collar; and I can remember thinking to myself, he doesn't actually *know* how attractive he is. How is that even possible?'

'He *completely* loves himself,' muttered Vinnie, but no one was listening.

'Anyway, one thing led to another and we . . . you know.'

'Bonked,' put in Maxine helpfully.

'Yeah. It was absolutely brilliant. The whole term was . . . magical. It just felt so *glamorous*. Like one of those Martini ads, you know, "Any time any place anywhere . . . "'

At this, the other four spontaneously leaned their heads together like glee singers and supplied the rest of the chorus: '"There's a wonderful world you can share, it's the bright one, the right one, that's Mar-tini."'

Stella found herself laughing again. This wasn't so bad after all. 'Yeah, so anyway,' she went on, 'at the end of term he told me he couldn't live without me and he wanted us to move in together in September. So like an idiot, I went straight out and put a deposit on a flat. He'd taken a summer job as a campsite courier, but he reckoned he could wangle me and Brid a free tent if we went out for a couple of weeks.'

'Yeah.' Bridget rolled her eyes. 'I wouldn't mind but we worked our arses off to get the cash. If you saw what really goes into Mr Kipling's cakes . . .'

'You worked in a factory?' Vinnie blinked in disbelief.

'Yeah, it was a laugh, wasn't it, Stell? I didn't fancy going home for the summer, so I stayed at Stella's and her dad put a word in for us with the—'

'Anyway, we're getting off the point,' Stella interrupted quickly. 'The point is, we got the money together and got ourselves over to France.'

'Oh, the crossing.' Bridget clutched her belly at the memory. 'Do you remember, Stell?' She puffed out her cheeks to mimic retching.

'But as soon as I saw him again,' Stella went on, 'I knew something had changed. He was kind of distant and he wouldn't look me in the eye. I told myself it was just shyness, but I was pretty devastated when he said I wouldn't be able to sleep in his tent or he'd get the sack.'

'You should have got off with some completely gorgeous French guy to spite him,' said Maxine.

'That's what *I* said,' nodded Bridget, 'but she wouldn't. There were these two blokes we met in the bar—'

'*Anyway* . . .' said Maxine.

'Anyway, just when I was giving up hope, he seemed to warm up a bit.'

'Guilt,' Vinnie said.

'He invited me to this beach barbeque on the Saturday night: bonfire, guitars, skinny dipping – back to Martini-land, I thought. It sounded so romantic. I spent ages getting ready and I blew the last of my francs on a bottle of Dubonnet. I thought I'd get him drunk and then drag him off to the sand dunes and, you know . . .'

'Shag him senseless,' supplied Max.

'Yeah, well, it didn't quite turn out that way.'

Vinnie topped up Stella's glass. Stella took a sip and swallowed slowly. The next bit was going to be the hardest, but it was time, and if her friends could bear witness without despising her, if *they* saw Matt as vain and vapid, then who was she to demur? Maybe he wasn't the love of her life. Maybe he was just another campus Don Juan. She put down her glass and took a deep breath.

'When we get down to Carnac-Plage, there's loads of people there. One of them's this girl Gisèle, who works in the campsite shop, and she plonks herself down right next to Matt – you'd have thought I was invisible – and *then*, she takes off her bikini top. I mean, it was half past eight – it wasn't like she was going to get a tan.'

'Amazing boobs though,' Bridget said reverently.

'God, don't you just hate really attractive women?' Vinnie exhaled a stream of cigarette smoke through her perfect vermilion lips.

'So then, right, it got properly dark and everyone started stripping off to go in the sea and I thought, I'm not just going to roll over and let this *bitch* steal my bloke, so I stripped off too. I was really glad it was getting dark, 'cause next to her I felt a bit . . . substandard, if you know what I mean.'

This provoked a howl of protest.

'Anyway, I go running into the sea with the rest of them, and for a while I manage to stick with Matt, but then he swims out really far and I'm not that good a swimmer. It's quite dangerous, Carnac-Plage, so I'm not that comfortable going out of my depth, but old Mark Spitz there's just a dot on the horizon by now, and guess who's by his side?'

'Gisèle,' Nell murmured, narrowing her eyes.

Stella sighed. It was starting to hurt now. Vinnie offered her a cigarette, and she took one, even though she didn't smoke. She found that if she didn't inhale, and just waved it around between her fore- and middle finger, it made a useful prop.

'The water's freezing so, after a while, I give up waiting for him to come back and I go and get dressed. Then we sit around for ages listening to these French lads *murdering* "Heart of Gold". No, don't laugh,' she cautioned, 'I've never been so miserable in my life!' And yet, suddenly, she found she could see the funny side and her own lips started twitching as much with the need to giggle as to cry.

'*Did* they come back?' asked Nell.

'Eventually,' said Stella. 'They came jogging up the beach, cool as anything. They'd swum round to the next bay and climbed back over the rocks. Stark naked. And the looks on their faces. You didn't have to be Sherlock Holmes to tell what they'd been up to . . .'

Vinnie took Stella's hand and gave it a squeeze.

'You should have slapped him,' said Nell.

'Cut his balls off,' said Max.

'Yeah, you're right. I didn't though, I just sat there. Worse than that – I let him pretend nothing had happened. He just strolled over with this silly grin on his face and sat down beside me. And she gave me this really super-ior sneery look, and then went back to her friends. But I was so pathetically grateful to have him back that I just *took* it.'

'I'd never let a man treat me like that,' announced Nell.

'You never know,' said Max. 'It's not that cut and dried. Sometimes you just keep hoping it'll be all right. Even when you know you're being a doormat. No disrespect, Stella.'

'No, you're right, Max. I'd have done anything. I'd have shared him with her. I'd have shared him with the whole *campsite*, as long as I was down for every third Wednesday. That's how desperate I was; clinging on by my fingernails.'

'So did you . . . you know, that night?' asked Nell.

Stella nodded. 'I knew it was the last time, so it was bitter-sweet, but he was amazing; so gentle and tender. It was like he had all the time in the world and it was just for me.'

Vinnie shook her head. 'God, don't you just *hate* a pity fuck?'

Stella recoiled a little. She had never heard of such a thing. Then again, if even Vinnie had been worked over by some guy, that somehow made it feel a whole lot better. The theme that was emerging here was that men were emotionally retarded fools, whose sole aim in life was no-strings copulation. Looked at like this, Stella's heartbreak had merely been an accident waiting to happen; certainly not a reflection of any physical or emotional deficit on her part. This was balm to her soul.

'We hitched home the next day,' said Bridget. 'You've never seen anyone cry so much.'

'No wonder the French think we're mad,' grinned Max.

'Who cares, you saved my life, Brid.' Stella flung an

66

arm around her friend and gave her a smacking kiss on the cheek. 'She saved my life,' she beamed at the others. 'Twice actually. If she hadn't offered me the room here, I'd have been stuck with all the no-hopers from Park Village. Can you imagine? I'd never have met all of you.'

'Arsehole's done us a favour,' said Maxine decisively.

'Who are you calling an arsehole?' Bridget bridled.

'I was talking about Matt Whatsisface, not *you*,' Maxine laughed.

'Exactly,' said Nell, 'his loss is our gain. Here's to Matt Whatsisface!'

'Abso-fucking-lutely,' Vinnie agreed, and they all chinked glasses. 'I can't imagine you not living here, Stella, it'd just be *wrong*.'

There was a reflective silence. The second bottle of wine was empty, the cigarettes all gone. Maxine picked up the fish slice and chipped a chunk of rice off the edge of the paella pan, but thought better of actually eating it. 'I'm starving,' she said. 'I wonder if the chippy's still open?'

Bridget

'Come on, Brid. Lecture starts in an hour.'

At this time of the morning, Stella's bright and breezy Midlands twang was more than Bridget could bear. She buried her head under the pillow, but she could still hear her roommate padding back and forth over the bare floorboards, humming under her breath. 'I'm trying to sleep,' she complained.

'It's on Plekhanov. The role of the individual in history. It'll come up in the exam.'

'Not going,' she mumbled.

'It's not like you to skive off, Bridget. I bet it's down to Steve, isn't it? I'd hate to see you throw away a first, what with finals just around the—'

'It's one lecture!' shouted Bridget, hurling her pillow in the direction of Stella's insistent voice. There was a long-suffering sigh and then the door clicked firmly shut. Poor Stella. She meant well, but sometimes sharing a room was . . . a drag. And that perfume she wore, just lately, it turned Bridget's stomach.

Bridget fell back into a fitful doze. She could hear pipes gurgling in the bathroom and a radio blasting out Haircut 100. Laughter and the smell of burnt toast drifted up to the attic from downstairs. On the landing, someone was accusing someone else of borrowing a belt without asking. The front door slammed three times at ten-minute intervals and at last all was quiet. The next time she woke, the clock on the bedside trunk said eleven fifteen. Shit! She had better get a move on. She dragged herself out of bed and pulled on her drainpipes. It was like hauling wet canvas up a shingle beach and by the time she had finished she was exhausted. She was permanently tired these days. Not just tired – bone-achingly weary. Stella was half right – some of that was down to Steve's sexual athleticism, but she hadn't seen him for a couple of days. He'd got to get his dissertation finished, he'd said, and she was sapping his energy. Steve was definitely on for a first. No doubt about that. But whereas before she met him Bridget had been aiming high too, now a first-class degree seemed a dry and dusty accolade, so far beneath the heady achievement, the sheer life-enhancing *coup* of falling in love, that she looked back with indulgent pity on the frigid little bluestocking she had been.

She finished dressing and went downstairs to the kitchen. Beneath the now pungent aroma of incinerated breakfast, Bridget detected the faint smell of curry powder and drains; a half-eaten bowl of muesli sat on the table and last night's dirty dishes lay in the sink, half submerged in a scum of coagulated grease. She felt the bile rise in her throat. She manoeuvred the kettle gingerly under the cold tap, averting her eyes from the mess, and then plugged it in. Usually a cup of Gold Blend was all it took to get her moving in the morning, but she didn't fancy coffee today. She rifled through Nell's collection of herbal tea bags, selected a peppermint one, added hot water and scalded her mouth on the first sip. She looked in the breadbin. There were two slices of Slimcea left in a plastic bag. She toasted one, smeared it with marge, forced herself to take a bite and gagged on it. Polystyrene would have been more appetising; she threw the rest away. The kitchen clock said eleven thirty. She slung her bag over her shoulder and was about to head off to catch the bus on to campus, when she heard a key turn in the front door.

'It's OK.' It was Maxine's voice. 'Everyone's got lectures on a Tuesday. We've got the place to ourselves.' Something about her conspiratorial tone stopped Bridget calling out to contradict her. Instead, she stepped out of sight behind the kitchen door, feeling like a criminal.

'Shame. I was hoping to meet your flatmates,' came an unfamiliar woman's voice; teasing, playful.

'Erm – not sure I'm really ready for that yet,' replied Maxine. 'Do you fancy a coffee?'

Bridget held her breath, willing Maxine's friend to decline. She would look like an idiot if they came into the kitchen now. There was a pause.

'It's not a coffee I fancy . . .' The girl's voice had dropped to a flirtatious murmur and Bridget had to strain to pick up their conversation. Wondering if she could have misheard, she peeped through the glass panel of the kitchen door. Maxine and her friend were in a clinch at the bottom of the stairs. Bridget gasped and ducked back out of sight, so quickly that she cracked her head on the wall and tears came to her eyes. Why had Maxine kept this from them? All those bawdy stories she'd told: blokes behind bike sheds; in her mum and dad's bed; in the refectory toilets . . . was it all a pack of lies? Or was she so sexually voracious that she'd take on all comers? Now Bridget came to think of it, though, it did explain the houndstooth jackets and the Doc Martens . . .

Anyway, she was probably making too much of it. Vinnie was always snogging girls and nobody seemed to bat an eyelid. Then again, Vinnie was histrionic, upper class, bohemian. Max was different – a normal provincial girl like herself. A bit loud; a bit of a character; but otherwise not unlike the girls she'd been to school with. Bridget felt close to her. Christ, they're shared a bed before. And there had never been any hint of . . . She didn't know whether to feel relieved or insulted. This was all a bit much. She stared in agony as the second hand of the kitchen clock sped round with no sign of movement from the pair in the hall. At last she heard giggling, followed by the creak of footsteps on the stairs. Bridget waited a moment or two, and then tiptoed through the empty hall and let herself out as quietly as she could.

She arrived at the bus stop in time to see the 47 pulling out into traffic. She swore under her breath. Now she would *definitely* be late, and if she missed her slot, she could end up waiting all morning, which would bugger her lunch with Steve – her one chance to see him this week. She wondered whether to pop into the library and warn him that she was running late. She knew his favourite corral in the philosophy section; she had taken a detour, many a time, just for the pleasure of seeing him hunched over Bazin or Foucault; but she hesitated, these days, to announce her presence. The look of bemusement on his face when she tapped him tentatively on the shoulder could be deflating, and their encounters seldom ended in the stolen kiss she had hoped for, but more often with a non-committal 'see you'. It was funny, she thought with a private smile, in bed he had no inhibitions, but get him back in his clothes, on the street, and he was too gauche even to hold her hand. She decided she didn't have time for the library and hurried straight across campus to the Portakabins that housed the student health centre.

Bridget had never been robust. As well as the asthma that had dogged her from childhood, she suffered periodically from eczema, gluten intolerance and allergies ranging in seriousness from mild strawberry rash to a terrifying bout of anaphylactic shock brought about by a peanut Revel. Since leaving home, things had eased up a bit, but a chance remark of her mother's on the phone a few weeks ago, regarding a family tendency to polycystic ovarian syndrome, had seen her once again beating a path to the doctor's surgery, urine sample in hand. Today was the follow-up appointment. The waiting room was packed. She gave her name to the receptionist.

'My appointment was actually for quarter to twelve,' she gabbled, 'but the bus was delayed and—'

'Take a seat please,' interrupted the cold-eyed young woman, plucking Bridget's notes from a filing cabinet and burying them at the bottom of a teetering in-tray. Her heart sank. She sat gingerly on the edge of the only vacant chair, which had a large blob of solidified chewing gum on the seat. Her fellow patients didn't look particularly ill to her. From across the room, she met the eye of a girl from her History seminar, whom she had overheard only last week, as she downed snakebite in Falmer Bar, announcing her intention to fake a nervous breakdown to get an extension on her thesis. One or two of the others looked as though they might require referrals to the drug rehabilitation unit, but good old-fashioned illness – the kind that wasn't self-inflicted or psychosomatic – seemed to be thin on the ground.

Bridget knew she ought to make the most of the waiting time by reading up on Plekhanov, but instead she plucked a well-thumbed copy of *Woman's Realm* from a nearby table and immersed herself in its problem page. Several magazines later, the waiting room was beginning to empty. All that was left to divert her now was an ancient copy of *National Geographic* or a CND flyer advertising a mass rally on 12 December. Bridget picked up the flyer.

'Embrace the Base,' it said, above a CND logo surrounded by a stylised ring of people holding hands. As a rule, Bridget didn't have much time for student politics.

Maxine had dragged her along to the occupation of the admin building last year, but when it came to chanting 'Organise! Occupy! Kick the Tories out!' she'd just felt foolish. Still, she supposed that the threat of nuclear annihilation was slightly more important in the scheme of things than a 20 per cent hike in campus rents. Greenham Common was a big issue. Her housemates were always banging on about it. No doubt they would all be going. But the flyer was advertising a women's-only coach chartered by the Brighton Women's Peace Collective. Bridget wasn't sure what she thought about that. The general idea seemed to be: men = warmongers; women = peacemakers; but how did Thatcher fit into that? Or Bridget's mother, for that matter?

Joan Rowland had been a hard woman to please and Bridget's had been an anxious childhood of flash cards, music lessons and school entrance exams. While her friends were reading *Bunty* comics and riding their bikes, Bridget was poring over *Look and Learn* and taking ballet lessons to improve her posture. In the early days, Bridget's father had tried to introduce a note of frivolity to this dour regime. He would bring Toblerones home on a Friday night, insisting that 'a little of what you fancy does you good'. On Wednesdays, when Joan studied local history at night school, he would let Bridget and her brother stay up and watch *Alias Smith and Jones*. One year he even surprised them all by booking a package tour to the Algarve, instead of Joan's preferred week in the Lake District. Despite her tight-lipped opposition to the plan, their mother had let her hair down in Portugal – she had even been seen on one occasion perched on a bar stool, sipping a daiquiri. Bridget had had high hopes that this giddy behaviour might prove a turning point for her parents' relationship, but, back in Harrogate, things only got worse. Her father stayed later and later at work. The Toblerones dried up, and on local history night Bridget and her brother would be left watching TV alone, while their father crouched in the dark hallway talking on the phone in a low, urgent voice, only hanging up when the headlights of Joan's Hillman Imp arced up the drive.

Soon after that, he packed a sports bag and left, to be with the woman Joan insisted on calling his floozy. Yet even whilst she hated him for leaving, Bridget had felt a grudging respect for her father's uncharacteristically decisive act. A respect which evaporated when, two weeks later, prompted by the eruption of Bridget's eczema from a scaly tidemark around her wrists to a full-scale biblical plague, he came back, unpacked his clothes and resumed the marriage as if nothing had happened.

How to equate her father's lily-livered behaviour with the machismo of the arms race? Or her mother's ruthlessness with the warbling emotion and rainbow-coloured banners of the women peace protesters? It simply wasn't that clear-cut, Bridget felt. Nevertheless, she put the flyer in her bag. She would see what Steve thought.

'Bridget Rowland, to room four please,' called the receptionist with an exasperation and volume that suggested this was the third or fourth time of asking. Bridget jumped up and grabbed her bag.

'Now then, Bridget, sit yourself down.' The doctor smiled, as warm and concerned-seeming as the receptionist had been peremptory. 'LMP?' she asked, cocking her head on one side beadily like an exotic bird.

'Sorry?'

'The date of your last period?' She was twirling a circular chart of some kind, which required the alignment of a number with a tiny aperture. Bridget felt irritated. She had been through all this with the Indian guy she had seen last week. Surely the point, with polycystic ovaries, was that you could never really be sure.

'I'm not a hundred per cent on that,' she replied. 'I think I had one in September, but then it just sort of petered out.'

'Yes, well, under the circumstances, a bit of spotting's not unusual,' said the doctor in a reassuring tone.

'Is it, you know, what we thought – the cyst thing?' she blurted out.

The doctor shook her head and gave Bridget a look of infinite sympathy.

'So what is it then?' Bridget clutched the edges of her chair and tried not to sound hysterical. She remembered that her mother's cousin had died of ovarian cancer at only thirty-nine and that her grandmother's rapid demise had had something to do with 'women's troubles'. Could she be next in line? 'It's not . . . ?'

The doctor was nodding slowly. 'I'm afraid so. But don't

panic. You're by no means the first undergraduate I've had to break this news to. I'll have to give you an internal to check just how far along things are, but even in the worst-case scenario, you'll still have options.'

Christ. This was moving fast.

'The next step would be referral to a counsellor. You're not Catholic, are you?'

Bridget frowned. 'No.'

'Good. Nevertheless, I'd advise you to think long and hard before making your decision. The knee-jerk reaction is often to just get rid of it as quickly as possible, but in my experience some women go on to have second thoughts. Only then, of course, it's too late.'

Second thoughts? Why *would* anyone . . . ? Unless it had spread so far that . . .

Bridget swallowed hard. 'Look, I'm sorry. I'm a bit confused. Could you just tell me where it is?'

'*Where?*' The doctor looked puzzled. 'Oh, I see, you're thinking ectopic. Goodness, young women are so well informed these days. But no, despite the bleeds, I've no reason to think it's anything other than an entirely normal pregnancy. Just hop up on the couch and we'll take a look . . .'

Bridget didn't hear the end of the doctor's sentence. She started to stand when she saw the doctor doing the same, but then she felt wind rushing in her ears and saw the mottled vinyl floor tiles rushing towards her. She heard a cry that might or might not have issued from her own mouth. Then nothing.

*

A pall of smoke hung over the tables in the library café. Everywhere there were students chain-smoking, drinking coffee, fretting about student stuff: deadlines, overdrafts, nuclear proliferation. Oh to be still in that happy place; what wouldn't she give to be waking up tomorrow morning to the prospect of a ticking off from her history tutor? A stern letter from the bank? The threat of Mutually Assured Destruction? She felt light-headed.

'What's so urgent that it couldn't even wait for me to finish my first draft?' Steve fidgeted on the vinyl bench across from her. Bridget sipped her tea, delaying the moment.

'I'm pregnant,' she said, putting down her cup and forcing herself to look him in the eye. She felt herself blushing.

'You're probably just late,' he said quickly. 'Stressed maybe? That can muddy the water.' He seemed very knowledgeable.

She shook her head. 'I've just come from the doctor's. I'm definitely having a baby.'

Steve shook his head slowly, then he clutched it in his hands as though the effort of keeping it upright were more than he could bear.

'I'm sorry,' she whispered.

'I thought you were on the pill.'

'I was. I am. Only I think sometimes if you take other things alongside it, it can, sort of, interfere . . .'

Steve winced. He stirred his coffee with a plastic spoon. He stirred and stirred until the swirling coffee threatened to breach the rim. He looked at her accusingly and she stared back at him. At last he seemed to remember himself. He put out his hand and touched hers lightly. 'Don't worry,' he said, 'I'm not going to do a runner. I know it's probably mine . . .' *Probably?* ' . . . We'll see it through together.'

She imagined them in grainy black and white, bickering over a carrycot in a bedsit, dishes piled in the sink.

'I haven't decided what to do yet.' She didn't want to force his hand; entrap him.

'What to do?' He looked incredulous. 'There's only one thing to do.'

'You mean get rid of it?'

'There's no need to use emotive language.'

'It's a baby, Steve.'

'A fetus.'

'Fetus is just the Latin for offspring.'

'Amo amas a-fucking-mat.'

Her eyes filled with tears and he seemed briefly repentant.

'It's up to you. Of course it is. It's the woman's decision.'

'But you'd have an abortion?'

'I would, yeah.'

'So when you said about . . . seeing it through together . . . ?'

'Well, I didn't mean a cottage with roses round the door.'

'What then?'

'I'll pay,' he said brusquely, and she could almost see him reaching into the breast pocket of his tail-coat, and unfolding a handful of crisp five-pound notes, like some hard-hearted mill owner out of Mrs Gaskell.

'You don't pay these days,' she said. 'They just give you some counselling and then they do it.'

'Oh.' He seemed disappointed. 'Well, I could come with you, if you want.'

'What for?'

He shrugged. 'Moral support?'

'Don't worry,' Bridget said. 'I'll be fine.'

Vinnie

'What do you think?' Vinnie twirled back and forth in skin-tight ski pants and a shocking-pink mohair jumper. 'Will he adore me?'

'Yeah, great,' said Maxine. 'Mind out of the way of the telly.' Everyone except Nell was sitting in a row on the brown elephant-cord sofa in the lounge, waiting for *Top of the Pops* to start.

'You look gorgeous,' said Stella. 'Are you going somewhere special?'

Vinnie hugged herself and nodded. 'You remember that boy who came to the after-show party? The politico with the amazing cheekbones?'

Stella looked puzzled.

'You know, Stell,' put in Max, 'the one who sells *Socialist Worker* outside the library.'

'*Oh*, the Woody Allen clone. Yeah, he's quite cute, if you like that sort of thing . . .'

'No, not *him*,' Vinnie recoiled. 'His mate. The good-looking one. Gorgeous green eyes, cropped hair. God,

I feel faint just thinking about him. Feel!' She thrust her hand towards Stella, who took it gingerly as if it might explode.

'She's shaking,' Stella confirmed.

'I am *literally* shitting bricks. Bridget, have you still got that bottle of Malibu in your room?'

Maxine smiled. 'Don't you think you ought to at least be sober when you get there?'

'It's OK, you can have it. I've gone right off it, anyway.' Bridget went upstairs to fetch it for her.

'*Thanks*, Brid,' said Vinnie. 'Just a little nip to still my beating heart. Honestly, it's the weirdest thing. He's not my type *at all*, and yet when he came up to me that night and started telling me how much he enjoyed *Chalk Circle*, I just *melted*. I think it's because he's the first guy ever who's been interested in what's up here.' Vinnie tapped her temple meaningfully. 'You have no idea how good that feels.'

'Funnily enough, I have every idea,' said Maxine drily. 'From my point of view it'd make a refreshing change if someone wanted me for my body.'

'Ah, shame!' Vinnie sat down on the arm of the sofa and flung a comradely arm around Maxine's shoulder. 'But I promise you, it's a curse, not a blessing. You can never trust their motives. It's like being really, really rich or something . . .'

'Another of life's terrible problems that I've managed to avoid,' Maxine said. 'God, Stella, you and me don't know how lucky we are, being plain and poor.'

'*Stella*'s not plain . . .' Vinnie protested. 'And nor are you, Max,' she added quickly. 'You're both very *striking*.'

'Vinnie, you're hopeless.' Max whacked her affectionately with a cushion. 'Now bugger off and let us watch telly.'

Vinnie sauntered up to the Barley Mow, deposited Bridget's empty bottle of Malibu in a litter bin and strolled into the public bar with a swagger that belied her nerves. It was a spit-and-sawdust sort of place and among the donkey-jacketed and Doc-Martened regulars she stood out like a flamingo in a flock of sparrows. There was a low satirical whistle as she walked in, followed by a few predictably sexist remarks, then the regulars went back to bellowing at each other above the pounding reggae bassline of 'One in Ten'. Vinnie recognised one or two familiar faces – a mature student called Wack, rumoured to be in the eighth year of his Ph.D.; Trevor the anarchist transvestite, downing pints in a tartan miniskirt; and a punk called Morag whose eyebrows resembled two angry hyphens crayoned on a white background. There was no sign of Nick.

Vinnie elbowed her way through the crowd towards the bar.

'You're slumming it, aren't you?' A bloke in a great-coat with lank shoulder-length hair winked at her. Vinnie recognised him from the after-show party. Determined not to recoil, even when she noticed a pet rat peering beadily from his pocket, she flashed him a smile and asked if she could get him a drink.

'Cheers, I'll 'ave an 'alf of Directors. No, make it a pint, if you're buying. Call it redistribution of wealth. Ha ha.'

The burly barman seemed to take pleasure in repeatedly failing to catch Vinnie's eye, and if rat boy hadn't had a vested interest in the outcome, she might never have been served. He staggered off as soon as his drink arrived, leaving Vinnie to down the double Jameson's and crème de menthe chaser which she had decided were necessary to quieten the butterflies in her stomach. She perched on a bar stool, wishing she could blend into the background, trying to ignore the amused glances of her drinking companions, whose clothes, in the warmth of the bar, gave off the unmistakable wet-dog whiff of the Oxfam shop. From the age of fifteen Vinnie had been told repeatedly that she'd look good in a sack, but this was the first time she found herself wishing she'd worn one. In all the time she'd been going out with men (and she'd started young) she had never given a fig what any of them thought of her, so naturally she had been adored. Tonight, for the first time, she looked at herself in the tarnished mirror behind the bar and saw a girl who had tried too hard.

Where the hell was he, anyway? She scanned the many scrawny Nickalikes in the bar, wondering whether she could have failed to recognise him. But no one here came close to his brand of consumptive glamour – the dazzling green eyes, the jutting cheekbones, the deliciously concave pelvis. Her stomach turned over at the thought of him and she decided, against her better judgement, to give him another five minutes . . .

Ten minutes and another crème de menthe later, Vinnie knew it was time to quit. She had resisted the temptation to buy cigarettes because she didn't want to taste of tobacco when he kissed her. Now it scarcely mattered. She fished in her pocket for some change and, climbing down off her stool, was surprised to find that her knees buckled under her.

'Wherssa cigrette machin?' she asked, keeping herself upright only by grasping the shoulder of the man next to her.

'Easy does it, love,' he said. 'It's through there.'

Vinnie picked her way across the floor as if negotiating a minefield and flung open a door giving on to a dingy corridor. She found the fag machine and after several attempts, her fifty-pence piece clunked home. She was about to retrieve her packet of Superkings when a girl in faded dungarees and red Kickers barged past, almost knocking Vinnie off her feet.

'Jeezchrissst, look wheregoin . . .' protested Vinnie, staggering slightly. She watched, open-mouthed, as the girl strode, two at a time, up a flight of stairs and disappeared through a door at the top. Slowly, very slowly, Vinnie digested the fact that the Barley Mow had an upstairs . . .

She made to follow the girl, but the staircase seemed to shift beneath her, making her lurch and grope wildly for the handrail. She paused on the half-landing, waiting for the hectic brown and orange wallpaper to stop jitterbugging before she could go on. Reaching a panelled door, she composed herself, took a deep breath and turned the handle.

'Make no mistake, comrades, this will be brought about not through the medium of bourgeois governments, but exclusively through the education of the masses . . .' Instead of the babbling camaraderie of an upstairs bar, a single voice boomed out in a cavernous function room. A middle-aged man with a tragic comb-over and a pair of NHS spectacles was slicing the air with his hand. '. . . through agitation, through explaining to the workers what they should defend and what they should overthrow . . .' he went on. Even in her befuddled state, Vinnie could tell that the earnest-looking group of people hanging on his every word were here for a grander purpose than a pint and a packet of pork scratchings.

'Oops, shorry!' she blurted. 'My mistake.'

'Aha, new blood!' The speaker beamed at her. 'Don't run away. Come in, come in . . .'

In Vinnie's dream, a man who looked uncannily like Stalin was trying to spot-weld her eyeballs to the back of her head. She writhed on the pillow, begging him to stop, and he melted away. Slowly, painfully, Vinnie came to, and realised that it had been nothing more than sunshine filtering through her closed eyelids. Some idiot had opened the curtains. She opened one mascara-laden eye and struggled to orientate herself. But which idiot? Which curtains?

'Good morning!'

She sat up and groaned. A figure, really just a blur,

against the intense light that was streaming into the room, was holding something out to her. It was a chipped white mug bearing the legend 'Viva la Revolución!' Nick. Despite her throbbing head, the vile taste in her mouth, the nausea; Vinnie felt a surge of pure happiness.

'Hello.' She smiled shyly.

'Careful, it's hot.' He handed her the tea and sat down beside her on the bed.

'I bet I look like shit.'

'You look beautiful.'

'Is this your flat?' She squinted around the room. Lime-green paint was peeling off the walls; the Dralon curtains sagged forlornly on their white plastic rail. A large poster of Lenin presided over the lethal-looking gas fire.

He nodded.

'It's nice.' She looked down. She was wearing her under-wear. 'Did we . . . ?'

He shook his head. 'You were a bit . . .'

'Oh God, don't remind me.'

He smiled at her. He was wearing pyjama bottoms. She could see his ribs through the translucence of his skin. He had his back to the window and his eyes looked huge. He leaned towards her and she put down her mug of tea.

'I haven't even brushed my teeth,' she said when the kiss finished. 'In fact, all in all, I don't feel you've seen me at my best.'

He smirked. 'You were very impressive last night.'

'What do you mean?'

'At the meeting. We were discussing Nicaragua and you said your cleaner was from Colombia, so you knew all about the suffering of the Latin American peoples.'

'Oh God!' Vinnie clutched her head.

'And you said that your dad and Bianca Jagger were like that.' He crossed his fingers. 'And your dad had organised a benefit for the Sandinistas and he raised so much money that he was on Noddy Holder's hit list.'

Vinnie frowned. 'Noddy Holder?'

'You meant Noriega.'

Vinnie pulled the duvet over her face and groaned. 'Anything else?'

'You agreed to join the party, and sign over ten per cent of your grant.'

'Oh my God. My parents will go ape shit!'

'Oh, and you said you'd marry me.'

Vinnie stopped laughing. She blushed with confusion – and something else. Pleasure. 'Just kidding!' he said, throwing a gentle punch at her upper arm. 'I don't believe in marriage. It's a bourgeois form of social control. You did join the party though.'

Vinnie nodded thoughtfully. She took another look around Nick's room. Piles of political pamphlets lay strewn across the swirl-pattern carpet; melamine shelves groaned under the weight of books by Marx, Trotsky, Kristeva and Derrida. A cork noticeboard on the wall was studded with dozens of badges expressing solidarity with trade unions and international causes Vinnie had never even heard of. Slowly, her gaze returned to Nick's face: his hollow cheeks, that tiny chip missing from his front tooth, those heavy-lidded green eyes.

'Best decision I ever made,' she said, tossing back the duvet and throwing wide her arms.

Maxine

Maxine lay back on the pillow and smiled. She felt she had come home. Daylight filtered through the half-closed Venetian blinds, giving the room a sub-aquatic feel and softening its brisk utilitarian character. It seemed right, this new softness. She had never been the type to go in for cushions or candles or incense, but for once the room seemed to possess its own romantic glow.

'So . . . that's what we do . . .' said Jo, propping herself up on one elbow and smiling down at her.

'What do you mean?'

'In bed. You wanted to know.'

Maxine gave Jo's shoulder a teasing prod. 'Cheeky.'

'I take it you approve?' Jo smirked. 'You seemed to be enjoying yourself.'

'I've never . . .' Maxine shook her head, lost for words. 'I don't know . . . it felt like I was in the right element for the first time ever. Like a . . . seal, or something. You know how they roll and flop and waddle on dry land, and then they get in the water and they're . . .'

'. . . grace personified?' supplied Jo, pushing a lock of Maxine's thick red hair behind her ear.

Maxine clapped her palms together appreciatively and honked. They both laughed.

She was surprised how much laughter there had been. That was almost the best thing about it. There was none of the *reverence* that men seemed to expect; nor any of that pop-eyed, frantic jiggling that made Max want to laugh. With Jo it had been conspiratorial and larky at first; like something that might go on after lights out at Malory Towers, and then it had become exhilarating and all-encompassing, like surfing. You were focused, but also abandoned; on your own, but part of something bigger; and after the tumult of the first breaker you were swept back to shore on a cavalcade of smaller, gentler waves.

'I don't even know if you like tea or coffee in the mornings . . .' Maxine bit her lip, as if this were some cataclysmic oversight.

'So much to discover . . .' Jo said, folding her hands religiously.

'You're bad!'

'I know.' They tussled under the duvet and kissed some more.

'I'm a tea woman,' said Jo, coming up for air.

'A tea lady, surely?' giggled Max.

'OK, a tea *lady*,' said Jo. 'So, go get me tea.'

Maxine gave her a look.

'*Please.*'

Maxine walked across the room self-consciously, hoping

the dappled shade would disguise her cellulite. She unhooked her candlewick dressing gown from the back of the door and wished she had given it a wash.

While the kettle boiled, she attacked the washing-up, squeezing generous amounts of Fairy Liquid into the grease-caked bowl and running the water as hot as she could bear. She felt like spring-cleaning the whole house; the whole world. She felt energy coursing through her veins like butane. She found herself singing Duran Duran under her breath. While the tea bags steeped, she threw open the door of the fridge, looking for inspiration. She would have liked to prepare Jo an exotic breakfast: quails' eggs and caviar; rum babas and lapsang souchong. But all she could find was a packet of soya mince and an out-of-date cherry yogurt. Never mind – it was nearly lunchtime anyway. They could go out. There was that greasy spoon near Seven Dials; or they could get fish and chips on the pier . . . Max's imagination ran riot. They had already missed a lecture each; might as well be hung for a sheep as a lamb. She fished out the tea bags, compressed them on to the spoon and lobbed them squarely at the centre of the swing-bin lid, where they plopped home, leaving a tan trickle in their wake. She sloshed in the milk, singing now. Unaccountably, she appeared to know all the words to 'Hungry Like the Wolf'. Funny the things you found out about yourself. She grasped both mugs in one hand, turned and almost walked straight into Nell.

'Ooh. Tea. Lovely,' Nell said, taking one of the mugs

from her and installing herself at the kitchen table. 'Sweet of you. I thought everybody had lectures this morning.'

'Yeah, I'm not er . . . feeling too good,' Maxine said with one eye on the open kitchen door. 'What are you doing back in the middle of the day?'

'You don't look very ill to me,' said Nell, ignoring her question. She looked Max up and down, and then looked again at the mug of tea she had commandeered. 'You sly dog! This wasn't for me, was it? God, I'm sorry. Here, have it back. I've only had a little sip. He'll never know.'

Max froze. It would be the easiest thing in the world to leave Nell's false assumption hanging in the air and slip back up to bed. It would also make a mockery of everything she had, in the last few hours, discovered.

'No. Really, Nell, there is no "he" . . .' she started to say.

'Great; in that case, pull up a chair. I'm in a bit of a quandary and I could do with some advice.'

Max opened her mouth. Then shut it again. She would make it quick: sip of tea; wisdom of Solomon; out the door.

'You see, I'm thinking of telling Mike's wife,' said Nell.

Oh God. Nell's affair. Now that she came to look at her, her housemate's eyes were a little wild. She seemed to be on a high.

'I think he wants me to. Really. Underneath. To force his hand. It's only the kids that have stopped me doing it already.'

Maxine perched one buttock on the edge of the chair, poised for a quick getaway. The trouble was, the more she looked at Nell, the more she could see the girl was out of her depth.

'Don't you think Mike should be the one to tell her?' Oh God, just see sense. *Quick!*

'To be honest, I think Mike's on the verge of a nervous breakdown. I think I have to be the grown-up here. I think I have to take responsibility for all our futures. I mean, it's not as though I don't care about Hector and Hermione. They're Mike's kids; his flesh and blood; of course I'm going to *care* about them. But this thing between us isn't going to go away. It's real. It can't be denied any longer. So why prolong the agony? That's my feeling anyway.'

'Listen, why don't you sleep on it? She's Sub-Dean of CCS. She could make life very difficult for you. Let's talk it through properly later . . .'

'I can't, Max. She's asked me to go and see her this afternoon. I think she's rumbled us. And I thought it might be more dignified just to, you know, come out with it, rather than let her do the whole *j'accuse* thing. What do you reckon? I would really value your opinion because, man-wise, you seem to have a helluva lot of exp— Oh, hello.'

Max turned round guiltily. Jo was standing by the kitchen door, fully dressed.

'I thought you were making tea,' she said to Maxine, glancing at Nell in a not entirely friendly way.

'Oh, yeah, sorry. I got – distracted.' This looked bad. It looked terrible. 'I was just . . . We were just . . . This is my flatmate, Nell. Nell, this is Jo. Joanna. She's my . . .

She and I are, well, we're . . .' Nell looked up enquiringly; Jo folded her arms and waited. '. . . both on the "origins of conflict" course together. We were just, er, comparing notes on the . . . origins of conflict,' she finished lamely.

'And now we're done,' said Jo. 'So I'm off. See you around, Max.' And before she knew what had happened, the front door had banged shut and Nell had picked up where she left off, droning on about Mike O'Meara. Max could hear her in the background, humming and hawing, but all she could think about was Jo, walking away from her. Out of her house; out of her street; out of her life.

She was like Judas. Denying her friend. Denying herself. And not even for hard cash – just out of fear. Fear of what, though? Or of whom? Whenever she had briefly entertained the notion of 'coming out' (and it had crossed her mind, on that last trip home, sitting at Paula's breakfast bar) she had known what her mother's response would most likely be: not 'Never darken our door again'; not 'What have I done to deserve this?' No. It would be 'What am I going to tell your Auntie Eileen?' If that was the worst that *Bolton* could throw at her, she should surely have been able to air her guilty secret in trendy cosmopolitan Brighton. How difficult would it have been to say, 'Nell, this is Jo, my girlfriend'?

'. . . wouldn't he? Don't you think? . . . Max?' Nell was leaning forward, all agog, awaiting her verdict.

'Yes. I'm sure he would. Look, sorry, Nell, I think Jo forgot her . . .' and she was out of there. Swinging the front door almost off its hinges in her haste to get it open, turning her ankle on the bottom step, panting and gasping her way barefoot down the street, the blood singing in her ears, her heart beating a tattoo in her chest. She reached the corner and there was Jo in the distance, moving fast downhill in that springy coltish way she had, her breath making little puffs in the chilly air.

'Jo!' Max called. 'Wait!'

She couldn't be sure, but she thought Jo quickened her pace. Maxine ran faster; her candlewick dressing gown flapped open and she half sobbed, pulling it back around her. In the end, she had gained so much momentum that she had to stop herself from running right past Jo by slapping her open palm against a lamp-post and swinging round it, so that they came face to face.

'You'll get yourself arrested,' said Jo coldly. Maxine pulled her robe around her and yanked the belt tight. Her hand smarted from the lamp-post and she had dog shit between her toes.

'I'm . . . sorry . . .' she panted. 'That . . . went . . . all . . . wrong . . . Can . . . we . . . start . . . again?'

'I don't know if I can be bothered, Maxine, to be honest. Seems like you've got a few things to work through first.'

'No. I'm fine with it. Really. It was just that . . . situation. I wasn't prepared – I haven't come out to my flatmates yet—'

'Look, Max.' Jo folded her arms across her chest and regarded her levelly. 'It's hard enough having relationships with women who know what they are. People think two women together must be twice as open, twice as caring, twice as emotionally sussed, but do you know what?'

Maxine shook her head miserably.

'They're twice as bitchy, twice as hormonal, twice as jealous . . . They never say what's on their minds; they sulk; they're promiscuous and if they're not getting their own way, they burst into tears. If you're in *any* doubt whatsoever about your sexual orientation, take my advice: stick with blokes.' She brushed Maxine aside and continued down the hill.

'I'm not!' called Maxine and, saying it, she realised it was true. 'I'm not in any doubt,' she called again and Jo stopped and turned round. Seeing the look on her face, Max realised that she hadn't just been angry; she'd been hurt.

'I'm gay,' shouted Max. 'I'm queer. I'm a lesbian!' An elderly lady dragging a shopping trolley pulled a sour face and made an elaborate detour to avoid her.

'Shhh,' Jo said, 'you're making a show of yourself.' But she started walking back.

'I'm a dyke! A lezzer! A ho-mo-sexual!'

'God, this is embarrassing,' said Jo, but her grin was getting broader. 'Shut up, can't you? Everyone's looking at us.'

They were standing on the same paving stone again, close enough that Max could see the pale blue flecks in Jo's light brown eyes.

'Make me,' she said.

Nell

'Great! Thanks, Max,' said Nell, aloud, to the empty room. She hadn't even shut the front door and now an icy draught was blowing through to the kitchen. Nell got up with a sigh, traipsed through the hall and shut it behind her. Max may have turned out to be a lousy agony aunt, but at least her brief presence had allowed Nell to voice the arguments and hear the force of her own inexorable logic. She would, she *must*, go and make a clean breast of it with Lesley Vicars. She hurried up to her room and changed her dungarees and granddad shirt for an antique petticoat, black boots laced with scarlet ribbons, and a greatcoat with military-style epaulettes. She drew her hair back into a soft topknot, framing her face, and then checked her appearance in the full-length mirror on the landing. Lara from *Doctor Zhivago* looked back at her. Poor Lesley in her Lady Di blouses and tea-coloured tights, she didn't stand a chance. She might be the one with the marriage certificate and the ear of the Vice-Chancellor, but Nell had sex and sex was power.

She was thirteen when this knowledge had been brought home to her. She'd been in the chicken shed at Home Farm, waiting to see if anyone else was going to turn up for the science lesson. Home schooling was like that. No stuffy classrooms, teaching was outside, weather permitting; hands-on; practical. It was very laissez-faire too; if you didn't fancy it, you didn't go – no questions asked. Most people did though, most of the time. But the poor attendance that day probably had something to do with the soaring temperature and the fact that no one had mucked out for almost a week. Nell's T-shirt was clinging to her back, her shorts were chafing her thighs and her trainers were mired in chicken shit. She knew she couldn't bear the ammonia stench much longer, but she didn't want to disappoint Richard, who'd agreed to pitch in with the teaching despite having no children of his own at Home Farm. His kids were at university, according to Caro, who had moved him in, with indecent haste, after her last boyfriend went off with a woman he'd met at Glastonbury Fayre. Richard seemed impossibly old to Nell, but he was very energetic and obviously thought himself pretty groovy. He built the kids a fantastic tree house and taught the boys the chords to 'Stairway to Heaven' on his guitar (although they took the piss out of him behind his back).

If he was disappointed to find only one pupil when he lumbered into the chicken shed that morning, he didn't show it.

'Any eggs?' he'd asked, walking over to where she stood in a shaft of sunlight, dust motes whirling round her head, sweat beading her top lip. She had shrugged and he had looked at her face, and then down at the place where her breasts made two barely perceptible bee-stings in her T-shirt. Then he had done an extraordinary thing. He had put out his hand and touched one of them. A strange expression had come over his face and then he had hooked one of his gnarled nicotine-stained fingers through the belt loop of her shorts and tugged her urgently towards him. His breath smelled sour and his stubble grazed her cheek as he tried to force his lips against hers and she stood, inert with shock as his other hand kneaded the bud of her nipple, as if she were some sex bomb off Pan's People, not a kid with grazed knees and a badly trimmed fringe.

'It's not wrong, you know, if you love the person . . .' he had breathed, and she had understood, then, what was coming next. 'Nobody has to know . . . it can be our secret.'

For a moment, Nell had wondered whether it might even be worth it – to get it out of the way; get one over on Clover and her mother; keep something in this stupid free-for-all of a commune that was hers alone. But then he had thrust his tongue inside her mouth and she had gagged, swiped his hand away from her breast and run. Away from the shed, away from the awful knowledge of what she had stirred in him. Back to her childhood.

Richard avoided her like the plague after that, delegating the science teaching to a drippy young woman called Alice and embarking on a lonely (and possibly exculpatory) project to build a new septic tank. If she walked into a room, he found some excuse to walk out of it.

At night, she would lie in bed, listening to the muffled sound of shouting and crying coming from Richard and Caro's bedroom, and wonder if he had confessed. She felt strangely powerful.

At the time, she didn't tell anyone what had happened. Now, looking back on it, she thought her mother must somehow have picked it up on the ether. She'd started behaving very strangely around the same time, exchanging her bell bottoms for miniskirts and tight cheesecloth blouses; ringing her eyes with kohl pencil; listening to Joni Mitchell and crying a lot.

But it wasn't until Richard hanged himself in the barn that things really started to unravel. The police came, social services got involved, the RSPCA threatened to prosecute over the condition of the pigsty, and Nell's mum attacked Caro with the bread knife and was sectioned. She must have been depressed for ages, Nell later realised. With Mum in the hands of the professionals, Dad spent a lot of time counselling Caro, who, not surprisingly, having just lost her boyfriend to suicide, was a bit of a mess herself. Nell's dad must have had quite a talent for it, though, because she perked up in no time, and when Home Farm imploded in the wake of the tragedy, they moved in together and he retrained as a Jungian therapist. After that, families left Home Farm like rats a sinking ship. The luckier kids got moved to Dartington Hall or the Steiner School in Totnes, but Nell and her sister Clover had to make do with the local comp. Eventually, her mother got back on her feet again, and made ends meet by taking in foreign students from the TEFL school in nearby Torquay. This enabled Nell to embark on a career of teenage promiscuity, which left her semi-fluent in three languages. She never forgot Richard, though, or that day in the chicken coop. If only she hadn't been such a prude . . . she might have saved a man's life.

Her heart beat fast at the thought of what she was about to do. Adrenalin surged in her. She had never felt more alive, or more certain that she was doing the right thing. She unhooked her hessian tote from the newel post, opened the door and tripped down the front steps to set about changing her life for ever. By the time she reached Lesley Vicars's room in Arts B, her stomach was churning. The door was shut and a sign on the outside said 'Do Not Disturb'. She popped her head round the secretary's door.

'Hello.' She smiled. 'I'm Nell Carpenter. I'm here to see Lesley.'

The secretary fixed her with a beady stare. She didn't smile. 'You can go in. They're expecting you,' she said.

They? Nell knocked tentatively and a voice said, 'Come in.'

The office smelled of coffee, books and new carpet. The first person Nell saw when she walked in was Mike. Despite the constraining presence of his wife, the sight of him stimulated the usual Pavlovian response: racing pulse, breathlessness, the conviction that if she were to take a step, she would collapse, Bambi-like, on the floor. He didn't make eye contact.

'Take a seat please.' This from Lesley. She was flanked by a man and a woman (divorce lawyers? Surely not on university premises). This was all very confusing. She felt out of her depth. Ambushed.

'First of all, can I just say . . . I know you know,' blurted Nell, 'and I'm glad. We never meant any harm. It's not Mike's fault, but there's no point pretending it's going to go away, because it's not—'

'Miss Carpenter.' The woman sitting on Lesley's left raised a warning hand. She spoke kindly, but with a professional distance. 'I think I should just explain why this meeting has been called. Why don't you take a seat? It's a lot to take in. I'm Jane Poynton from Student Welfare and this is Alan Eckersly from the AUT – that's Professor O'Meara's union. Professor Vicars is here in her capacity as Sub-Dean of your school of studies, rather than, er . . . anything else.'

Lesley regarded her, stony-faced.

'He hasn't done anything!' Nell blurted. 'We haven't even had sex yet. You can't blame him! It's just something that happened – I'm an adult, I knew what I was getting into.'

Mike pinched the bridge of his nose between thumb and forefinger and closed his eyes.

'Nell,' said Jane Poynton sharply, 'no one is suggesting that Professor O'Meara has behaved improperly. We have asked you here to address your conduct towards him. You should know that your recent behaviour constitutes sexual harassment.' She put a bundle of envelopes on the table and Nell gasped and looked accusingly at Mike.

'They were private!' she said. 'I can't believe . . .' She trailed off. She was starting to feel nauseous. This was horrible. Why was Mike letting them do this? And why wouldn't he look at her?

'And this,' said Jane Poynton, putting a photocopied sheet on the desk, 'is a list of phone calls made to Professor O'Meara's home number between October the ninth and November the twenty-eighth. The number from which these calls were made is billed to 14 Albacore Street, Brighton. That's where you live, isn't it?' Nell shrugged and jutted her chin. 'On November the eleventh, you rang this number fourteen times in ten minutes. At three in the morning. In a house where two young children were trying to sleep. Do you understand that this is serious, Nell?'

'No, no, you're making it all sound really sordid, but it's not like that. He loves me. Tell them, Mike . . .' She turned to him, and he shook his head, not unkindly.

'OK then.' She could hear her voice starting to crack. 'What about what you said that night when you were dropping me home after babysitting?'

Lesley Vicars threw Mike a sharp glance.

'She was getting distraught in the car,' said Mike wearily. 'I pulled over because it was dangerous. I tried to calm her down.'

'You said you loved me!' Nell said, her eyes blazing with indignation. 'You tried to kiss me.'

'Nell,' he said gently, 'I told you you were a very intelligent and attractive student, but that I was married and that it would be unethical for me to have a relationship with you because I'm your teacher. And she tried to kiss *me*,' he added, turning to Jane Poynton.

'OK then, explain this!' Nell had been scrabbling in her bag. She pulled out several sheets of closely written A4 with green annotations in the margin and slapped it on the desk so hard it made her hand smart.

'What's that?'

'It's my essay on Hegel,' she said. She was having difficulty keeping the note of triumph out of her voice.

'What about it?' asked Lesley Vicars, darting another of those inquisitive glances at Mike. He shrugged back at her, apparently puzzled.

'Read Mike's comments.' Nell sat back in her chair, arms folded, and Jane Poynton read aloud the comments scrawled down the left-hand margins.

'Read them in order,' said Nell.

'"Impressive beginning. More could be made of Hegel's dialectic in this section. Unclear in paras three and four. Save your summing up for the conclusion. Try not to use emotive language. Halve the number of footnotes. Avoid lifting arguments wholesale from other commentators. Feuerbach is fairly tangential to this argument. You would be better off looking at Weber."' She frowned and turned the sheets back and forth, between her hands. 'Seems like a run-of-the-mill essay to me. Is this your writing, Mike?'

He nodded.

'Give me a pen.' Nell fluttered her hand impatiently and Lesley Vicars gave her a red Biro, unable, in spite of herself, to disguise her curiosity. Nell drew an angry ring around the first letter of each sentence except the last one, where she ringed the whole word. 'There you go.' She thrust the paper back at them. They looked baffled. 'It's a message,' Nell said. '"I Must Have You." See? Couldn't be much clearer, could it?'

'"Haf you,"' corrected the man from the AUT, who had been silently scribbling notes until now. 'It actually says, "I must haf you". F for Feuerbach.'

'Oh, as if that makes any difference,' said Nell, snatching the essay back. 'It's perfectly clear what he meant. Mike, why don't you just tell them? I know you're probably scared for your job, but I'm freely acknowledging in front of all these people that you didn't seduce me, or abuse your position as my tutor. We just fell in love.'

A complicit look passed between the members of the panel; a look that made Nell feel as though she was at a McCarthyite show trial.

'There's no case for my member to answer here,' said the AUT man, *sotto voce*, to Jane Poynton. 'The girl's obviously a bit . . .' He raised his eyebrows meaningfully.

Nell opened her mouth to protest, but Jane Poynton cut her off before she could utter a word.

'That's enough!' she said so sharply that Nell flinched. 'On behalf of the university administration and in the presence of the Sub-Dean of your school of studies, I am issuing you with a verbal warning. You must stay away from Professor O'Meara and his family and cease all verbal and written communication with hi—'

'What about my teaching?'

'Please don't interrupt. I'll come to that. You will cease all written and verbal communication with him. You will be transferred into Dr Jenner's seminar group and you will not attend any of Professor O'Meara's lectures . . .'

'I'll fail my degree!' wailed Nell.

'Well, you should have thought of that before you started behaving like a little tart!' retorted Lesley Vicars, finally losing her cool. 'Sorry, sorry . . .' she said to Jane Poynton. She ran a forefinger nervously around the front of her pie-crust collar. Jane Poynton pursed her lips briefly and then went on.

'Failure to comply will result in you being asked to leave the university and would not preclude the possibility of legal action. Do you understand?'

Nell nodded. A tear trickled down the side of her nose. Mike O'Meara coughed awkwardly.

'Good. There are some phone numbers here that you might find useful.' The Poynton woman handed her a printed sheet. 'Student counselling service, medical centre, that sort of thing. You can go now.' Nell stood up shakily. There was a palpable air of relief in the room: a vexatious issue had been efficiently dealt with; filed away under 'H' for hysteria. Lesley Vicars stood up and brushed down her skirt, the AUT man and Jane Poynton murmured to each other about filing reports.

Only Mike watched Nell go, giving her a last look of tender admonishment; the sort of expression she imagined he might use when sending Hector or Hermione to stand in the naughty corner. Her top lip was wet with mucus and she felt a sob rising up in her chest, but she held it back for long enough to mouth the words 'I love you' before she left.

Carry Greenham Home

Dawn broke over Brighton on 12 December like a tear in a skein of black fabric. For Bridget, it was the last beautiful thing to happen that day. She had been awake all night (or that's how it felt). Her eyes were gritty and her head ached. She was supposed to be 'Embracing the Base' today with the others. She had stayed up till one thirty helping to paint the banner, but she had known all along that she wouldn't be there to carry it.

It had been fun, at the time. They had drunk a bottle of cooking sherry and realised, too late, that they had spelt 'abolish' with two bs. But by that time the banner was so over-decorated with flowers and rainbows and butterflies that you could barely decipher the words anyway. They had sung 'Imagine' by John Lennon in what sounded to their ears like three-part harmony, and they had waved their arms in the air. They had felt giddy with pride in their handiwork and optimism about the demo. At the time Bridget had almost got carried along with it.

But this morning she couldn't even say she would be there in spirit. She didn't feel remotely optimistic about the Greenham women's chances of influencing government policy. She could understand their anger; she shared it. But it was naive to think that you could face down the unstoppable force of patriarchy just through the strength of your collective emotion. The men had the big guns – literally and metaphorically. They had the suits and the robes and the badges of office; they had the keys to the executive washrooms and their fingers on the button of annihilation. You had to play the game their way or they would take their ball home. Thatcher had cottoned on, so why not the Greenham women? All this trilling about peace and freedom; all the balloons and kazoos and stripy knitted jumpers; all the tearful testimonials on TV: they just weakened their case.

So today Bridget would stage her own protest, albeit a bleak and nihilistic one. How could anyone bring a child into a world so intent on destroying itself? It seemed to her now that her thoughts had been blood red and scary for weeks. Even before she had actually known about the baby. She kept having nightmares. One morning she had woken up drenched in sweat, having just managed to crawl out of a tiny cave, before a guillotine came down to chop off her head. It had been her head in the dream, but also the baby's. The thought of actually going to term filled her with dread. She pictured the midwife handing her a squirming bag of gristle like the baby in *Eraserhead*. She didn't think she could bear it.

Then again, imagine if you could overcome the temptation to leave it in the nearest phone box. Imagine you overcame your revulsion and kept it, long enough for its skull to stop throbbing and its hair and teeth to grow. By that time you'd have bonded. You'd be head over heels in love and it would be your job to keep it from harm. And there was so much harm out there. Not just the small stuff, like nuclear annihilation; *big* stuff. Big, *big* stuff, such as no one to play with at playtime and bullies on street corners and perverts in cars and adults who hadn't the tiniest clue how to love each other, never mind their luckless progeny. Christ, no, she wouldn't wish it on her worst enemy.

'Brid, get a move on. We're going in ten minutes,' Maxine called up from downstairs, her voice full of confidence and optimism. No qualms for her about joining in with silly songs or telling the police where they could stick it.

'Be right down . . .' Bridget called, lying perfectly still.

'She does know the coach leaves at nine, not half past?' Stella fretted.

'We might as well just go,' muttered Nell. They were in the hall, banner furled, rucksacks stuffed with sandwiches, flasks and cagoules. They had heard that you were supposed to take stuff to pin on the fence, but they weren't quite sure what. Vinnie had copied out a poem by Sylvia Plath; Nell had stolen a drawing by one of Mike's kids; Stella had a pair of bootees from when she was a baby; Max had some keepsake or other, she wouldn't say what.

'Well, I'm going to go on ahead,' said Vinnie. 'We're meeting Nick and Dan at the Level.'

'You do realise . . . ?' Maxine called, but it was too late. 'She does realise it's a women only coach? You'd better go after her,' she urged the other two. 'She's going to freak when she finds out. I'll go and round Bridget up and we'll follow on.'

Vinnie, Stella and Nell reached the Level to be told that two coaches had already left. The third was filling up fast. A huge banner saying 'BRIGHTON WOMEN FOR PEACE' filled the whole of the back window, but there was some sort of altercation going on at the front end.

'Nick!' said Vinnie, panting up beside him. 'What's wrong?'

'This demented feminist is trying to tell us she'd rather the coach left half empty than with me and Dan on board,' he said, his face ugly with incredulity.

It was true that there were a number of empty seats at the front of the coach, but the atmosphere on board was buoyant. The women, old and young, hippies, housewives, grannies and punks, were all wrapped up against the cold and couldn't wait to be on their way. A few of them jeered Nick and Dan. The 'demented feminist', a calm middle-aged woman in waxed jacket and slacks, was trying to defuse the situation.

'I'm sorry. It's nothing against you, but this coach was chartered by Brighton Women's Peace Collective, and it says in our constitution—'

'Oh, better stick to your constitution,' sneered Dan. 'Never mind that we're on the brink of nuclear annihilation, as long as you're following paragraph five, clause three.'

'Greenham *is* predominantly a women's protest,' the woman added patiently. 'Some of us believe that that adds to its symbolic power.'

'Symbolic power?' snorted Nick. 'What good is "symbolic power" when they're going to site imperialist death machines on our soil? You need *real* power. You want to be talking to the trade unions, trying to mobilise the workers in the army and the police...'

Some of the women on the coach were getting restive now and had begun singing:

> 'So tell me which side are you on?
> Which side are you on?
> Are you on the other side from us?
> Which side are you on?'

'Shit!' Stella muttered in exasperation, half to herself, half to Nell. 'This is getting out of hand. Trust Vinnie to cause a scene. She's going to miss the coach if she's not careful. And God knows where Bridget and Max have got to.' The last thing she wanted was to spend a day at Greenham Common with just Nell for company – she didn't have much to say to her at the best of times and ever since her run-in with Lesley Vicars Nell's behaviour had been stranger than ever.

'Come on, Vinnie,' she muttered, craning her neck to get a better view of the row on the pavement. Nick's companion seemed to be the one causing most of the trouble. If she hadn't been so worried about Vinnie missing the coach, she'd have got off and given him a piece of her mind. She knew the type – middle-class leftie, never done an honest day's graft in his life (as her dad would no doubt have said). She'd run rings round his sort more than once at the school debating society. Their faces when they found out they weren't the only ones who'd heard of Gramsci...

'Are you on the side that likes to hunt?' sang the women lustily. 'Are you on the side that calls us...?'

The coach driver started the engine. Vinnie, still on the pavement, darted an anxious look at the vehicle as it shuddered into life.

'Look.' She turned her fifty-megawatt smile on the waxed jacket woman. 'I completely see your point, but could you not just let these two come along as a goodwill gesture? They could be mascots,' she added hopefully.

Dan's face was a picture.

'They can come if they cut their dicks off,' shouted a woman near the front to howls of mirth from the rest of the coach.

'I don't know why they don't just let them on,' said Nell wearily. 'What does it matter? None of it's going to make any difference anyway.'

'Don't say that!' said Stella. 'Of course it's going to make a difference, it has to. But if those two were so keen to be involved, they should have organised their own coach.'

'I can't see the problem,' shrugged Nell, 'there are seats going spare.'

'Not when Max and Bridget get here . . .'

'You still think they're going to make it?' Nell looked sceptical.

'Of course they will. They'll be here in a minute.' Stella stood up in the aisle and peered anxiously through the rear window, but a cloud of exhaust fumes obscured her view.

'All aboard that's coming aboard,' shouted the driver, prompting a burst of whistles, cheers and Red Indian whoops. All the women on the near side of the bus started beckoning madly for Vinnie to join them. It had become more than a point of principle. It had become a battle of the sexes. Stella watched Vinnie looking from the men to the women and back again in an agony of indecision.

Come on, Vin, she willed her and as if Stella had said it out loud, Vinnie seemed suddenly galvanised. She gave Nick a regretful kiss on the cheek, leaped aboard to an almighty cheer and the doors hissed shut. The women's singing didn't die down until they reached the M23.

'Bridget, you're not even dressed!' Max chided, breathless from running up two flights of stairs.

'That's because I'm not coming,' said Bridget, rolling over in bed to face the wall.

Sensing that this wasn't mere laziness, Max adopted a playful tone.

'Course you're coming. What if we can't embrace the

base because we're one short?' Max pulled the duvet off her.

'You won't be.' She pulled it back. 'Please, Max, I've got . . . something else I need to do.'

'Ooh, very mysterious. What's that then, painting your toenails for peace? Shaving your pubes into a CND sign?'

Bridget turned round. 'I'm having an abortion,' she said.

The colour drained from Max's cheeks. She felt as though she'd been punched.

'Shit!' she mouthed. She put out her hand to touch Bridget's shoulder, but stopped short. There was a long silence.

'Is it Steve's?'

Bridget nodded, dumbly.

'How far . . . ?'

'Only eight weeks.'

'Where will you . . . ?'

'I'm getting the five pas ten to Victoria. There's a clinic right near the station.'

'I'm coming with you.'

The train rumbled out of Brighton station over the viaduct. Bridget looked down at the rows of little terraced houses below her and wished she could swap places with any one of their inhabitants. How she would love to be getting on with a normal day; drinking tea; listening to Radio 1; cleaning the lav. She thought she could put up with pretty much any other problem: unemployment; drug addiction; maybe even a little tumour, as long as it was treatable.

What she couldn't cope with was the thought of being herself for the duration of this most wretched of all days.

'Penny for them,' said Max.

'It's raining,' she said. 'They'll be getting wet.'

Max looked at her watch. 'They'll still be on the coach,' she said. 'How are you feeling?'

'Sick,' said Bridget.

'What, like you're going to *be* sick?' Max leaned forward, concerned.

Bridget shook her head. 'No, sick with nerves, shame, self-disgust . . . you know how it is? Oh no, you don't, do you? 'Cause you weren't daft enough to get yourself knocked up six months before finals.'

'Well, actually—' Max started to say.

'And come to think of it, you won't be getting knocked up any time soon either, going by what I saw the other week.'

'What's that supposed to mean?'

'Forget it,' muttered Bridget, 'I'm all on edge. None of my business.'

'What's none of your business?'

'Who you snog.'

Max blushed. 'How did you know?'

'I was in the kitchen, a couple of weeks ago. I heard you come in. Then I sort of . . . saw you . . . by accident, with that girl. I wasn't spying,' she added hurriedly. 'Don't get me wrong, I'm fine with it.'

'Big of you.'

Bridget laughed for the first time that day. 'No, I mean I was just a bit surprised. I thought you liked blokes.'

Max shrugged. 'I did.'

'So do you, you know, "swing both ways"?'

Maxine shuddered. 'God, no, I'm definitely a lesbian.'

'Good decision,' said Bridget bleakly.

Vinnie was convinced that Nick was going to chuck her when she got back. Luckily for Stella, this provided them with a lively topic of conversation. By the time they reached Pease Pottage, she had managed to persuade Vinnie that political differences were good for a relationship. Her mother and father had never seen eye to eye, she told her. Her mum was a *Daily Mail* reader, her dad a left-wing firebrand, but they had just celebrated their silver wedding, so it went to show . . . It felt good to give Vinnie advice. It put them on a more equal footing. In fact, she was starting to suspect that Vinnie wasn't as Teflon-coated as she appeared. Just occasionally, she forgot to be the girl about town who'd been there, done that, got every last T-shirt going, and betrayed a girlish naivety that Stella found as endearing as it was unexpected.

The coach swished on through the driving rain. Every so often, an overtaking car would beep its horn in support, prompting another round of singing from the women. Stella liked the one that went 'She goes on and on and on, you can't kill the spirit'. She could imagine her dad rolling his eyes in mum's direction and saying, 'Amen to that.'

Once they had sorted Vinnie's relationship, they moved on to discuss Nell, who had fallen asleep, head lolling against the window opposite.

'She's in a bad way. I've never seen anyone go down-hill so fast,' Vinnie whispered. 'Look at her hair. She hasn't washed it in days.'

'I know and have you seen the colour of her tongue?' agreed Stella. 'She's drinking loads of black coffee and smoking like a chimney, and yet she can't seem to stay awake.'

'She'll get over it,' said Vinnie. 'I had a crush on my art teacher at school. It's just a phase.'

But Stella wasn't so sure. A couple of nights ago, she had been woken up by what sounded like the keening of a wounded animal coming from the floor below. She had wanted to go down and comfort Nell, but didn't really feel equipped. She ought to have been able to help, being lovelorn herself, but she couldn't help feeling that hers must have been a minor-league skirmish if this was what real heartbreak sounded like. She was starting to wonder whether what she had felt for Matt had been infatuation rather than true love. Certainly, since the night of the disastrous paella, their break-up had seemed less calamitous. She might even, she thought, be ready to move on.

'That boy with Nick?' she said to Vinnie.

'Dan, you mean? The one with the bad skin and the tragic parka? What about him?'

'Oh, nothing . . . just thought I'd seen him around, that's all . . .'

By the time the coach had reached the outskirts of Newbury, Stella and Vinnie had discussed the foibles of each of their housemates, exchanged potted histories of their own love lives to date and addressed the vexed issue of how one knew when one had found the real thing. Finally they had fallen into a companionable silence. This was progress, Stella realised; at this rate, she would soon be able to count Vinnie a proper friend. But before she could get too dewy-eyed, a cheer went up on board. Someone had spotted a sign for the air base, and whooping had recommenced. Nell woke up and they all began gathering their belongings together. The driver couldn't park for ages because the line of coaches was so long. They seemed to have come from everywhere; big, obvious places like Cardiff, Dundee and Manchester, but also obscure quaint-sounding ones like Ely and Shoeburyness and Godalming.

'God, this is amazing,' said Vinnie, stepping off the coach straight into an icy puddle in her winkle-pickers. It was sleeting slightly, but the mood was upbeat. It seemed to Stella like a medieval fair; there was an air of excitement and purpose but also a surreal quality that reminded her of a Brueghel painting. Women seethed all around them: stout WI types with pudding-bowl hair and sturdy shoes; androgynous girls in berets and ankle boots; intellectual viragos in muesli-coloured headgear; meek-looking housewives pushing buggies. There were mothers and daughters and sisters and grannies and dozens and dozens of friends. Everyone seemed slightly stunned by the turnout. What had started as a symbolic gesture suddenly seemed like a political coup. Surely this many women could not be ignored?

The Brighton contingent shuffled along in the direction of Blue Gate, which, rumour had it, was their designated 'Embracing Point'. Every so often, with the spontaneity of a football crowd, a chant or a song would start up, accompanied by tom-toms, whistles and tambourines. At the main gate, they passed a row of policemen and reprised their chant of 'Which side are you on?' Most of the coppers remained hatchet-faced, except one, who, when Vinnie clopped past just inches away from him, leaned forward and said, in a not unfriendly tone, 'Give us a blow job,' to which she responded with scandalised laughter.

But if Stella and Vinnie had entered fully into the spirit of the day, Nell seemed aloof and preoccupied. Stella wondered if she was in any fit state to be here. She had dark rings under her eyes and, although you couldn't tell in her afghan coat and pixie hat, she had grown incredibly thin. Stella wondered whether she was taking something, she seemed so spaced-out all the time, but she was pretty sure Valium was meant to cheer you up, and Nell had just got more and more down. Nevertheless she shuffled along beside them and took her turn holding the banner aloft until they reached their destination (though none of them was actually certain when they had, as all the gates appeared to be the same shade of gunmetal grey).

'Oh my God, you two, look at these.' Vinnie had clambered up the steep grass verge and was fingering some of the tributes that had been attached to the perimeter fence. There were babygros and photos of children, teddies, flowers and ribbons. Shredded plastic had been woven in and out of the wire to make rainbows, CND symbols and pleas for peace and love. Vinnie put a hand over her mouth, blinking back tears. 'It really brings it home, doesn't it? I mean, we're just day-trippers, but some of these women have left their families – their *babies* – to set up camp here.'

'Come on, let's put our things on,' said Stella.

They both rummaged in their bags for the keepsakes they had brought to add to the nine-mile shrine. Stella dug out her tiny yellow booties and tied them on by their flimsy ribbons. She'd meant to save them for her own first child, but who knew, now, if the world would last that long?

'Nell, what about your picture?' Nell fished in her pocket, her face unreadable. She unfolded Hermione's felt-pen masterpiece and fastened it in place. It fluttered there for a second, before a spatter of raindrops sent rivulets of colour coursing down the page and obliterated it. Stella saw a look of anguish cross Nell's face and thought she heard her suppress a whimper, like an animal in pain. But Vinnie's demand for safety pins distracted her momentarily and when she turned back, Nell had gone. Meanwhile Vinnie had pinned up her Plath poem and was reciting it aloud, quickly attracting an appreciative audience, intoning the words in her actor's voice, until she was drowned out by a disturbance at the gate.

'Take a seat please,' the receptionist said. Bridget and Max sat down side by side on two moulded plastic chairs and looked around the poky first-floor waiting room. There were three other women there: a whey-faced girl in stonewashed denim and chipped bubblegum nail polish; a young Indian woman whose world-weary expression suggested she had done this before; and an older woman with her husband, smart, well-to-do. Bridget could scarcely fathom *her* motives until Max nudged her and indicated a poster on the wall: 'Five ways to aid conception', it said.

'Do you think they *want* a baby?' she asked incredulously.

The idea that the clinic might provide fertility treatment as well as terminations seemed brutal beyond belief, like dangling cream cakes just beyond the reach of a starving child.

'They look pretty broody to me,' Max whispered back. 'Shame you can't come to some arrangement . . .'

Bridget turned round indignantly in her chair. 'Is that supposed to be funny?'

'Not really.' There was a silence; then Max added, 'It's what I did.'

'What's going on?' Stella asked of no one in particular. She and Vinnie stumbled back down the verge, alarmed by the air of panic. They could hear shouting, running feet, the wail of distant sirens.

'Trouble at Blue Gate,' they heard someone say. 'The pigs are there.'

The peaceful atmosphere of moments ago had given way to chaos. Women were surging around Blue Gate and it was impossible to see what was going on. Rumours multiplied: wire cutters; police provocation; mass arrests.

'Where's Nell?' asked Vinnie, clutching Stella's arm. 'We need to find Nell.'

'I don't know,' Stella shouted back. 'She was here a minute ago . . .'

'What do you mean "it's what I did"? hissed Bridget angrily.

'I got pregnant, when I was fifteen. I had it adopted,' Max said.

'I don't believe you.'

Max fished in her pocket and handed Bridget a tiny pink wristband. Bridget turned it over. 'Baby Greenhalgh Female 12.3.76,' it said. She gawped.

'What's it doing in your pocket?' Her tone was suspicious.

'I was going to fasten it to the fence at Greenham.'

'A girl?'

Max nodded, her head bowed. Bridget couldn't see her face. When Max started to talk again, Bridget could barely hear her.

'I wanted to keep her so badly, but my mum was dead against it. She wanted me to go to university. I was supposed to be the clever one.'

'How old would she have been?'

'Not would have been, *is*. She *is* six. She'll have started school . . .'

'Oh Max!'

*

'Excuse me, please. Sorry, can we just . . . ? We've got to find our . . .' A cordon of police was trying to hold back the women now, but Stella and Vinnie pushed determinedly through. An unmarked police van with a black grille on the front was slewed across the driveway to the gate. Two Black Marias blocked the lane in both directions. Some women were crying, others shouting. More sirens sounded in the distance and the crackle of static from walkie-talkies was all around.

'Fucking pigs fucking mowed her down,' one woman sobbed, barely coherent, her face wet with tears.

'No, no, I saw it. She jumped. She jumped right in front of the van,' another woman said. 'I saw her face. She did it on purpose. She did it for Greenham.'

'I wanted to tell you. So you know there's a choice. I think of her *every day*. I regret giving her away *every day*. If this is what you want, then fine; but I don't want you to end up regretting it like I did.'

'Why couldn't you have told me before? Why wait till now? Jesus, Max. I mean . . . Jesus!'

The receptionist looked up from her desk. 'Bridget Rowland?' she said pleasantly.

Bridget clenched and unclenched her fist around Maxine's wristband.

'You can go through now. Room Three.'

'Nell, *Nelly*, where are you?' Stella yelled, her face white, strained.

'Scuse me, sorry. Can you just . . . ?'

'We've got to find our friend. Sorry. Sorry. Would you just please *move*!'

With a last desperate push the two of them were through to the front, in time to see two paramedics handing a stretcher into the back of an ambulance. Jutting out from under the blanket, a pair of black lace-up boots pointed skywards, their scarlet ribbons caked in mud.

1992
Ireland

The Rayburn was playing up again. It was early February and mist lay on the fields outside. Vinnie had lit a fire in the living room, but it kept going out. She could already feel a bone-chilling damp beginning to seep out of the foot-thick walls and take over the whole house. If the kids were to have something more nourishing than jam sandwiches for tea, William would have to fix it pronto. She would ask him when he dropped Niamh home after playgroup, before he could disappear back up to the big house. She slammed the ashpit door closed and the handle fell on the floor and cracked another of the slates beneath. Vinnie cursed.

She gathered up her sheaf of proofs from the kitchen table and carried them through to the parlour. Stray bits of Playmobil crunched underfoot as she picked her way between empty cereal bowls and discarded socks to the busted chintz armchair beside the fire. The cat's litter tray was overflowing, but the smell was somewhat masked by the aroma of stale tobacco. Last night's empty wine bottle still stood in the grate. She took the packet of Old Holborn from her dressing-gown pocket, tipped the last few strands into her hand, rolled them into a meagre cigarette and smoked it whilst prodding the fire in the vain hope that it would suddenly roar into life. She was in no mood for proof-reading, but she was already behind on the dead-line. If she didn't finish it before Niamh got home, it would be another day late, and Hanson Fothergill would lose patience with her and stop sending her work. She put on her glasses and traced her finger along the title: 'Boundary Layer Separation and Vortex Creation in Superflow through Small Orifices' she read. The letters were already transposing themselves before her eyes and she hadn't even got to the body of the article with its mathematical formulae and brackets within brackets. She marked up the first page, her writing geriatric with the cold. She yearned for a cup of scalding tea to nurse, and briefly considered abandoning her task and trudging over to Brenda's to scrounge one, but that would mean getting dressed. She was four pages into 'Boundary Layer Separation' when she heard the rattle of the letterbox and, eager for distraction, went into the hall to see what the postman had brought. There were three envelopes lying on the liver-coloured lino: a letter from BTE telling her the phone was about to be cut off; a Kodak freepost envelope; and a thick cream missive, addressed to Ms Lavinia Napier-Geddes and redirected via her parents from her old address in Bethnal Green. This was intriguing. Vinnie frowned and slipped her thumb under the flap. She took out a weighty piece of deckle-edged card. Christ almighty! *She* was getting married.

Vinnie felt a rush of emotions: excitement at the thought of seeing everyone again; apprehension at how she might come across; envy at the sophistication of the venue and the glamour of the match. But mostly she just felt a visceral tug back in the direction of her old life, her old self. They *would* all go, surely? She would hate to be the only one. She supposed there might be a question mark over Stella in view of what had happened, but it wasn't every day you got invited to the nuptials of one of TV's leading anchorwomen and an international media mogul and Stella was too soft-hearted to bear a grudge. It was just what Vinnie needed to shake her out of the doldrums. She'd have to see if Brenda would have the kids for a couple of days. She must remember to take some snaps of them to show off. They would make up for her somewhat under-whelming career. Of course William would be a feather in her cap too. Wait till she told him . . .

'You're living in cloud-cuckoo-land, Lavinia,' he said when she buttonholed him, an hour later, all thoughts of the Rayburn forgotten. 'There's no way I can leave Colebrooke to run itself for two days. There's an aromatherapy massage course booked for that week. You go, if you think we can afford it.'

'Where are you going, Mummy? Can I come?' Niamh threw her arms around Vinnie's knees and gazed up at her adoringly.

'Nowhere, darling. How was nursery?' Vinnie replied absently.

'It was top notch, wasn't it, Niamhy? She made a roller-coaster out of toilet rolls, and Christy tried to copy her, but his fell apart,' said William, hanging up Niamh's book bag for her and straightening the wellington boots she had shucked off carelessly.

'You shouldn't do everything for her, it just makes it harder for me when you're not there,' protested Vinnie.

'Ach, she's only a baby. You're only a baby, aren't you, Naimhy? Now give your da a kiss. I've to get back up to the house now, but I'll see you at bedtime.'

'Oh Will, before you go, could you take a look at the—?'

'Tonight, sweetheart,' he called. 'I've to go over the menus with Catriona now, and I'm late already.' And he was back in the Land-Rover, powering up the driveway towards the house.

'Mummy, what's for dinner?' asked Niamh, running ahead of Vinnie into the kitchen, impervious to the cold.

'It's juice and biscuits, Niamh. Apparently your daddy's more interested in feeding the guests . . .' complained Vinnie.

'I don't know what "apparently" means,' said Niamh, helping herself to fistfuls of chocolate Hobnobs from the tin.

That house had a lot to answer for. He was forever up there, in a huddle with Catriona and Jason, planning the 'curriculum'. William only had to get a sniff of a profit and he'd lay on a course in anything. Transcendental meditation had been a winner; 'Trace your family tree' went down very well with the Yanks (none of whom left without a certificate proclaiming their distant kinship with Bernadette Devlin or Bobby Sands); then there was astrology, yoga, gestalt therapy, macrobiotic cookery, you name it. None of them made serious money, though; or not enough to pay the upkeep on the house. Colebrooke was haemorrhaging cash. It needed a new roof and the back of it was subsiding into the bog it was built on, but William wouldn't hear of putting it up for sale. It was 'the family seat', never mind that the family was a bunch of English brigands who'd built it with blood money.

Five years ago, the house had saved Vinnie's life. She still kept a copy of the ad she had answered in *The Lady* after Nick had left.

COUNTY KERRY
HOUSEKEEPER AND AIDE-DE-CAMP REQUIRED
FOR LARGE COUNTRY ESTATE HOSTING
ARTISTIC/PERSONAL DEVELOPMENT EVENTS.
REPLY P.O. BOX 436 EIRE

'Housekeeper', you had to laugh. But she had scented something unorthodox, and she had been right. When William had met her and Leon off the ferry in Dun Laoghaire, they had clicked straight away. They had a lot in common: she was the daughter of theatrical bluebloods;

he was the descendent of Anglo-Irish aristos who had fallen on hard times. His charming Irish brogue, she soon discovered, was laid on with a trowel – he had actually been educated at a minor public school near Bath – but by the time Vinnie cottoned on, she was infatuated with him. The punters loved it too, especially the Americans. It went with the crumbling house, the half-baked new-age courses and most especially with the devastating good looks of the host. It was all a far cry from her dour life with Nick in Bethnal Green: the concrete tower block; the tenants' meetings; 'the toddler group' that amounted to a bunch of whey-faced women sitting round a draughty community centre while their children fought over broken plastic toys. Compared to all of that, Colebrooke was heaven.

Vinnie fell in love again; and this time in the satisfying knowledge that she had reverted to type. She knew enough about psychology to recognise that her relationship with Nick had been little more than a delayed adolescent rebellion; a kicking over of the traces. There had been a large dollop of lust in the mix too, she couldn't deny, but that hadn't lasted long. Nick's idea of foreplay had been to read out snippets of rousing good cheer from *Socialist Worker* as they lay together under their thin duvet. 'Workers seize industrial plant in Bolivia; Defiant dockers strike on; Biggest-ever CND rally,' he would pant, turning to her at last, eyes alight with zeal; only to find her snoring away. William's technique was more up Vinnie's street. She would scarcely notice the rhythmic plop of raindrops leaking into the pan at the end of the bed, because Will would be stroking her pubic hair as he recited Yeats from memory.

> 'Beloved, gaze in thine own heart
> The holy tree is growing there . . .'

It wasn't long before Vinnie was pregnant again. William, resourceful as ever, encouraged her to team up with Brenda, the midwife from the village, who was just a couple of weeks behind her in the baby stakes. Together they held natural childbirth classes in the Great Hall at Colebrooke ('In the kingdom of the blind, the one-eyed man surely to heaven is king,' Brenda had said). In the event, neither of them practised what they preached. Dervla was born by emergency Caesarean, and Niamh was dragged out with the aid of forceps and an episiotomy. Vinnie had had to sit on a rubber ring for the first six weeks and by the time the pain of the stitches was easing, she had succumbed to mastitis. It was as much as she could do, in the months that followed, to cope with the children and the lodge, never mind the big house; which she now visited so seldom that it seemed less bricks and mortar than a mirage occasionally glimpsed through the mist, like Manderley. William brought Catriona in on a trial basis, and for a while Vinnie felt usurped, but she concluded in the end that her rival couldn't be much more competent in the role than she had been herself, or William wouldn't have to spend so much time up there baling her out.

All day, Vinnie kept finding herself drawn back to the hall stand and that fat cream envelope.

'You'd not mind staying with Auntie Brenda for a couple of days while Mummy and Daddy went for a little break, would you, Niamh?'

Niamh, by now installed in the living room, watching Nickelodeon, replied with a distracted, 'Uhuh?'

'You'd like to go and sleep over with Dervla, wouldn't you? While me and your da go and visit some old friends?'

Niamh dragged her attention away from the screen and fixed her grey-blue eyes on her mother's face.

'It's not for a week or two,' Vinnie wheedled. 'We'd bring you a present.'

Niamh considered. 'Could it be a Sylvanian Families windmill?' she asked.

'I don't see why not, if we can find one.'

This really didn't need to be the big deal that William was making out. Flushed with success, Vinnie vowed to try the same tack when Leon came home from school.

'I don't really like the idea of you and Will being abroad,' he said gravely (he had always had a neurotic streak, which Vinnie blamed on his father's abandonment).

'It's not abroad, darling. It's London,' laughed Vinnie. 'We'd be back in two shakes of a lamb's tail.'

But Leon's face was pinched and anxious, a look that Vinnie knew presaged tears. She fought the irritation that was rising in her. He could be such a histrionic boy at times. And he really was getting a bit too big for this sort of thing.

'Come on, Leon, Niamh is fine with it and she's only five. Don't tell me I'm to ask her to hold *your* hand, now.'

'Can I not come with you? Maybe I could stay with Daddy. My proper daddy, I mean.'

Vinnie turned on him angrily. '*William* is your proper daddy, Leon.' He's certainly made a better job of it than Nick ever did. He doesn't even remember your *birthday*. And anyway, he doesn't live in London any more, he lives in Barnsley . . . Oh, darling, don't cry.'

Vinnie gathered him to her and stroked his springy brown hair. His face was hot and he shuddered as he struggled to keep back the tears.

'I'm sorry, I'm sorry, I'm sorry. I know it's hard for you, Leon darling, but it's hard for me too. I just need to have this break, sweetie. You'll understand when you're older. How about if I ask Bren to come and stay here, with Dervla, and then you'll have your Nintendo and everything and you'll hardly miss us at all. How about that?'

Leon looked up at her and shrugged, his eyes shimmering with tears.

'Come on now. Be my big boy. You can do this for Mummy, can't you?'

He sniffed two candlesticks of mucus back into his nostrils and forced himself to smile.

'That's my boy. I tell you what' – Vinnie took him by the shoulders and moved him to one side so that she could make her way to the kitchen – 'you'll have your favourite tea tonight for being a brave little soldier. You'll have a mashed potato volcano *erupting* with baked b— Oh *fuck*, the fucking Rayburn's fucked! Damn! Damn! Damn!' And she slammed her fist into the wing of the busted armchair, making her little tin ashtray jump off the arm and shower dog ends all over the floor.

'It doesn't matter, Mummy,' said Leon quickly, 'I can go down to the village for some chips, or—'

'No, no, my angel.' Vinnie's words were kind, but her face was grim and she was already in the hall, jamming her feet into Will's work boots and shrugging her coat on over the top of her dressing gown. 'I've had enough of this. I'm going up to Colebrooke and tell your daddy that it's the middle of winter and his children need a hot meal inside them. Mind Niamh for Mummy,' she called over her shoulder, leaving the front door wide open and Leon biting his lip in the hall.

She took the direct route across the fields instead of following the meandering drive, but with every step, the boggy ground sucked Will's boots away from her thread-bare socks and her ankles soon started to chafe. She distracted herself from the discomfort by murmuring under her breath the speech she planned to make when she got there. She imagined his contrition when she appeared wraith-like at the French windows; how he would cut Catriona off in mid-sentence with an imperious gesture, embrace his poor neglected wife, bundle her into the back of the Land-Rover and hurtle back down the drive to mend the Rayburn, stoke the fire, gather his little family into his protective embrace. Then, when she had cooked a delicious meal for everyone, she would pack the kids off to bed and they would make love in front of the fire. She would work him up into a frenzy of desire and when he was putty in her hands, she would mention the wedding again . . .

She panted her way to the brow of the hill and Colebrooke lay before her, grey and austere. A light shone from the servants' quarters in the east wing; the rest of the house looked blind in the gathering dusk. Vinnie broke into a galumphing run, tripping over tussocks of grass, and starting when a bird flew up in her path. She no longer cared about giving William a bollocking; she just wanted to get there. She skirted the parterre and picked her way through the neglected vegetable garden, up cracked and weed-infested stone steps towards the kitchen, where she could see lights blazing and hear the sound of a radio blasting out the theme tune to *PM*. She burst in. The room was empty but there were signs that a meeting had taken place – used mugs on the table, a ringbound folder, spreadsheets; Catriona's leather shoulder bag hung over the ladderback chair. Vinnie switched off the radio and before silence could completely engulf the room, she heard a faint scuffling and what sounded like whispering coming from the old scullery. She tiptoed over, twisted the door handle and walked in. At first she could only see her own reflection in the Georgian window panes of the scullery as the light from the kitchen leaked into the poky space, but she knew at once that she was not alone. She felt for the light switch and snapped it on.

The tableau that met her eyes was not the one she had feared. It made no sense. Her husband was fumbling to fasten the top button of his jeans, his unbuckled belt dangling free, while Jason, the youth he employed as chief cook and bottle washer, was half crouched in the corner, glancing back guiltily over his shoulder, his cheeks crimson, his shirt-tails half in and half out of his cord trousers.

'Lavinia. It's not what you think!' William shouted as she backed out of the room and shut the door after her. She scrambled across the kitchen as though a pack of dogs was after her, half gasping, half retching. She flung open the kitchen door and ran down the steps, but her jelly legs wouldn't support her, and she fell against a stone urn at the bottom and grazed her thigh.

She was halfway across the vegetable garden when William caught her by the elbow and swung her round to face him.

'Lavinia, stop. You're making too much of it. I know what it looks like, but it doesn't mean anything. I don't even like the fellow.'

Vinnie could hardly speak. She bared her teeth like a horse, her face white, flecks of saliva gathering at the corners of her lips. 'You do *that* with someone you don't like?' she spat.

'This is nothing to do with you; with *us*. This is just . . . just something that happens. I don't know. I don't know why. Because I'm weak, I suppose, and venal. But it's nothing; just an aberration. You wouldn't understand. This is a . . . a kind of habit you get into; some men get into.

It doesn't mean I'm queer. It doesn't mean I don't love you.'

Vinnie laughed mirthlessly. 'I thought *Nick* was spine-less. I thought he'd sunk pretty low, but he's a fucking paragon compared to you. At least he told me what was going on; wept and wailed and gnashed his teeth. At least I didn't walk in on them shagging like animals. At least he left me for another *woman*.'

'Ah sure, he's a paragon that one. Big fucking socialist he turned out to be. You have to laugh – leaving you for a *miner's* wife. You couldn't make it up, could you? Fair play to the fellow; solidarity doesn't get much more fucking solid than that, does it? Sod your flying pickets and your collecting buckets, why not go the whole fucking hog and screw the missis?'

'Sh-u-u-u-u-t U-u-u-u-up!' shrieked Vinnie, clamping her hands over her ears. She turned and ran again, this time heading round the front of the house and climbing into the Land-Rover. The keys were still in the ignition.

When she reached the lodge, she killed the engine and paused for a moment, pressing her head against the cool glass of the driver's side window.

'Mummy's home,' she called, her voice only wavering a little. 'Pack your things. We're going over to Brenda's for a day or two.'

While the children ran upstairs to gather together pyjamas, toothbrushes and Nintendo games, she took a last look around the dingy hallway. She wouldn't miss this shit-hole, that was for sure. Her eye fell on the smart wedding invitation propped on the hall stand – so out of place under the bare lightbulb and trailing cobwebs. The card was so thick it took her two attempts to rip it in half.

Brighton

'I see that friend of yours is getting married. The one off the telly,' Paula said to Maxine. 'Are you going?'

Maxine darted an anxious look at Shona. She hadn't broached the subject yet. 'Maybe. Haven't decided.'

'She comes across a bit stuck up to me,' said Graham. 'I wouldn't have thought she was your type, Maxine.'

'Who's this, Max?' Shona put down the menu and sat forward in her seat.

'Oh, just someone I lived with at college. We lost touch. Big poncy wedding in London. Not our sort of thing . . .'

'Sounds like *my* sort of thing,' said Shona, 'or am I not invited?'

'Of course you are. Plus guest, it said. That's not the issue. Anyway, look, shall we order? Graham and Paula must be starving.'

They were in Mange Tout, a new restaurant, which had been favourably reviewed in the *Evening Argus*. This was the first time Paula and Graham had made the trip from Bolton, and Maxine wanted to show her appreciation. She also wanted to soften them up. The waitress came over and they gave their orders.

'Wine?' she asked.

'Oh, I think so, don't you?' said Graham expansively. 'What's it to be, ladies? Bottle of Sancerre, I think?'

'Actually, we're not drinking.' Maxine blushed scarlet. 'Can we have a bottle of mineral water?' she said to the waitress.

'Bloody hell, our Maxine . . .' Paula didn't bother to disguise her amazement.

'Well, I'm just doing it to support Shona, really,' explained Maxine hurriedly.

Her sister and brother-in-law exchanged glances.

'Max! They'll think I'm an alky or something.' She tapped Max on the wrist in mock admonishment. 'It's nothing like that. It's just that I'm hoping, *we're* hoping, to get pregnant.'

Graham, who had been tasting the Sancerre with rather too much ceremony, now spat it back into his glass in astonishment. Maxine swivelled round in her chair and gave Shona an incredulous look.

'Dive in feet first, why don't you?' she hissed.

'Well, they might as well know,' replied Shona. 'It's what we're here for.'

Now it was Paula's turn to bridle. 'I thought we were here for a nice meal out,' she said. 'If I'd realised you had an agenda . . .'

'We are, we don't,' Max said. 'We just wanted you to know our plans. It could have waited till the main course, but . . .' She gave Shona an exasperated look.

'So that's it, is it?' said Graham, taking a swig of wine. 'Men are officially surplus to requirements? What's the deal then? A poofter and a turkey baster?'

Paula kicked him under the table.

'I'm only kidding,' he said. 'They know I'm only kidding. I'm a thoroughly modern man, Paula, I know my place. Pardon my ignorance, but how do you decide, in a set-up like yours, which of you's going to be Mummy?'

There had, in the end, been no decision to make. Maxine was the one who had been desperate for a baby (the child she had given up for adoption would be sixteen by now, a year older than she had been when she got pregnant). It had taken her six months to win Shona round to the idea and another two to find a prospective sperm donor – Graham's assumption about the poofter and the turkey baster, whilst insensitively put, was nevertheless spot on. A gay friend, Anthony, had stepped forward, but a row between Maxine and Shona as to the appropriateness of requiring him to take an HIV test led to a further six-week hiatus in proceedings, by which time he had met a chartered surveyor and moved to Hemel Hempstead. When talks resumed, three months later, it was decided they should take some of the heat out of the issue by going to a clinic, but preliminary fertility tests to determine Maxine's suitability for the programme revealed her fallopian tubes to be badly scarred from her early pregnancy. Her only chance of conceiving was through IVF. Now began an expensive and emotionally crippling rollercoaster of raised and dashed hopes. Every month Maxine dreaded the arrival of her period; every month, the inevitable clot of red on toilet tissue would drive home her failure: as a woman; as a mother; as a person. One year and a near nervous breakdown later, Shona declared that enough was enough. If motherhood meant everything to Max, then she would *be* a mother – to Shona's baby.

'I can't have children,' Maxine explained, twisting her napkin into a corkscrew in her lap.

'Yes you . . .' Paula started to say, and then bit back the words with an uncertain glance at Shona. 'I mean, I'm *sure* you probably could. You're only thirty-one.'

'No, really, I can't,' said Max, a little more vehemently than she intended. 'It's not me saying that, it's the doctors. Shona's going to do it instead.'

'I see,' said Paula, eyeing Shona's Armani jacket with some scepticism. 'And you've talked this through, have you? Only you give the impression of being more a career woman, Shona, if you don't mind me saying.'

'Christ, Paula, *you* worked when the twins were little,' Max burst out.

'Yeah, in the dry cleaner's. Once they went to school,' said Paula. 'I wasn't a big shot.'

'I'm not a big shot either,' Shona soothed, 'but I will have to go back to work after the baby's born. We blew all our savings on Max's IVF. If this project is going to be viable, we need to have an eye on the bottom line.'

Max glared at Shona. How did she expect to convince

the world's most conventional couple that she was a prospective earth mother when she kept coming on like Gordon Gekko in a dress?

Luckily the arrival of their starters enforced a polite, if strained, silence for a minute or two.

'Well,' said Graham, tucking his napkin into the front of his Pringle sweater, 'if it's a loan you're after, we might be able to sort something out. My BT shares are doing very nicely—'

'Graham!' Paula hissed. 'Don't you think we ought to discuss it first?'

'It's all right, Paula,' said Maxine, 'we're not after your money. It's not about that.'

'Well, what the hell is it about, our Maxine? 'Cause it's about summat,' Paula snapped, her refined visitor's inflection finally giving way to broad Lancashire. 'I knew it was too much to hope that you were just being nice, inviting us down for the first time in ten years. I should've known there'd be an exterior motive.'

'Ulterior,' Maxine corrected automatically, and then wished she had bitten her tongue.

'*Ulterior* then. The point is, you haven't got us down here for a stroll on the pier, have you?'

'You could have come down any time you wanted. It's you that's stayed away, not us that's not invited you.' Maxine pushed her deep-fried Camembert to one side. She didn't feel like eating any more. The whole evening seemed to be careering away from her like a runaway train.

'Girls, girls,' said Graham. He poured another glass of

wine. 'Have a drink, Maxine. I'm sure Shona won't mind under the circumstances, will you, love?'

Shona raised her hand graciously.

'Well, it gets on my wick,' muttered Paula. 'She does her own thing all this time, hardly bothers with the twins, doesn't visit me mam in hospital, and then as soon as she needs summat, blood's thicker than water.'

Max flinched at this. She took a hasty mouthful of wine. It was true that she had only gone home a handful of times since leaving university, but the reason certainly wasn't indifference. She had hoped that it would get easier, seeing Paula's boys grow up, but every time she encountered them, wobbling round the close on their new bikes, watching children's TV with their grandma, warbling along tunelessly to Christmas carols in the school nativity play, she wanted to weep for the girl cousin they would never know; *she* would never know.

'Come on now, Paula, that's water under the bridge,' said Graham. 'Give the girl the benefit of the doubt. She's *said* she doesn't want anything . . .' Max gave Shona a complicit look, and realised too late that her brother-in-law had seen it. As he looked slowly from one to the other, the truth dawned. 'Bloody hell!' he said.

'Bloody hell what, Graham?' asked Paula, more agitated than ever, but he was shaking his head in stunned silence. 'Bloody hell *what*?'

Maxine was relieved to go back to school on the Monday. Taking 9W for history was usually the low point of her

146

week, but for once their insolence and time-wasting was a welcome distraction from the knowledge that she and Shona had blown their last chance of parenthood. Sunday morning had seemed to last for ever. They had eaten breakfast with their guests in an atmosphere of chilly politeness, and then shared out the various sections of the Sunday paper and hidden from one another. When the time came for Graham and Paula to catch their train, they had gone through the barrier without so much as a backward glance; this in a family famed for its *Sound of Music*-style send-offs, even if you'd only dropped in for a cuppa. To Maxine it felt terminal.

So when the phone rang on Wednesday night, the last person she was expecting to hear from was Paula.

'Maxine.'

'Paula, er, hi. You got back all right then?'

'Obviously.' Paula's voice was clipped and businesslike, but Max sensed an underlying nervousness. 'We've had a talk. Me and Graham. He'd like to help you.'

Maxine, who had been stirring pasta sauce whilst holding the phone in her free hand, now stopped and watched the wooden spoon subside gently into the sauce. 'You mean he'll give us his . . . ?'

'Yes,' Paula said quickly. 'You might as well know I've got a lot of reservations about same-sex parents, but I'm prepared to go along with it to make you happy.'

Maxine's eyes welled up. Never had such a grudging concession evoked a more heartfelt rush of love and gratitude. 'Oh Paula, that's fantastic. Unbelievably generous.

I can't wait to tell Shona. She's going to be over the moon. Tell Graham he's my hero. That's really big of him – especially when she's not even family.'

'Well, that's *why*, really,' said Paula.

'What do you mean?'

'To be honest, if you'd asked me if *you* could have Graham's baby, I don't think I could have handled it. Every time I looked at it I'd have thought of you and Graham . . . you know, but if *she's* having it . . .'

'You do know that it doesn't involve having sex, don't you?'

'Bloody hell, Maxine, do you think I'd casually ring up and offer my husband as a stud? Of course I know. I'm just saying it seems a bit less . . . icky, if you know what I mean.'

'I see,' said Maxine, although she didn't. Her mind went into overdrive. 'We'd better get together again, ideally in about a fortnight when she's ovulating. There's a lot to discuss. I'll need to explain to Graham how to—'

'We know all that,' interrupted Paula brusquely. 'Sterile jars, room temperature, minimal time lag between harvesting and' – she paused delicately – 'insemination.'

'Blimey, you have done your research.'

'Just because I haven't been to college doesn't mean I'm thick.'

'I know, I know.'

'I've got some jam jars I can put in the steriliser. Lucky I kept it.'

'Jam jars? Mightn't Graham feel a bit . . . overwhelmed?' Maxine struggled to keep the giggle out of her voice.

'Don't worry, they're those miniature ones; Mum's been saving them from Whiteley's caff. I knew they'd come in handy.' Max could detect a corresponding snigger behind Paula's businesslike reply, but neither of them dared acknowledge it for fear of demolishing the carefully established neutrality of their conversation.

'Well, look, this is fantastic news. I'll talk to Shona. Can you come down again the week after next?'

'You can come up,' retorted Paula. 'It's Auntie Eileen's birthday that weekend, so you can crack on that's what you're coming for.'

Paula was clearly enjoying having the whip hand, but Max daredn't demur, even though Auntie Eileen's attitude to lesbianism was only slightly more enlightened than Queen Victoria's.

'So . . . we're not telling Mum yet then?' she asked timidly.

'Let's see if it works first,' said Paula. 'Give my best to Shona,' and she rang off.

'Eeh, that feels good,' said Janice Greenhalgh, clasping her daughter against her easycare polyester jumper. Maxine breathed in the scent of hairspray and Nivea. It felt good to her too. 'And you must be Shona,' she said, shaking hands a little stiffly.

'Lovely to meet you, Mrs Greenhalgh,' said Shona. 'I like your garden.' She nodded through the Everest double glazing towards the immaculate plot outside, where early daffodils and grape hyacinths bobbed optimistically in the freezing east wind.

'Are you a gardener?' Maxine's mother asked.

'Not really. We've only got a balcony. It overlooks the marina though, so we get a nice view. You must come down and stay.'

'Sounds posh,' said Maxine's mother. 'I'll put the kettle on. We'll not be having tea till the others get here. Do you want a biscuit to put you on?'

'I'm fine, thanks. Can I do anything to help?'

'No, you're all right. It's nothing special; cheese toasties and salad. The boys' favourite,' she added apologetically.

Maxine avoided Shona's eye. She knew that if she met it, she would read amusement there and she didn't want to be complicit in patronising her mother.

'Are these your grandsons?' asked Shona, picking up one of the many framed photos dotted about the room.

'Aye. Little terrors,' she said affectionately. 'First picture from secondary school. I can't believe it, can you, Maxine?'

'They're like their dad, aren't they? Lovely brown eyes.' Shona was scrutinising the photo a little too avidly for Maxine's liking. She took it from her and placed it back on top of the television.

Graham's navy-blue Vauxhall pulled up outside and the rest of the party got out, Paula marching ahead like a woman on a mission, the boys scrapping over a hand-held games console, Graham escorting Auntie Eileen with exaggerated courtesy up the drive.

'Hiya,' Paula said, giving Maxine a brisk hug and ignoring the enquiring glance her sister gave her.

'Hiya, Auntie Maxine.' The boys submitted to a kiss each from Maxine.

'Good to see you again, ladies,' said Graham with a meaningful wink.

'Happy Birthday, Auntie Eileen, this is my partner Shona,' gabbled Max.

'Hello, Maxine love. Nice to meet you, Sheena. I'll just go through, Janice, if you don't mind, my lumbago's giving me gyp.'

Once everyone was installed in the through lounge and the television had been turned on to placate the boys, Maxine's mum started bringing in a variety of nibbles, pickles and table sauces to accompany the toasties and arranged them fussily on the smoked-glass coffee table. When everyone was on their second cup of tea and the babble of background conversation had risen to a suitable level, Max tapped Paula meaningfully on the arm, and Paula, keeping her eyes fixed pointedly on the football results, reached into her handbag and transferred her precious cargo surreptitiously into Max's bag, which sat conveniently next to it on the sculpted carpet. The conversation turned to the subject of work, and Steven and Daniel became restive and were ordered out on to the drive to kick a ball while Grandma pottered in the kitchen, Graham outlined Warburtons' expansion plans and boasted about the new company car he would be getting at the end of the tax year. Auntie Eileen asked Shona what sort of business it was that she and Max were in. Shona was puzzled at first, but when she realised the old lady had mistaken the deliberately ambiguous term 'partner', she started to explain the true nature of their relationship. This, Max realised, must be avoided at all costs.

'Oh, Auntie Eileen, I forgot, I've brought you a birthday card,' she said, scrabbling frantically in her bag. Shona frowned at her and carried on.

'It's something people say, my generation anyway,' she was saying, 'when they're not actually married, but—'

'It's here somewhere, I know it is,' Maxine almost shouted. Where was that blessed card? She was emptying out her bag now, in a frenzy, lining up lipsticks, keys, tissues, everything, on the edge of the coffee table. 'Here it is!' she said, triumphantly unearthing it from a zip compartment she had forgotten about.

'Oh Maxine, I wish you hadn't, love. At my age you don't want to be bothered.' Auntie Eileen's gnarled hands trembled as she wrestled with the envelope. By the time everyone had admired it, the conversation with Shona had been forgotten and Janice had returned carrying a plate piled high with toasted sandwiches.

'Plymouth Argyle one, Stockport County one,' intoned the announcer on the Saturday sports round-up. Otherwise all was quiet except for the munching of sandwiches, the slurping of tea and the occasional request for someone to pass the salad. It wasn't until the mountain of toasties had been reduced to a single dainty triangle, and the table was spattered with Piccalilli and ringed with brown sauce, that Maxine noticed a miniature glass jar at its far corner, the carefully sterilised lid unscrewed, Auntie Eileen's knife balanced precariously on the top of it. She gasped in horror and nudged Paula.

'Last toastie for the birthday girl?' asked Maxine's mum, offering the platter across.

'I've had an ample sufficiency, thank you, Janice,' replied Auntie Eileen, probing one of her molars with her tongue for a strand of cheese. 'That was a veritable feast, but I have to say, I don't think much to your salad cream.'

Clapham

Amber pushed the bowl of Coco Pops away from her and rested her sandy-coloured head on the kitchen table. Stella knew the game was up. She had been kidding herself her daughter was fit for school, but looking at her now, all limp and lethargic, she knew she had a problem. Chicken pox was doing the rounds; just Stella's luck for it to strike between nannies.

'Dan,' she called, 'Amber's not well.'

'Poor baby.' Her husband popped his head round the kitchen door and pouted sympathetically at his daughter whilst patting the pocket of his jacket for his house keys. 'You have yourself a lovely pyjama day and I'll bring you a treat home from—'

'Oh no you don't,' said Stella. 'I can't stay off. I've got a big meeting this morning.'

'So have I,' said Dan.

'Well, my lot are coming from Seville. I've had to book a translator.'

'Spanish trade unionists?' grinned Dan. 'They probably

won't turn up till tomorrow teatime. I've got to brief Derek on Maastricht, so he doesn't make a prat of himself on *World at One*.'

'Can't you do it from home? *Please?* I can be back for one.'

'No can do, sweetheart. Don't want to look like a quiche-eater, do I? Why don't you ask Barbara?'

'Dan! Just because she doesn't work doesn't mean we can take advantage. She's a friend.'

'Beats me why,' said Dan. 'You've got nothing in common.'

'Actually, we did the same subject at university.'

'I don't know why she bothered if all she was going to do was pop her kids and then watch daytime TV all day.'

'Maybe she didn't want to run round like a headless chicken when one of them got ill,' muttered Stella.

'Anyway, love, I've really got to dash. Good luck with the dagos – give 'em what for!'

'We're all on the same side,' called Stella as his footsteps receded down the hall. "Workers of the world unite", remember?' The front door slammed. 'No, you don't, do you?' She snatched Amber's cereal bowl off the table and dumped it in the sink. 'You go back up to bed, sweetheart,' she said. 'I'll bring you some honey and lemon in a minute. I've just got to make a quick phone call.'

'Her daughter paused in the doorway. 'Are you and Daddy going to get divorced, Mummy?' Stella put the telephone handset down abruptly and turned round.

'Of course not, sweetheart. Daddy and I love each other

very, very much. *Nearly* as much as we both love you. What on earth made you ask that?'

Amber shrugged her shoulders and a flash of pot-bellied midriff appeared above her Boden pyjama bottoms. Stella felt an overwhelming surge of love and guilt. She was so little still. Maybe it was too soon to have gone back full-time . . .

'Just checking,' said Amber, and then shuffled out of the room. Out of the mouths of babes . . . thought Stella. She made a mental note to talk to Dan about it when he got home. Except, increasingly, that seemed to be after nine, or later if there was an evening meeting; and if he didn't have one, she did. She never would have believed they'd become one of those couples who got their Filofaxes out to book a rendezvous in their own kitchen . . .

She remembered watching Dan cradle Amber in his arms when she was ten minutes old, tears in his eyes. Never mind two days' paternity leave, he had taken a six-week leave of absence so that he could bond with her; had worked short days for six months. He was the talk of the NCT coffee mornings: no man had ever been more at home with a muslin cloth slung over his shoulder; he pushed Amber's buggy with the same insouciance most men reserved for their 3 Series BMW. He knew about cradle cap and colic and the latest findings on phthalates in teething toys. But in those days he had been a humble parliamentary researcher, whose airy-fairy sexual politics had been indulged because it made his more senior colleagues look good. A couple of promotions later, he was PPS to an ageing, ineffectual Geordie MP in a safe Labour seat. He was one heart bypass away from the backbenches. His priorities had changed.

Funny to think that when Vinnie had first introduced them, Dan had called *Stella* a bourgeois reformist for being a Labour Party member. What a turn-on it had been, trading political insults in the Barley Mow before tumbling into bed at Albacore Street. How privileged she had felt to be admitted behind Dan's chippy façade to glimpse the sentimental idealist underneath. Even his nerdy persona soon stopped seeming like something she had to excuse and became an asset – an emblem of his character. And how refreshing that, contrary to expectations, he kept his egalitarianism out of the bedroom, taking a firm hand with her between the sheets. He made Matt look like an amateur . . .

At Albacore Street, Dan and Nick had been affectionately known as Stalin and Trotsky. They had kept in touch after graduation, until the miners' strike created an ideological rift between them. Nick had defended to the hilt Scargill's refusal to hold a secret ballot, Dan had seen it as a catastrophic tactical error that split the union and doomed the strike to failure. He broke with the SWP and, under Stella's influence, joined Labour, just as a new pragmatism was beginning to stir in its ranks. Stella, meanwhile, had got herself elected shop steward in the branch of Marks & Spencer where, under her mother's influence, she had reluctantly taken a job. Bliss was it in that dawn to be alive.

She picked up the phone and tried to round up an emergency babysitter. Dan's mother would have loved to help, but she was volunteering in the hospice. Old NCT pal Morag was all set to bring her toddler over for the morning until Stella mentioned chicken pox, when the offer was swiftly withdrawn. In the end she resorted to ringing Barbara next door, who was only too happy to oblige – after she'd had her facial at ten thirty. Stella calculated that with a fair wind and the full co-operation of London Transport, she might just make her meeting. She accepted Barbara's offer gratefully and went to check on Amber, who had drifted into a feverish sleep. Stella turned back the duvet and smoothed the hair tenderly away from her daughter's clammy forehead, before tiptoeing downstairs again. She now found herself in the unusual position of having time on her hands. She had not expected to be off this morning, so had left all her papers at work. There seemed to be nothing else for it but to take a leaf out of Barbara's book. She made herself a coffee, plumped herself down on the Laura Ashley chesterfield and turned on daytime telly.

'Next, we meet the man who donated a kidney to save the life of his wife's lover . . .' Christ, it was *her*; coiffed to within an inch of her life; ditsy smile; perky, dumbed-down demeanour. You'd never have known she had a first in Philosophy. Stella picked up the remote to zap her away again, but found herself mesmerised. The last time she'd been eyeball to eyeball with those improbably blue peepers had been on the picket line at TV-am in 1987. She'd never forget it.

Stella was a communications officer for the ACTT by then. She hadn't lasted long at Marks and Sparks. Making sure the freezers were full in the food hall was never going to compete with manning the barricades in the class war. Her mother was disappointed to see her jeopardise a nice steady career for a job as a rabble-rouser, but her dad was all for it. You didn't just lie down and let big business walk all over you, they agreed; you put up a fight. So when TV-am sacked 229 technicians for striking over pay and conditions, it was time for the ACTT to prove its mettle. Fleet Street was finished by then, and Eddie Shah had given the National Graphical Association a bloody nose, but the TV technicians hadn't yet faced their Waterloo. Who was to say they weren't in with a shout? What could the management do? Reinstate the test card?

It turned out they had something else up their sleeves.

It was still dark and freezing cold when she'd turned up at Camden Lock, bristling with self-importance in her high-visibility steward's tabard. The building looked like a toy fort with its supposedly witty eggcup castellation – it certainly came under siege that day. Stella warmed herself for a while around the pickets' brazier, exchanging a few pleasantries with the regional organiser, then moving away tactfully when she sensed she was cramping their style. Her instructions had been to monitor the situation and try to make sure that any confrontation between strikers and scabs was defused before it could turn violent, but so far only a handful of technicians had attempted to pass the cordon, provoking scuffles and the odd jeer but not requiring Stella's intervention. Several TV news crews were hanging around, but they seemed uninterested in the run-of-the-mill blacklegs. There was a rumour afoot that the suits were going to try to run the show themselves. Stella had just bought herself some breakfast from a nearby van and had an egg and bacon bap in one hand and a cup of tea in the other when a voice shouted, 'Here they come!' Before she knew it, she was being propelled forward by a surge of pickets and her tea had deposited itself all over the turquoise suit of a woman who had just emerged from a sleek Rover.

'Get out of my way!' the woman shouted, her hysteria out of all proportion to the level of threat. She stared wildly into Stella's face, her eyes so close that Stella could see the cobalt eyeliner on her inner rim.

'Nell!' Stella's face broke into a smile of genuine pleasure, before her brain had computed the meaning of their encounter. It was definitely her, she'd have recognised that retroussé nose anywhere, and those intense blue eyes. And yet in every other respect Nell had been made anew. Her long straight hair had been dyed, permed and teased into a doll-like wig, her pale, freckled skin was caked in foundation, her hippy clothes replaced with shoulder pads that could take your eye out.

Nell looked back at her, first with recognition, then confusion, and finally embarrassment. 'Excuse me,' she said, and pushed her way past.

'You're not going in there, are you?' Stella clutched desperately at her sleeve. 'Nell, it's me, Stella. It's a picket line. You don't cross a . . .' But Nell had swept on with her flunky and Stella was swallowed back into the seething mass of pickets, scarcely able to believe that the encounter had really happened.

Yet here, years later, was the proof that it had. Nell's image had softened a little since then, to go with the lime-green sofa and the orange gerberas, but otherwise she looked much the same. She had been promoted from the news desk and was now anchoring the whole show, along-side a smarmy bloke in a coloured V-neck. Otherwise not much had changed. For once you were a television person-ality, what did change? Barges might chug down the Thames through the picture window behind your left shoulder; police helicopters might throb in the skies, causing the soundman a headache; but the world went on out there while you stayed cosy and warm in your bubble. Stella watched Nell emoting for England, pursing her lips, furrowing her brow, crying crocodile tears over the self-lessness of the poor stooge who'd just spilled his guts for the cameras, and shook her head.

The conventional wisdom was that Nell's 'accident' had changed her. You didn't spend ten days in a coma and wake up unscathed. No wonder, it was felt, she had turned into this hard-faced, go-getting media monster. No wonder she had cut herself off with ruthless efficiency from her past life (though she continued to exchange Christmas cards with Max; no one could quite bear to dump Max). But what struck Stella, comparing the Nell on her TV screen to the sweet-faced hippy of yore, was that, despite outward appearances, she hadn't really changed at all. She had always had an alarming solipsism and an uncanny knack of turning life's vicissitudes to her advantage. She had always nodded and smiled in all the right places. She had always allowed you to think that you were on her wavelength, and then said or done something that made you realise she was actually on another planet. And yet . . . and yet . . . underneath it all there was a sweetness, a vulnerability that made you want to give her just one more chance.

Stella was jolted out of her reverie by a persistent high-pitched bleeping sound. Dan must have left his pager behind. She rummaged under cushions to no avail, then she hurried out into the hall, but by the time she had been through the pockets of his various coats, it had stopped. Served him right if he'd missed a call from Number Ten, she caught herself thinking; he shouldn't have been so quick to run away from his domestic responsibilities. No sooner had she sat back down in front of *The Morning Show*, than the phone rang.

'Seven nine six three.'

'Stella?' said the voice at the other end. 'Hi, what are you doing home?'

'Brid, hi. Amber's off sick. I drew the short straw. Why are you ringing me if you thought I wasn't here?'

'Oh, er . . . just checking what time you want us on Saturday.'

'About eight, I suppose. But that still doesn't—'

'Have you had yours yet?' interrupted Bridget eagerly.

'My what?'

'Your invitation to Nell Carpenter's nuptials?'

'You're kidding. That's spooky. I'm watching her now on *The Morning Show*. I thought she was married to her career.'

'Oh, it's a great career move.'

'Why, who's she marrying?' Stella asked.

'Des Percival.'

'But he's *ancient*. What on earth can she be thinking?'

'Well, let me see . . . TV presenter marries multi-millionaire media mogul. Gosh, you know, I can't imagine . . . I tell you what, though, it'll be a hell of a do. I must say, now I've got my head round the idea, I'm quite looking forward to it. Posh frock. Champagne by the bucketful. Chance to catch up with everybody. Max is going with her new woman, apparently, and she thinks Vinnie might even come. It's not to be missed, Stell. Definitely hatchet-burying time.'

'She won't invite *me*. Not if she's got any shame.' Stella tried to sound indignant, but she actually felt a little left out. 'Not that I'd dream of going.'

'Oh, don't be ridiculous. Nobody takes that stuff seriously any more. If Neil Kinnock can go, I reckon you can.'

'Who says Kinnock's going?'

'Oh, I . . . heard a rumour. It's not just him, though, loads of big names'll be there. Rupert Murdoch, Harold Evans, Ted Turner.'

'All men, I notice. Since when were you in thrall to the patriarchy?'

'Oh come on, Stell. Get off your soap box for a minute and admit you're impressed.'

'Impressed or not, I haven't had an invite—'

'Listen, I'm going to have to go. My boss is giving me the evil eye. I'll see you on Saturday. And if you haven't had your invite by then, I'm going to ring her.'

'Don't you d—' But Bridget had gone. Stella returned, with renewed curiosity, to *The Morning Show* where Nell was now helping the resident chef to ring the changes with sun-dried tomatoes.

Hackney

'Don't wear those trousers. They look cheap,' Bridget said.

'They were cheap,' said Nigel cheerfully. 'Ten pounds ninety-nine Mr Byrite. I thought you said it was just us going.'

'Yeah, us, Stella and Dan.'

'Well, they won't mind.'

'*I* mind,' Bridget snapped. She closed her eyes briefly. She sounded like her mother. 'What I mean is,' she went on, 'I like you so much better in your chinos. Why don't you wear your chinos with a T-shirt and a V-neck over the top?'

Nigel shrugged. 'Whatever turns you on.' If only, Bridget thought.

He was a lovely guy. Everybody said it. 'Great bloke, Nige,' they said. And they were right. He was clever; easy-going; not drop-dead gorgeous, but by no means unattractive – he had a bit of the Old English Sheepdog about him, shambling, scruffy, lovable. It was what had first attracted Bridget to him; it was what she had needed after the string of bastards she had dated since leaving university. Steve Pinder had been the blueprint, but there had been no shortage of imitators. Lean, mean heartbreak machines. They were nearly always creative types, film buffs, artists, musicians. They would pursue her madly at first, intrigued by her air of independence and her slightly off-beat style; but the minute she let her guard down, they would go all chilly and unavailable, citing deadlines, psychological breakdown, problems in the band. At one stage she thought of having some business cards printed with the slogan 'It's not me, it's you' so that she could hand them out on first dates.

Nigel had been the antidote to all that, the bridge over her troubled water. Meeting Nigel had been like coming home; better than coming home actually, because Bridget had never been happy at home, but she was happy with Nige. They bought a first-floor flat in Stoke Newington for £34,000 and furnished it with it second-hand finds from Portobello. There were Hitchock film posters on the walls; brightly coloured kilims on the floors, a mismatched selection of 1930s china in the cupboards. By day, they did valuable work in a small housing association in Islington, she in research, he in finance; by night they went to subtitled films at the Rio in Dalston or ate cheap curries on Brick Lane; then they made love under their Habitat duvet. It felt cosy and safe. The gnawing fear in her belly was gone. So, it seemed, was her ability to reach orgasm. It didn't really bother her at first; she could sort herself out after Nigel had fallen asleep. But it bothered him. He was forever wanting to slow things down, light candles, massage the soles of her feet. It got on her nerves.

'Nice dress,' Nigel said. 'Is it new?'

'No,' Bridget lied. She had bought it from French Connection in her lunch hour.

'Sexy.' Nigel came up behind her and folded his arms around her waist. She could feel his warm breath on her neck. She thought if he didn't move soon she might scream.

'Thanks,' she said. She gave him a chaste kiss on the lips and extricated herself from his embrace. 'I'll be a few minutes putting my face on,' she added, 'can you sort out a bottle of wine to take? I think a red would be best. Preferably not Chilean.'

'Yes, ma'am!' He saluted and left the room.

Bridget busied herself at the dressing table. She hadn't just bought the dress. She had bought new eyeliner and lipstick as well; not to mention underwear. Though quite why she was wearing it tonight, she didn't know. There was no chance of anything happening; far too dangerous. And the worst of it was, when they got back, after a couple of bottles of Merlot and a spliff, Nigel would think it was for him. She smiled at herself ruefully in the mirror. She could remember having a dingdong row with Stella once about sexy underwear. They had just got back from picketing the Duke of York's cinema in Brighton because it was showing *The Postman Always Rings Twice* – the remake with Jessica Lange and Jack Nicholson. None of them had seen it, but it was supposed to have a dodgy scene in it, where Nicholson's character raped Lange's and she enjoyed it, and that was reason enough for all the Albacore Street women to pile down there and shout at the punters until they were hoarse. It was a good laugh, but then when she and Stell were getting ready for bed, later, they had started discussing the difference between eroticism and exploitation. Stella had said, a little shame-faced, that she thought it was OK to wear sexy stuff in bed, provided you really loved each other and it was a relationship of equals. Bridget had got very indignant and accused her of colluding in her own oppression. At the time, the only sexy lingerie Bridget had come across was the sleazy Ann Summers stuff, rather than the infinitely subtler Charnos combo she was wearing this evening, but she still recognised when she was skating on thin ice.

'Come in, come in,' Dan said jovially. He embraced Nigel in a gruff, mannish way and kissed Bridget fondly on both cheeks.

'Hello,' she mumbled, staring at his Converses like a love-struck teenager. She would have to do better than this.

'Stella's in the kitchen massacring the starter,' said Dan casually. 'Come on through.' He ushered them past the sitting room, where Amber was watching *Blind Date*. Bridget stuck her head around the door.

'Hello, cutie pie. How's my favourite . . . ? Oh, you poor thing, you're covered.' Amber was a mass of chicken pox; her chocolate-box features covered in blisters.

'It's really, really itchy,' grimaced Amber, 'but Mummy

says if I scratch I'll be scarred for life and I won't be able to model.'

'*Does* she indeed?' laughed Bridget. 'I shall have to go and ask her about that.

'So you're putting Amber up for child modelling now, are you?' she said, walking into the kitchen with a mischievous grin.

'Hi, Brid.' Stella went over and embraced her warmly. 'It's just this week's fad,' she said. 'Last week she wanted to be a ballerina. I just thought it might stop her scratching her spots. Talking of models, you look amazing. She looks amazing, doesn't she, Dan?'

Bridget blushed and took a glug of the wine that Stella had poured for her.

'Always does,' said Dan in the sort of gentlemanly tone that he might have used to a maiden aunt. God he was good, Bridget thought. No wonder he was in politics. You'd never have known that two days before they'd been in a hotel in Bayswater, her ankles wrapped around his neck, him thrusting into her until the headboard twanged.

'I feel really fat,' she said lamely. 'What are we having? Ooh, quiche, lovely.'

'Individual goat's cheese tarts actually,' corrected Stella, wiping a floury finger across her cheek, 'only I don't know if I've caramelised the onions properly.'

'I'd say you'd incinerated them, judging by the smell,' grinned Dan.

'I'm sure they'll be delicious,' said Nigel.

They took their seats around the kitchen table. The men

talked football and politics. Bridget and Stella discussed work. Once they had made inroads into the first bottle of wine and Stella had served the starter, everyone began to relax. The conversation broadened out into a general discussion about what they had all been doing in the few weeks since they had last got together, and ended up dwelling for far too long, in Bridget's opinion, on whether David Lynch had a plot in mind for *Twin Peaks*, or whether he was just winging it. She opted out early, sat back in her chair and watched Dan surreptitiously over the rim of her wine glass. She didn't dare stare for too long, not only in case she was rumbled, but also because the sight of him made her breathless. She wondered, not for the first time, what might have happened if she had noticed how attractive he was when they were still at university. She could see now that Dan was one of those men who grow into themselves as they age. He had been gangling and ill at ease as a student, with bad skin and a political conviction that had come across as aggression; an all-round eruption of a boy. But in maturity he had grown in confidence and developed a gaunt, vulpine grace. He had found his milieu and it suited him. Nige, on the other hand, had been his ideal self when she had first met him at twenty-five – dog-like, both in his demeanour and his devotion to her. He would only go downhill from now. He might still have an unruly mop of hair, but she could already see exactly where it would eventually recede, as well as precisely how his open, attractive face would grow slack and jowly.

The conversation had moved on to DIY and when Stella dragged Nigel off, between courses, to demonstrate the power shower they had recently had installed, Bridget found herself alone with Dan. A brooding silence prevailed for several moments, then he spoke, his voice low, conspiratorial.

'This is doing my head in.'

'I know.'

'I don't think you do, or you'd have made some excuse.'

'You mean not come? Wouldn't that just look suspicious?'

He shrugged. 'I don't know, but this is awful.'

Bridget sighed. He reached across and stroked her wrist. Her stomach plummeted like a lift in freefall.

'I don't want to be doing this,' he said, his eyes locked on hers. She felt a spasm of fear. 'I mean, I *do*. God, I so do. But you being here, with Amber next door in her PJs and Nigel and Stella discussing the bloody *plumbing*, and all the time I'm thinking about what I'd like to be doing to you. It's just . . . wrong.'

'You don't have to tell me, Dan. She's my best friend. I never meant for this . . . It's not as though we went looking for it, is it? We fought it hard enough . . .'

And they had. A full six months had elapsed between the spark igniting between them and the full-blown conflagration. During that time, they had done everything they could to stamp it out. They'd all been on holiday together in Dorset when it started. Stella had taken Amber horse riding and Nigel was sleeping off a hangover. Dan and Bridget had decided to go for a jog to clear their heads. They had left the house in unsuitable footwear and a slightly hysterical mood of self-mockery, neither of them really having much of a clue. The first slight incline left them doubled up and gasping for breath – too winded even to laugh at themselves, so they had walked after that and then stopped to admire the view. Nothing had happened – no stolen kiss, no fumble in the bracken; only a look that passed between them and changed everything. Afterwards the conversation had become suddenly stilted and fraught with meaning at the same time. They had tried to pretend nothing had happened, but denying it had only made it worse; more dangerous. There had been agonising moments along the way: a kiss under the mistletoe that had been too chaste for credibility; an awkward arm's-length slow dance at a party (because Stella was dancing with Nigel and it would have looked funny not to). Then one day she had bumped into him at the opening of a new arts and media centre in Islington. The Chardonnay had been flowing and, before they knew it, they had slipped away from the throng and were writhing around on the floor of its state-of-the-art, fully sound-proofed recording studio, while the great and the good swapped business cards outside. After that, they had met weekly, or fort-nightly, during their lunch hours or after work. It had almost become routine – compartmentalised. Some days she even forgot to feel bad about it. Until they all got together, like this . . .

'Well, next time I'll make an excuse, then,' murmured Bridget miserably, 'but I can't not see Stella, can I?'

'I'm not asking you to boycott Stella, obviously. I'm

just saying I can't do this *Thirtysomething* thing where we all hang out on a Saturday night.'

'No, I know what you mean. It's a mess.' Bridget returned his haunted look, but no sooner had their eyes met again than his lips were on hers and she was half rising out of her seat to return his kiss. For a few precious seconds, nothing else mattered but the intoxicating chemical rush. He pulled her clumsily towards him, bumping her leg against the edge of the table. His hands were just beginning to find their way down over her hips, swirling the silk of her dress against her thigh, when the power shower, which had been thrumming in the new wet room above their heads, abruptly stopped. They leaped guiltily apart and sat back down. Footsteps and laughter could be heard on the stairs. Dan picked up the wine bottle and refilled Bridget's empty glass, picking up as he did so the tail end of some imaginary anecdote.

'. . . and do you know what he had the cheek to say to me?'

'What?' Bridget pressed the backs of her hands against her hot cheeks.

'He said if I wanted to stick to my principles, I shouldn't have gone into politics!'

'Sounds about right to me,' said Stella, walking in and laying a friendly hand on Bridget's shoulder. 'Is he boring you senseless with shop talk? I've told you about that, haven't I, Daniel? By the way' – she waved a thick cream envelope in front of Bridget – 'my invitation came.'

'You see, I *knew* you'd be on the guest list. You *will*

come, won't you? Imagine: an Albacore Street reunion, ten years on. We'll all get to meet each other's other halves and . . .' She caught Dan glowering at her. '. . . everything,' she finished lamely.

'Well, I don't know. I'm torn,' Stella said. 'It would feel like I was condoning Nell's behaviour. I know it was a long time ago, but she crossed a picket line. And not just any picket line, *my* picket line.'

'Frankly, I'm surprised you'd even consider it,' said Dan.

'Really?' Stella furrowed her brow. 'I thought you'd say forgive and forget. You're usually such a pragmatist. It's going to be full of movers and shakers – Kinnock might even be there. It could be good for your career, Dan.'

'Oh, I can get Kinnock's ear any time, if I need to,' said Dan, 'I don't need to go to some rarefied media wedding. It sounds fantastically boring, if you ask me.'

'Personally, I'd jump at the chance,' put in Nigel, ever cheerful, ever ingenuous. 'Not for the big wigs, but just to meet the famous Albacore Street women. The way Bridget talks about it makes it sound like Woodstock and the Algonquin Round Table rolled into one.'

Stella laughed. 'Blimey, that's going some,' she said. 'I mean, don't get me wrong, it was good. One of the best times of my life, actually, looking back . . .'

'It was *fantastic*,' agreed Bridget. 'I've never talked so long or stayed up so late or laughed so much.'

'And we danced sometimes . . . do you remember, Stell? When Maxine used to DJ and we boogied so hard we scratched half her singles.'

'Served her right for owning the Bee Gees,' said Stella. 'God, it was fun though.' Her eyes misted over. 'Nothing's ever quite lived up to it . . .'

'Thanks a lot,' said Dan.

'Oh, I don't mean you, sweetheart. Or this . . .' She waved a complacent hand to indicate domestic bliss and in a flash all Bridget's goodwill evaporated and she wanted to slap her. 'But it was something special, wasn't it, Brid?'

'Yes.' She glanced at Dan. 'I'm not sure we could ever recreate it, though, Stell. I mean, don't get me wrong, I would *love* you to come to the wedding, but it would be a real shame if it didn't live up to your expectations.'

Everyone's eyes were on Stella. 'It *would* . . .' she said, waving the thick envelope back and forth playfully so that it sent a gust of chilly air across the table. 'But you know what? In the interests of long-lost friendship and sheer nosiness, I'm going to take the risk.'

Chelsea Harbour

Nell walked into her closet and the concealed strip lighting flickered on, illuminating rail upon rail of suits, dresses and coats. She shucked off her silk kimono and gave herself a long appraising look in the floor-to-ceiling mirror. Her face, free of make-up, looked small and fragile, her fair eyebrows and gingery lashes barely visible. Her slender shoulders, gently curving tummy and slightly low-slung hips reminded her of a Kewpie doll. She traced her finger down the length of the sunken yellow groove that ran, like a dried-out riverbed, from hip to knee. This scar, she was stuck with. The one inside, she liked to think, had healed.

From the moment she had opened her eyes and blinked up at the duck-egg-blue ceiling of the high dependency unit at Berkshire Royal Infirmary, she had seen the future with dazzling clarity, and the future was work. Looking back, she sometimes wondered whether she had really been in a coma at all, as everyone insisted, or residing in some Platonic parallel universe. Had she glimpsed her ideal self? That sometimes seemed like the most rational explanation for the conviction with which she came to and announced that she needed her books.

Her body was a battlefield of bed sores and wasted muscles. Her leg had been reconstructed around a titanium plate. She would walk with a limp for the rest of her life, but her mind was as sharp as a cheese wire. The university had been co-operative. She had received transcripts of all the lectures she had missed and a special dispensation entitling her to postal library loans. She was given an extra six weeks to hand in her thesis on Cartesian Dualism, which, in the end she didn't need. She got the highest first of her year. Professor Jenner had recommended that she dispense with a masters and go straight for her doctorate, but at the last moment funding had been withdrawn. She was told that if she deferred for a year (by which time Mike O'Meara would, conveniently, be on sabbatical), she would be assured of a fully funded place. They needn't have worried. She was completely over Mike. She could see her obsession now for what it had been – an Oedipal infatuation; an attempt, simultaneously to replace her absent father and atone for Richard's suicide, for which she still felt culpable.

'Nell?' Desmond's voice called from the adjacent bathroom. She could hear the impatience in his tone, above the gushing taps and the background inanity of Radio 2.

'Coming,' she called back. She had barely scrambled into her underwear when his call came again. It was asking for trouble to keep him waiting. She hurried through.

'What is *with* this . . . ?' He sounded exasperated. 'Sort it out, can you?' He waved a can of shaving foam at her. He was standing in front of the wide, glass basin with a towel round his waist, one side of his face lathered up, his lean, upright frame showing his age only in the slightly yellowish tinge of the flesh and the springiness of the white hairs on his back.

'Sort what out?' Nell looked blankly at the can of foam.

'It's hissing at me. I can't get the bloody stuff out,' he said, for all the world as useless as a toddler, but much, much angrier. Nell shook it.

'It's empty, darling,' she said.

'It can't be. I only started it a couple of days ago. Give it to me.' He snatched the can back from her and forced the aerosol button down so hard that it broke off and pinged across the bathroom. Des brought his fist down hard on the glass sink-surround and Nell flinched.

'I'll get you another one,' she said, clicking open a cupboard and deftly searching among the piles of fluffy flannels and expensive unguents. Panic rose in her as she realised that she wasn't going to find one. As she squatted down awkwardly to rummage through the lower shelves, she struggled to keep her bad leg from splaying awkwardly, for she knew from experience that that would enrage him still further.

'Brilliant!' he shouted. 'I've got a board meeting starting in forty fucking minutes and I look like a fucking caveman. It's not like you had to go shopping yourself, is it? You only had to tell the fucking help.' He stepped towards her, his fist clenched, and she felt an adrenalin rush of fear and excitement. His voice dropped to a menacing murmur, 'But I suppose you think you're too good for that, do you? Too good to keep house? Too fucking clever to be a proper woman?' He loomed over her and as Nell shrank back, she was acutely aware of the slice of blue-green glass just inches from the back of her head. If he should lose it now . . .

'I'm sorry, Des, I really am . . .' she panted. To look him in the eye was, she knew, a calculated risk. She parted her knees a fraction further so that he could glimpse the crotch of her skimpy pants, jutted her lip in a moue of contrition and lifted her gaze . . .

'Get up you silly cunt,' he said, his voice avuncular now, indulgent. Suddenly it was a game again. Clumsily she hauled herself to her feet and they stood face to face. Nell put her hand on his cheek and started to spread the excessive amounts of shaving foam that he had applied to the left side of his face gently around to the right. 'You see,' she murmured gently, 'there's plenty here. You use too much.'

He jutted his jaw and she braced herself, but then his face broke into a grudging smile. 'Well, I'm very fucking hairy,' he said. Relief mingled with disappointment.

'There you go,' she said when his face was fully foamed. She squeezed his cheeks together affectionately and pouted her lips at him in a cartoon kiss.

'Not so fast . . .' he said as she made to leave the room.

'What?'

'Finish me off,' he said, closing the toilet lid and sitting down.

'I beg your pardon?' Nell feigned a Lolita-like coyness.

'Shave me!' he said.

'But . . . Mac will be here any minute,' protested Nell uncertainly.

He handed her the razor. 'Do it!'

'It won't look good if I'm late for your flagship show.'

'I don't give a fuck,' he growled. 'They can wait for you. Go on. Do it for Daddy.'

Nell glided the razor as smoothly as she could over her fiancé's thick weekend stubble. She gasped in shock as Des grabbed her buttocks in his big hands, but she didn't flinch. Now began a battle of wills, his hands exploring her flesh through the thin fabric of her underwear, her hand remaining steady, her eye focused, aware that if she so much as nicked the skin, he would have his revenge. He pummelled and probed; she kept her touch surgeon-steady, until, with her task almost done, she allowed her hand to slip and a bead of blood bloomed near Des's right earlobe. He met her eye and, as he winced in pain, she glimpsed triumph in his eyes.

He left for work, grimly smiling, a shred of tissue covering his cut. She left twenty-five minutes late, in her trainers and dressing gown, her suit slung over her arm; her patent shoes dangling from her middle finger.

'You look like the cat that got the cream,' said Mac, meeting her eye in the rear-view mirror.

'Yup!' She grinned and settled back into the comfy leather seat, wincing slightly as she crossed her legs.

Mac had been her driver for years now. He'd seen her stressed out before a tricky interview and blissed out afterwards; he'd seen her lucid on coke and incoherent on alcohol; he'd seen her dolled up to the nines and bedraggled the morning after. And gent that he was, he pretended he hadn't seen any of it. Nell sometimes thought he was the only person in her new life that she really liked. He had earned his spurs that first morning in 1987 when he had picked her up from her Putney flat-share to drive her to TV-am. She had barely noticed him until they got to Euston, when she had looked up from her script and caught his eye in the mirror.

'Nervous?' he'd said.

She'd nodded.

'You'll be fine,' he'd said, 'I can feel it in my water.' And she'd believed him.

Then they'd reached Camden and she'd realised that the 'bit of a protest' the producer had warned her about was in fact a mass picket.

'Greedy beggars,' Mac had muttered, 'striking for overtime when there's all them unemployed.' Nell could have kissed him. With a phrase, he had turned her from blackleg to freedom fighter; his *Daily Mail* pieties the perfect salve for her troubled conscience. He'd pulled up outside, turned round and winked, and before she'd known it a private security guard was bustling her out of the back of the Rover and past a wall of hostility.

'Scab!'

'Scab!'

'Scabby bitch!'

'Shame!'

The taunts had come thick and fast. She had felt the seethe of the crowd, seen flashing blue lights and heard the static from police intercoms. She had staggered forward, head swimming, heart thumping. Her knees began to buckle, like the last time; just as at Greenham.

'Get out of my way!' she had shouted shrilly, but the sound had seemed to come from somewhere else. Then a flash of searing heat on her arm had brought her back. She'd looked uncomprehendingly at the dark stain spreading on her turquoise sleeve and then indignantly into the face of the silly bitch who'd thrown hot tea at her. 'Nell!' Nell had stared at her assailant, confused. For a split second she'd almost smiled back, happy to see a friendly face among the hostile ones. But there was the plastic cup in Stella's hand and here was the scald on Nell's wrist and those two things didn't add up to friendship at all. Not in Nell's book.

'Excuse me!' She'd barged past, not seeing; not wanting to see.

'You're not going in there, are you?' Stella had tugged at her sleeve. 'Nell, it's me, Stella. It's a picket line. You don't cross a—' But Nell didn't care. If this was how pickets behaved – how *friends* behaved – Nell was happy to defy them. She'd had enough of all the hypocrites: the hippies who preached peace and love, but spread misery and chaos; the lefties who were for the underdog, but acted like yobs. She fought her way up the steps, through the glass doors, into the comfort of the lobby, with its chrome and glass and its shiny lift, waiting to take her onwards and upwards.

The rest, as they say, had been history. The informal camaraderie of those strike-hit broadcasts, with executives operating the cameras and wardrobe working the autocue, had flattered Nell's breezy off-the-cuff style. She may have started off a minor player, but the camera loved her and her handovers from the news desk were characterised by a wit and irreverence that the anchors had trouble matching. As Des had said to her, when he took her out to dinner to break the news of her promotion, she was the best thing to happen to TV-am since Roland Rat.

When Nell got to the studio, the director was tearing his hair out. They were supposed to have done a pre-recorded gardening spot on the roof terrace and now there wasn't time. Unable to let rip at Nell because of her lofty connections, he took out his annoyance on her co-presenter, Mark, who, Nell knew, would exact his own subtle revenge as soon as they went on air. To make matters worse, make-up discovered a lurid bruise on Nell's neck that no amount of Max Factor would hide, and she had to put on a Hermès scarf, which ruined the line of her suit. Finally, the running order having been rejigged so that the missing gardening spot could go out live at the end of the programme, she and Mark were left bantering inanely for two whole minutes while that day's human-interest guest was prepped for the show; but he still came on looking, as far as Nell could tell, several sandwiches short of the full picnic.

'Welcome back.' Nell put on her 'serious' face and with an encouraging smile to their guest: 'And thank you, Clive, for agreeing to share your story with us. I know it can't be easy for you.'

On the contrary, Clive appeared to be raring to go.

'So,' Mark purred. 'Let's go back three and a half years to when you thought you were in a happy, monogamous marriage.'

'I didn't *think* I was happily married,' said Clive. 'I was. Still am, as it happens.'

'That is incredible.' Mark shook his head, with an expression that mingled pity and admiration.

Nell cut in: 'But then you discovered something that shattered your world, didn't you, Clive?'

Clive looked slightly perplexed for a moment. 'Oh I did, aye,' he said.

'Can you tell us what that was?'

Clive coughed awkwardly. 'Well, I found out my Audrey was seeing someone.'

'How *did* you find out?' Mark leaned forward almost imperceptibly.

'It were her moods. She got very withdrawn and depressed. And she was weepy. It's not like Audrey to be weepy – she's the life and soul, normally.' He smiled fondly. 'In the end I got it out of her.'

'She'd been having an affair...' Mark's voice dripped sympathy.

'Aye, she had. But it weren't just that. He was very sick. That's how they'd got together. She's a nurse, you see.'

'Audrey's lover, Peter, had been on dialysis for a number of years,' Nell explained for the viewers' benefit.

'And that's where you came in,' Mark said. 'Not that you weren't in already, so to speak, being Audrey's husband.' Nell rolled her eyes off-camera.

'If Peter didn't find a kidney donor,' she interrupted, 'within the year, he'd be . . .'

'Dead, aye,' supplied Clive baldly.

'So, instead of letting nature take its course,' Nell went on, 'which is what many of us mere mortals might have done under the circumstances, you decided to do something very extraordinary and selfless indeed, didn't you, Clive?'

Clive looked at her blankly, then cottoned on. 'Er yes, that's right. Well, I couldn't bear to see the wife so upset, so I said if we were a match, like, he could have one of mine.'

Nell laughed her tinkly 'how adorable' laugh and said in mock reproach, 'You say that as if you were offering him your second-best lawnmower, Clive, but let's get this clear, you were volunteering to undergo a life-threatening operation to donate one of your own kidneys to your wife's . . .' And now she faltered. She found herself suddenly hoarse; the bridge of her nose was prickling. ' . . . to your own wife's lover.' She threw Mark a pleading look, hoping he'd take over, but he didn't seem to notice. Nell pressed on, her voice cracking: 'I'm sure I'm not alone in thinking that that's rather unusual. Rather *exceptional*. Can . . . you . . . explain . . . why you did it?'

Clive shrugged matter-of-factly. 'I love 'er,' he said. The camera zoomed in on Clive's face, but to the irritation of the director, he was dry-eyed. Nell's tears on the other hand were brimming over.

She was at a loss to know why exactly she was crying, but now that she'd started, she couldn't stop. The cameraman caught on quickly and her red-rimmed eyes and quivering lip could soon be seen in lurid close-up the length and breadth of the country.

'I suppose that's almost the definition of unconditional love, isn't it?' Mark said gently. 'It's the sort of love we expect between a mother and child; the sort of love we all aspire to in our relationships . . . but which few of us actually *achieve*.' Nell shuddered with pent-up emotion.

'Attagirl, Nell, keep 'em coming,' the director murmured into her earpiece.

'Well, I don't know about that,' Clive was saying. 'I just thought, this way, there was a chance she'd be happy again. I know there's some men'd think it's not manly; that I should have punched his lights out, but I'm not a violent person. I were upset, don't get me wrong. It weren't a decision I took lightly, but I knew if I were a biological match and I just, you know, let him *go*, the wife'd never get over it. And I'd never forgive meself. Not if he died, like.'

By now Nell was having trouble keeping herself together.
Mark leaned forward intimately. 'And what's the situation between you and Audrey now, Clive?'

'We're still man and wife,' he said, a little defensively. 'Still the best of friends an' all.'

'And er . . . Audrey and Peter?'

'They packed it in.'

'Conscience got the better of him, did it? Would have been a bit off-colour, really, if he'd used his new-found vim and vigour to, you know . . .' Mark mugged shamelessly to camera.

'Aye,' muttered Clive, by now looking thoroughly miserable.

'So,' Mark summed up as the clock on the monitor counted down to the advert break, 'Clive's selfless gesture saved his marriage. I just love a happy ending, don't you, Nell . . . Nell?' He turned towards her and feigned surprise at her dishevelled state. 'Oh dear, it seems to have touched a nerve. You old softy you.' He clamped a comradely arm around Nell's shoulders and looked back to camera. 'After the break, if Nell's up to it, it's over to *The Morning Show* kitchen, where we'll be finding out why Mediterranean cookery is so much better for our health. Don't go away.'

En route to the post-show meeting, Nell ducked into the Ladies to freshen up. She still felt raw from the Clive and Audrey débâcle. By the time she walked into the conference room, the air was thick with recrimination. A round of coffees and a plate of pastries stood untouched as just about everyone from the director to the runners attempted to pass the buck for the fiasco that had been today's show.

'Glad you could join us,' said the producer tartly as Nell muttered an apology.

'Late again, *quelle surprise*,' murmured Mark under his breath as she sat down.

'We were just trying to get to the bottom of what went wrong in the kitchen. That tomato tart looked like an abortion!'

'Tasted like one too,' put in Mark feelingly. 'I wouldn't have given it to my dog.'

'It was supposed to cook for an hour, that's why,' protested Vernon, *The Morning Show* chef, 'but if you remember, we were shunted up the schedule without a by-your-leave. There was nothing I could do. I'm a chef, not a bloody Time Lord . . .'

Nell had just opened her mouth to take the blame, when Des burst in.

'What the fuck was that?' he said, standing, arms akimbo, in the doorway. Everyone, including Nell, shrank down slightly in his or her seat.

'The show, you mean?' asked the producer with a nervous smile.

'Show? Shambles more like!' bawled Des. 'I've seen headless chickens with more sense of purpose than you lot. It was an embarrassment.'

'I concede,' piped up the director, 'that we got off to a shaky start. We had a few er . . .' He glanced pointedly at Nell. ' . . . timing issues, but I felt that by the second commercial break we were back on top of things, thanks to the consummate professionalism of—'

'Professionalism?' roared Des. 'Don't make me laugh. Sue Lawley reading the news while Nicholas Witchell wrestled a lesbian under her desk, *that* was professionalism. With the honourable exception of my fiancée here' – he put his hand on Nell's shoulder and the hairs stood up on the back of her neck – 'you lot were about as professional as Kettering fucking United! Get it together, or I'll terminate your contracts and replace you with Bungle and fucking Zippy!' And with that he slammed out of the room again.

There was a lengthy pause, and then the director took a deep breath. 'Croissant anyone?' he said.

By the time the platter made its way round to Nell, there was nothing left but a morsel of stale vanilla Danish, but she had lost her appetite anyway.

St Bride's Fleet Street

On the day of Nell's wedding, Maxine wore an aubergine trouser suit over a lime-green and aubergine striped shirt. She had had her hair restyled for the occasion in a tousled auburn crop. The finishing touch was a pink silk corsage, which perfectly matched the shade of Shona's dress.

Stella bought two new outfits for the wedding and ended up wearing neither of them. After an hour of twirling and bottom-lip biting in front of the wardrobe mirror, she dumped them both in favour of a tea dress and pashmina combo that had seen her through three previous dos.

Bridget was having a crisis of conscience over Dan. Determined to keep him at arm's length on the day, she chose a demure drop-waisted dress with nautical over-tones, an oversized blazer and low-heeled, round-toed shoes. A sleek, fringed bob completed the austere look. She was dismayed (but perhaps not to her very core) when Nigel told her she looked like a sexy schoolgirl and suggested they keep the taxi driver waiting for five minutes. They did not.

Vinnie, as always, dressed for herself, in a figure-hugging black jersey dress, emerald-green fishnets and a matching pillbox hat, complete with veil. She was still blonde, though not quite such an improbable shade as in her student days. The hat disguised the fact that her roots hadn't been re-touched for a while, the veil concealed the dark circles under her eyes and the bias cut of her charity-shop dress camouflaged the extra inches on her hips.

As each one of them arrived and located the others, their squeals became a little louder.

'God, you haven't changed a bit!'

'You look stunning.'

'It's *so* good to see you. How amazing. How fucking amazing!'

It was left to Stella to point out that they were in church and ought perhaps to moderate their language.

Among the bland, designer-clad conformity of the rest of the congregation, their eccentric garb marked them out as 'the college friends' as conspicuously as if they had stood in the pulpit singing karaoke to Depeche Mode.

'What a shame your husband couldn't come,' Stella gushed to Vinnie, 'I was really looking forward to meeting him.'

'I know, it's too bad,' lied Vinnie, 'but the business is just taking off – he couldn't get away. And you're with Dan . . .' She shook her head in disbelief. 'You're a dark horse, Stella. I must say he's worn very well . . .'

'Ah well, sold out to the bourgeoisie, you see,' shrugged

Stella, 'not like Nick. I dare say he's still living on the breadline somewhere, fighting the good fight?'

'I wouldn't know,' said Vinnie sniffily, 'we're not really in touch any more. Bridget's boyfriend seems jolly,' she added in a brighter tone.

'Nige? He's great. We see a lot of them, me and Dan.'

'Is Dan OK?' Vinnie asked hesitantly. 'He seems a bit . . . tense.'

Dan did indeed appear distracted. The luck of the draw had found him seated between Stella and Bridget, but he seemed to have forgotten his manners and, rather than make small talk, he was gazing up into the vaulted ceiling of the church, as though contemplating the nature of the divine.

'He's fine,' smiled Stella indulgently. 'He's probably just planning his networking strategy. There's a lot of bigwigs here. Don't look now, but Jeremy Isaacs is two rows behind us.'

'Oh God, celebrities. Spare me.' Vinnie stifled a yawn. 'The reason I love Ireland so much is that people are just people over there.'

'Is that the groom, then?' Maxine whispered to Bridget, pointing towards the front row where Des Percival was slouched rakishly beside his best man, as though waiting to watch the three twenty at Chepstow. 'I thought he was her dad! Do you think they're in love?'

Bridget shrugged. 'I suppose so. He doesn't do anything for me. You can just *tell* he drives a Beemer and listens to Phil Collins.'

'God knows what he makes of Nell's record collection,' laughed Bridget. 'Do you think she's still into Beefheart?'

'Who knows *what* she's into,' mused Bridget, 'she's an enigma.'

Max nodded in agreement. 'I know. Who'd have thought, from our lot, it'd be *Nell* that made the big time.'

They both looked instinctively towards Vinnie, who was chatting away animatedly to the devoted audience of one she had always had in Stella.

A preparatory belch of air from the organ, followed by a flurry of familiar notes, prompted the congregation to rise as one to its feet.

'"Jesu Joy".' Stella clutched Vinnie's wrist excitedly. 'My favourite!' Everyone craned their necks to catch the first glimpse of the bride and, as she walked down the aisle ahead of a gaggle of pint-sized bridesmaids, a collective sigh passed around the wedding guests. Despite her slight limp, Nell managed to look positively ethereal. She had had the good sense to revert, on her wedding day, to the favoured style of her youth. Sleek tailoring had been eschewed in favour of pure romance. She looked like a pre-Raphaelite nymph. Her dress of artfully draped cream chiffon flattered her small frame and offered a glimpse of pert bosom, as fleeting and subtle as a mirage. Her shoulder-length hair had been crimped and crowned with a simple headdress of ivy and hellebores. Stella looked from the innocent young bride to the dissolute old roué she was marrying and back again. She shuddered. It had the feel of a ritual sacrifice.

Until now, Nell's day had passed in a blur, like land-scape glimpsed from a speeding car, but as she set off up the aisle on Mac's arm (her father having a prior engagement at an ashram), it lurched into slow motion. The music seemed to slur like a gramophone winding down; every step she took felt like wading through treacle. Friendly faces beamed their approval. Friendly faces, but not the faces of friends. *The Morning Show* had turned out in force, and there were movers and shakers by the score – people from Des's world, on whom the scent of Business Class still lingered – but friends, *real* friends, were thin on the ground.

Then she had glimpsed Maxine, grinning from ear to ear at the end of one of the pews, and her heart had leaped. They had come! Vinnie too, to her surprise. Even Stella had let bygones be bygones. They were a motley crew, with their ragbag of outfits and ill-assorted partners. She had added their names to the guest list almost on a whim, when Des had goaded her about not having a past, but now that they were here, she realised how very pleased she was to see them. She fluttered her fingers prettily as she passed and they nudged each other and giggled like spinsters on a Sunday school picnic.

Afterwards, at the Dorchester, they gathered anxiously in front of the seating plan. 'Great! We're all together. Table seventeen,' said Bridget.

They peeped through the doors into the ballroom, where round tables draped in dazzling white cloths were laid with a bewildering array of silverware.

'Lovely,' murmured Stella doubtfully.

'It's terribly ostentatious,' complained Vinnie, 'like releasing those doves when we came out of church. Terribly naff, I thought.'

'Oh, I thought that was rather sweet,' Stella said, then she added, 'Though of course it's very cruel.'

'Fancy her promising to obey,' clucked Maxine. 'In this day and age.'

Vinnie had had enough of hovering on the threshold. Sweeping a glass of champagne from a side table as she passed, she led the way across the sprung wooden floor to table seventeen.

Though each of them affected a casual sophistication as they settled in, hanging their handbags on the backs of their spindly gilt chairs, unfolding napkins the size of sheets across their laps and daintily sipping their champagne, each secretly felt a little out of her depth. Max had feared Shona would feel left out, but no sooner had she let slip the fact of her pregnancy than she had become flavour of the month and everyone was asking impertinent questions about due dates and birth plans. Thank goodness it was so early on, or they would no doubt have pawed her belly into the bargain. This was her baby too, Max wanted to remind them; and the very fact that Shona had volunteered her slender, androgynous body as its unlikely incubator was a testament to their love.

Vinnie was fast weaving a web of deceit, not only regarding her marital status, but also her professional life.

By the time she was on her second glass of fizz, she had promoted herself from humble proof-reader to commissioning editor of a leading Dublin publisher; a white lie she was to regret when Nigel asked if he could send her the first draft of the novel he'd been writing in his spare time.

As usual, Bridget's antennae were trained on Dan. It was amazing how animatedly you could converse, how genuine could be the laughter, while you were actually tracking your best friend's husband around the room. In this, the Dorchester ballroom offered the advantage of being mirror-lined. At one point he caught her eye as he chatted with Glenys Kinnock, and held it for just that moment longer than necessary. Bridget felt the usual calamitous lurch within her pelvis.

Despite her handsome husband and high-powered job, Stella had only been among her old friends for a few minutes before she felt, once again, like the last pick for the netball team. It was thrilling to see everyone and she'd been delighted to find her place card next to Vinnie's on the table, but she still felt as gauche and clumsy as she had that first day at Albacore Street. It didn't help that she was underdressed. She wished now she'd opted for the turquoise harem pants and tunic, never mind that Dan had told her she looked like Princess Jasmine. And though she knew it didn't really matter that she had poured water into her wine glass and used her dessert fork for her amuse-bouche, she couldn't quite muster the insouciance required to get away with it.

As venison followed seafood followed vichyssoise, with a different wine accompanying each, the conversation flowed with less and less inhibition. By the time they were on the dessert course, Vinnie, Maxine, Stella and Bridget were mired in nostalgia. They all thought they remembered the definitive Albacore Street party, but no one could agree about when it had taken place.

'It was Christmas.'

'No, we were outside.'

'Neil Critchley smoked his entire stash of home-grown in one night and puked in the chicken brick.'

'No, he passed out in the bath and someone puked on him.'

'Boy George was there.'

'It was a lookalike.'

'Do you remember that mob that Ben Fairweather brought? What a bunch of tossers. I swear one of them actually had the same frilly shirt my mum got from Richard Shops!'

'I know, and to think I used to fancy Tim Ellis . . .'

'Was he the one with the Flock of Seagulls haircut?'

'Can you believe men actually got themselves up like that and we didn't laugh them off campus?'

'You were too busy trying to get into their jodhpurs,' observed Dan with a hint of bitterness.

'Not me.' Bridget blushed. 'I hated all that New Romantic crap.' Although now he mentioned it, she could recall an unfortunate dalliance with a boy called Ollie who had insisted on borrowing her styling wand the next morning. What a lot of time she had wasted on the wrong men . . .

Emboldened by drink and a desire to prove that, pashmina or no pashmina, she could tell it like it was, Stella was now relating the story of their landlord Trevor Cunliffe and his secret pornography stash. Dan rolled his eyes; he had heard it a dozen times before. He muttered something about a post-prandial cigarette and stalked off. And if his wife was indifferent to his departure, Bridget, he noticed, was not.

The meal was drawing to its conclusion. The speechmakers were starting to swot up on their jokes. Waiters hurried between tables, supplying new glasses for the toasts, but Stella was hurtling, oblivious, toward her punchline. In drink, her Birmingham accent and slightly nasal intonation gave her already strident voice unparalleled reach and penetration. 'I mean this wasn't just any old sleazy landlord,' she went on, 'this was the course convenor for Women's Studies . . .' The MC was on his feet by now and all the other tables had adopted a reverent hush, but, despite warning glances from the others, Stella had failed to notice. 'The sheer hypocrisy of the man,' she was saying, 'One minute he's giving lectures on the objectification of the female form, the next he's wanking off to *Playboy!* We got our revenge, though, didn't we, Max? Remember?' She grasped Shona's arm confidentially. 'We invented a new nickname for him and graffitied every women's toilet on campus. Goodbye Trevor Cunliffe . . .' The MC struck his gavel once, twice, three times on the table and into the answering hush, Stella bellowed, 'hello TREVOR CUNTLIPS!'

A female guest on a distant table tittered nervously. Two hundred and four others swivelled in their seats and stared with undisguised distaste at the foul-mouthed harpy on table seventeen.

'*Ladies* and gentlemen,' said the MC with a reproachful glance in their direction, 'pray silence for . . . the groom.'

Stella stared at the weave of the linen tablecloth until she thought it must burst into flames.

Des Percival rose from his seat with the air of a man very much accustomed to public speaking. The room was already quiet, but, with a showman's instinct, he took possession of the silence, and waited until every member of his audience was watching him intently before beginning.

'Ladies and gentlemen, boys and girls, thank you for being with us today. I can't speak for Nell, but I can honestly say that this is the happiest day of my life.'

The audience ah-ed in unison, Nell smiled coyly up at Des and mouthed. 'Me too.' The women on table seventeen smiled politely.

'Happier,' he went on, 'than the day I made my first million.' There was a ripple of indulgent laughter. 'Happier than the day my son graduated from Harvard; *considerably* happier than the day of my first marriage!' The laugh got bigger. 'Happier than the day I got my decree absolute.' The audience erupted. 'And this is the big one' – he came in on the tail end of the laugh, raising his voice slightly to be heard, 'I can honestly say that I am even happier today than I was last Thursday when a little company I own merged with MTC Media Corp. and allowed me to stop worrying about how I was going to pay the caterers!' The audience (amongst whom MTC Media Corp. were well represented) burst into sycophantic applause.

'This is making me ill,' muttered Maxine.

'God, he's a creep,' whispered Vinnie. 'I feel sorry for Nell.'

'Shhh!' urged Stella, keen to avoid any further public disgrace.

'Seriously' – Des held out his hands, palms down as if to quell the adoration of his fans – 'that's enough about me. Now I'd like to tell you some of the reasons I fell in love with my *wife*.' (More indulgent aahing.) 'Though of course, two of them will be immediately obvious to the gentlemen in the room!'

Table seventeen recoiled in disbelief, but he was already compounding the sin, by mouthing 'Sorry, darling!' at Nell, and then to the audience *sotto voce*: 'She used to be a bit of a women's libber, you know!'

The speech went on in a similar vein for some time. If the Albacore Street women had wondered, on first recon-vening, if they still had anything in common, Des Percival's speech gave them their answer. Looking aghast at a roomful of people for whom this sort of rugby club banter appeared to pass for Wildean wit, the years fell away and the sense of being a clique, a cohort, a *coven* reasserted itself. Perhaps theirs had been the last wave of feminism; it was certainly years since any of them had declared herself a feminist without adding some propitiating disclaimer, but after Des's speech, the torch of their collective indignation burned as brightly as it had when they'd raised petitions to ban page three from the campus newsagent or marched behind banners demanding 'A Woman's Right to Choose'.

'Not a word about Nell's first in philosophy,' muttered Maxine.

'He hardly *mentioned* her career,' fumed Stella. 'You'd have thought we were back in the fifties. God, if Dan had told everyone at *our* wedding that they shouldn't be fooled by my gorgeous exterior because I was really just the girl next door, I'd have filed for divorce. Where *is* Dan, by the way?'

Bridget feigned surprise at his absence, though she had been timing it with the second hand of her watch. 'Probably calling the office. You know what he's like.' She shrugged and then blushed, but Stella didn't seem to notice the overfamiliarity of her tone.

'No one could have called *our* wedding sexist,' Stella added smugly. 'It was so right-on I'm almost embarrassed. D'you remember, Brid? Bridget was my best woman,' she added, for Vinnie's benefit. It had always rankled with Stella that Vinnie hadn't turned up.

'It was still a wedding though,' Maxine pointed out. 'Why get married at all if you don't agree with the traditions?'

'*Exactly* what I said,' nodded Stella, 'but it was Dan in the end. He was worried about the legal position, you know, with Amber and everything. And to be honest, I was concerned I might not get his pension.'

'You old romantic you!' teased Vinnie.

'There you are, social control!' Maxine slapped the table emphatically. 'You didn't do it for you. You did it for the State.'

'It felt like more than that though,' protested Stella. 'I know it sounds corny, but when Dan said his vows, I was moved to tears. It felt very solemn, pledging fidelity in front of all the people we love. He had a lump in his throat too, I could tell.'

'Gosh it's hot in here.' Bridget got up suddenly, almost knocking over her chair in her haste. 'I think I'll just go and get some air.'

'Don't be long,' Max warned, 'they'll be starting the dancing soon.' Even now, the lights were being dimmed, a mirror ball was working its kitschy magic and, at the request of the groom, the DJ was cueing up 'In the Air Tonight'.

Bridget cast her eye around the lobby for possible clues to Dan's whereabouts. A liveried flunky gave her an enquiring glance.

'I don't suppose you've seen my husband? Tall, dark, little round specs. Probably clutching a packet of Silk Cut.'

'The smokers tend to congregate in the Knot Garden, madam. Through the double doors and turn left.'

'Thank you.'

Following the signs, she hurried round a corner and came face to face with Dan heading back the other way.

One glimpse of his lean, intelligent face, his bow tie flopping undone around his neck, his wire-rimmed glasses, which saved him from looking like a cad, and Bridget's resolve crumbled.

'What the fuck . . . ?' He grinned at her. His breath smelled of whisky.

'We need to talk,' she said, avoiding his eye. He darted a glance up and down the corridor, then, satisfied that they had not been seen, he took her hand and led her through a glazed panelled door into a small courtyard.

Nell was beginning to enjoy herself. For the past two hours she had been knocking back champagne as if it were lemonade but it had had no effect whatsoever. Now, at last, she was starting to feel fuzzy round the edges. It was a relief to have the formalities over with. If Des's speech had been a little old-fashioned for her liking, at least she was satisfied that he was well and truly hooked. He had used the word 'love' seven times; she had counted. And that was seven times more than he had ever used it to her in person. She had minded very much at first. She had always suspected some ulterior motive in his courtship (although she knew the casting couch was supposed to work the other way – her sleeping with *him* to get promotion, not him sleeping with her to sign her up). But their relationship continued long after she'd become a fixture on Des's flagship show, and although he seemed intriguingly aloof, she knew he wasn't seeing anyone else. The first time she had blurted out the 'L' word, their love-making had been fuelled by drink and poppers. He had been a little rougher with her than usual and she had cried, at first in pain, then, when he had cradled her in his arms and kissed the tears from her cheeks, in gratitude.

'Don't cry, baby, Daddy's here,' he had murmured, over and over, and she had felt so safe and so cherished that she had just come out and said it, without thinking. He had smiled down at her, unfazed, but disinclined, apparently, to reciprocate. Well, now he had said it in front of a room full of people – in front of the man who, in just a couple of weeks' time, looked set to be the next Prime Minister, for goodness' sake. So it must be true. She twisted the dainty gold and platinum band on her finger. In the heat of the room it chafed uncomfortably. She bit her lip. Des had spent a fortune having it custom made; he'd go mad if he found out it wasn't a perfect fit. She resolved not to tell him.

After they had cut the cake and thanked Mac and the best man and the bridesmaids, Des announced that it was time to mingle. While he sauntered over to the BSkyB table and started back-slapping, Nell hurried, with mounting excitement, towards table seventeen. 'Nell, you're a picture!' cried Vinnie, whirling her round.

'Well, if it isn't our Nelly off the telly! Come here and give us a kiss,' grinned Max. Stella said nothing, for no words were needed. As Nell approached her, she rose from her seat and they embraced.

By now the DJ had dispensed with the rock'n'roll stand-ards that had brought Des and his buddies twisting and jiving on to the dance floor and was pandering to the next generation down. As 'Tainted Love' segued into 'Girls Just Want to Have Fun', the Albacore Street women scrambled towards the dance floor and formed a ragged circle, arms draped around each other's shoulders, high-kicking in time to the music with such clod-hopping exuberance that Nell's disability was barely discernible. Then just as they were making their way, eyes shining, chests heaving, back to their seats, the opening chimes of Sister Sledge drew them back again.

'Where's Bridget?' Max said, looking around urgently. 'Quick – tell her they're playing our song!'

With 'We Are Family' ringing in her ears, Stella hurried obediently towards the lobby.

'No, Dan, I came to find you to tell you this had to stop,' Bridget protested as he tugged her out of sight behind a topiaried yew and pushed her roughly back against the wall.

'It will stop, it will . . . you're right,' he said, burying his face in her neck so that his words were scarcely audible, and then pulling the fabric of her dress aside roughly and kissing her collarbone, 'just . . . not . . . quite . . . yet.'

'Don't, Dan, not here. It's too . . . oh God! Oh God.'

The bright lights made Stella's head reel. She stood for a moment, looking around, disorientated. The doorman took a solicitous step towards her.

'Can I help you, miss?'

'Probably not.' She smiled. 'Unless you've seen my friend. Small, pretty, short hair, sailor dress?'

He shrugged and shook his head. 'Sorry.'

Stella felt ill. She had given up on finding Bridget before the record ended. Her more urgent need now was for a sit-down and a glass of water. Unsure where she was going, she blundered through some double doors and down a corridor. She could feel a rejuvenating blast of fresh air coming from somewhere. She followed it.

'Dan, we can't . . . this doesn't feel right,' Bridget protested.

'Feels bloody right to me,' he muttered, hoicking her higher up the wall and grinding his pelvis against hers, all the while kissing her into submission. Deftly, Bridget slipped her hand under her dress. She had her knickers hooked halfway off when she heard the sound of high heels running on paving stones and then the unmistakable sound of someone vomiting into the nearby flowerbed.

Stella wiped her mouth on the back of her hand and shivered. She looked up, appalled to see that she wasn't alone. Shrinking back into the shadows, and somehow contriving by their furtiveness to make themselves all the more conspicuous, was a courting couple. The temptation was to run, head down, back to the corridor and pretend she hadn't seen them, but her route took her within feet of them and, as she drew level, Stella felt compelled to acknowledge the absurdity of the situation. Her eyes flicked up, taking in their panic-stricken faces.

'I won't tell if you . . .' she started to say. Then her voice trailed away.

2002
Vinnie

'Shhh!' Vinnie whispered, one finger over her lips, the other clutching at her companion's sleeve. She tottered down the steps into the open-plan living room, but lost her footing on the last one and cannoned into the glass coffee table. Leon, who had nodded off, fully clothed, on the sofa, stirred and his eyes flickered open.

'Niamh?' he said. 'Is that you?'

Vinnie aimed a light-hearted slap at her accomplice, a gaunt middle-aged man dressed in jeans, cagoule and aviator sunglasses. 'Now look, you've woken him up,' she remonstrated, giggling. 'Shhh! Go back to sleep, baby. It's only Mummy.' She sat beside her son on the sofa and patted his chest fondly, then remembered something hilarious and started tapping him awake again. 'D'you know what, though? It's the funniest thing. This fella we were out with, he's with the band, whassis name again?'

'Tommo,' supplied her friend.

'Tommo, thassright. Well, he had this little dog with him, this funny little whippety thing it was, with a cute little neckerchief, such a darling little doggy. Well, you'll never believe where it came from, Leon. Leon? Are you listening . . . ?'

'Uhuh?' Leon forced his eyes open again.

'Bjork!' Leon's eyelids flickered shut. Vinnie took his face between her hands and squeezed gently. 'Bjork, Leon. You know, that crazy bint from Iceland? It was Bjork's little dog, but she couldn't keep him because – and this is the mad part – apparently it is illegal – to have a pet – dog – in Iceland!' She said this with several emphatic nods of the head and then sat back the better to digest her son's reaction.

'OK, Mum, yeah, whatever,' muttered Leon.

'Anyways, this is what she told them backstage in Reykjavik, apparently. You remember, the Scandinavian tour, Leon, back in the spring ? (I didn't think Iceland was even part of Scandinavia, but there you go.) So Madam gets this little pup out of her bag and she tells them she's going to have to have the poor little thing put down if the authorities find out. I mean, what kind of country bans pet dogs? Anyways, meladdo from the band, you know . . .' She clicked her fingers at her companion.

'Tommo.'

'Old . . . *Tommo* smuggles the little fella back to Ireland on the tour bus and now he's the band mascot. How d'you like that? I'll have to get Tommo to bring him round. You'd go mad for him, Leon. He loves dogs,' she said to her friend. 'What a sad, sad country,' she added mournfully to herself, 'no wonder their music's shite.'

'What time is it?' asked Leon, sitting up and darting a hostile glance at Vinnie's companion.

Vinnie squinted at the over-sized Bakelite clock above the mantelpiece. 'Well, if the little hand's on the two and the big hand's on the five, that makes it . . .'

'Nearly half past two, babe, I'm gonna do one. Be seein' you, Louis.'

Vinnie pouted her disappointment, but now that she was sitting down, she didn't feel like arguing the toss. 'Bye bye . . .' She struggled for the name. '. . . sweetie. Great craic. Be seein' yous.'

She turned back to Leon, who had swung himself upright and was massaging his eye sockets with the heels of his hands. 'Sweet of you to wait up, baby. Don't suppose you could roll your mammy a little fagerette, could you?'

'I was waiting up for *Niamh*,' said Leon. Nevertheless, he reached for the rolling tobacco and spread a cigarette paper out on the coffee table. 'Are you not concerned that your fourteen-year-old daughter's roaming the streets at half past two on a school night?'

'Christ, if she's got school, that means I've got *work*. Jesus, Mary and Joseph, Leon, I feel like a great big bag o' shite. Pass me that cig, will you?'

'Mum!' Leon glared at her in disbelief.

'Ach, she's probably stopped the night with Niall or Deirdre. She'll have sent me a text. She's a good girl. Do us a favour, Leon, and check me phone.'

Leon took Vinnie's mobile out of her bag. 'The battery's

dead,' he said in disgust. 'She could be anywhere. I'm going to call the Garda.'

This focused Vinnie's mind at once. 'No, Leon, don't be so silly. Let me just ring her friends first. She's been doing so well lately. Let's keep it between these four walls for once. I just know she's all right. A mother has an instinct for these things.' She drew needily on her cigarette and they sat in silence for a minute. 'Christ, I'll kill her when she gets in. She's no right to send us demented with worry like this.'

The next day, leaving for work, late and hungover, Vinnie was first irritated and then relieved to trip over Niamh's trainers on the stairs. She was less pleased to find her daughter's keys dangling in the lock on the outside of the front door. Lucky this was Dublin 4, she thought, else they could all have been murdered in their beds. As it was, the keys would, in all probability, have remained where they were until Mrs Hayden from next door used them as an excuse to pop round and eyeball Vinnie's latest outré departure in interior décor. ('It's very nice, dear, I'm just not sure it's in keeping.') Much as Vinnie loved the comfort of her life here, her one cavil was the irredeemably bourgeois character of the neighbourhood. She could have wished for a bit more 'edge'. Then again, she thought smugly, that was what *she* brought to the party. She yanked her daughter's keys from the lock and, thrusting them into the pocket of her coat, set off across town towards the office.

Unusually, the sun was shining, and by the time she arrived, she was feeling almost human. It was surprising what a bottle of spring water and a line of coke could do to mitigate the ravages of a night on the tiles. She ran up the steps to her office, pressed her code into the entry system, and in the second or two it took for the buzzer to sound and the heavy mahogany door to yield to her body weight, she admired the gleaming brass plaque.

O'Donoghue, Driscoll, Napier-Geddes
Literary Agents

It just went to show where a bit of chutzpah could get you. If she hadn't told that little white lie at Nell's wedding and pretended to be a publisher instead of a lowly proofreader, Nigel never would have sent her his manuscript. Terrifying, really, to think that she had left it gathering dust behind the futon in Brenda's spare room for six weeks, before coming across it by accident and starting to read. Of course, to him, the time lapse had betokened credibility. No publisher worth their salt got back to you within the month. It had taken all Vinnie's improvisational skill to make that first phone call to him.

'Really very promising . . . not our sort of thing, but I have some contacts in the business who might just see its potential. Give me a week or two's grace to talk them round . . . and please God don't make me look like an eejit by signing with someone else in the meantime . . .'

It had been Nigel (God bless him) who'd insisted on giving her a cut when the rights were auctioned, telling her she was his lucky charm and requesting that she handle all his work from then on. And with such a prestigious author in her stable (in truth, it was a stable of one) O'Donoghue and Driscoll had welcomed her with open arms – had given her, at times, a little more deference than even *she* felt she deserved. The truth was, she'd been able to do pretty much as she pleased – a mixed blessing, as things had turned out. Did she feel a twinge of conscience, now, when she looked back on that first big fib? Not really. She'd earned it. If she hadn't bitten the bullet and rung Daddy to ask for David Puttnam's number, Nigel's film rights might still be languishing unsold. Instead, the movie of the first book in the trilogy was in pre-production, with Colin Firth slated to take the lead role. And it had cost her dear, ringing home after all the years of estrangement. Mind you, Daddy soon warmed up when he realised the black sheep of the family had come good. He and Mummy couldn't get over fast enough at the prospect of some schmoozing in Dublin's artiest postcode.

No, Vinnie firmly believed that fate had played a hand in guiding her towards her natural vocation. At the end of the day she didn't have a theatrical bone in her body. Business was what she excelled at. She had the knack. She could spot a bestseller in the slush pile at fifty paces. She had a sixth sense for the zeitgeist and a talent for closing a deal. Within the year she had poached a highly lucrative chick-lit novelist from another agency and acquired the backlist of an important Irish playwright just as his work was reappearing on the school curriculum. Her portfolio had grown steadily ever since. She was charmed, so she was, and they were lucky to have her. In fact, for quite a few months now, she had been wondering whether she hadn't outgrown the Irish literary scene. If she hadn't had her eye on the lead singer of the band, and Niamh hadn't just settled into St Ursula's, she would have moved back to London. Then again, the agents in London were probably a bit more rigorous in their business practices than O'D & D, and though she might come trailing glory, they'd be taking a long hard look at the bottom line . . . What a bore.

'Morning, Denise.' Vinnie breezed into the elegant reception area. 'Could you be a darling and fetch me an Americano from Costa? I've a got a dozen calls to make and my head feels like it might explode at any moment.'

'Reeled him in yet?' grinned Denise, whose prurient interest in her social life Vinnie slightly resented.

'I'm sure I don't know to what you're referring, Miss Fletcher,' said Vinnie in mock outrage. She gave Denise a conspiratorial wink and went into her office, surprised and not a little irritated to see Tony O'Donoghue sitting in *her* leather chair behind *her* desk.

'Hello, Tony,' she said. 'I know we said we'd talk ancillaries this morning, but I've a couple of calls that won't wait, so if you can give me twenty minutes . . .'

'No problem, Lavinia. The ancillaries can wait. It's the auditors that are chomping at the bit.'

Vinnie blanched. 'Auditors?'

'Apparently there were some discrepancies between our

end-of-year accounts and the tax returns filed by some of our authors.'

'What sort of discrepancies?' she asked, turning to hang up her coat so he couldn't see the expression on her face.

'I've no idea. You know what these bean-counters are like. Some jobsworth in accounts probably just put a decimal point in the wrong place. But it's just to warn you that the Department of Trade are sending in their people on Monday, and we need to have everything ready for them. I know it's a pain in the arse, with Frankfurt round the corner, but there it is.'

Vinnie shrugged resignedly. 'It's not that I object to the scrutiny, that's only right and proper,' she said, 'it's the thought of having to breathe the same air as a bunch of *accountants*,' She shuddered theatrically and Tony laughed.

'You cheer me up, Lavinia, you really do.' She shot him a winning smile. When the door had shut behind him, she slumped down into the still-warm chair and stared numbly into space.

On the way home, she stopped off at Brown Thomas and bought Niamh a couple of T-shirts. She liked to think she knew the sort of thing her daughter preferred – a bit grungy, a bit street. When she got back to the house, Niamh was slumped in front of the television with a can of Tango and a block of chocolate. She was still wearing her bomber jacket over her school uniform and the curtains were drawn.

'Hello, my darling,' said Vinnie, pulling them back so that her daughter recoiled like a vampire at the sudden inrush of sunlight. 'How was school? Are you not boiling up in all those layers, Niamhy? It's summer out there in the real world, if you did but know it.'

Niamh's hair hung in two lank skeins either side of her face. Vinnie itched to sweep it up into a ponytail and give her poor skin a chance to breathe. She could be a stunner if she only took the trouble, but she didn't seem to care. It frustrated Vinnie. She remembered all the fun she had had herself as a teenager, roaming round Highgate on the pull, dating the boys, playing them off against each other. Niamh could have a bit of that, if she just made the best of herself, instead of hanging around with catatonic Niall and brain-dead Deirdre. It made Vinnie feel tired just looking at them. The sum total of their aspiration seemed to be a bit of inept shoplifting. And even then they didn't pinch anything good. What self-respecting teenager stole a *toaster* for goodness' sake? One that wanted to get caught, she supposed, if you looked at the record. She really couldn't fathom the girl. Even now, her daughter was staring, as if transfixed, at a cartoon meant for four-year-olds.

'I'm cold,' Niamh said distractedly, reaching each hand into its opposite sleeve and scratching manically. Niamh was always cold. Or claimed to be. Vinnie sometimes wondered if her daughter might be developing anorexia or bulimia, so fond was she of concealing herself in shapeless layers of clothing. Then again, the amount of junk food she consumed seemed inconsistent with that diagnosis.

Sometimes she would stand at the door of the downstairs cloakroom, when Niamh was in there, listening for the sound of retching; but so far her detective work had proved inconclusive.

'Here; little present.' She tossed the carrier bag on to the sofa, but Niamh barely turned her head.

'Thanks,' she said.

'Aren't you going to look?'

Niamh tore her gaze away from the screen and looked inside the bag. 'Yeah, thanks,' she said.

Vinnie snapped. She tore around the sofa and shook its contents into Niamh's lap.

'There, look. T-shirts. Two of them. Chosen by me, with a mother's fucking care, and they weren't cheap either.' Niamh recoiled slightly, but her expression hardly changed. 'Honestly, Niamh, it's punishment you should be getting, not presents, after you kept me and Leon up half the night with worry.'

'Sorry,' mumbled Niamh, 'I sent you a text.'

'Well I didn't get it.'

'Sorry.'

'God's sakes, leave her alone. You always do this.' Vinnie's shouting had brought Leon in from the kitchen.

'Do what? Expect my daughter to exchange two words with me when I've been out all day working to keep a roof over your heads? It's not easy, you know, being a single parent.'

'Oh for Christ's sake, spare us. I can buy the single bit, but *parent*? I don't think so. You were so off your face last night when you came in with your fancy man, you didn't care if Niamh was alive or dead.'

'He's not my fancy man. He's just a friend.'

'Oh, like all your other "friends", you mean? Seano and Johnno and Tommo. Do you think any of them'll remember your birthday? Because I don't. You're just a pathetic old groupie. It's *embarrassing*.'

Vinnie gasped; her eyes stung with tears.

'I'm sorry. I didn't mean it,' said Leon. He touched her gently on the shoulder and Vinnie threw her arms around him and sobbed.

'You're right. I'm a crap mother. I'm erratic and selfish and irresponsible and you both deserve better. But you have to know that there's nothing and no one in my life that means more to me than you two, Leon. Tell me you believe me . . . Niamh, do you hear . . . ?' She turned round, but Niamh had gone.

Maxine

'When did this come?' asked Maxine, trying her hardest to show Robin only her pleasure at the letter's contents and not the creeping suspicion that Shona had deliberately kept it from her. It wasn't as though Shona was careless by nature. It was Max who was always disrupting her 'systems' with slovenliness; mixing up bills with junk mail; forgetting to sort the laundry into whites and coloureds; leaving piles of marking on the kitchen table so there was no room left to eat dinner. No, Shona's world was neat and orderly, a place for everything and everything in its place; and letters from school did not mysteriously get 'filed' inside telephone directories. 'Dunno,' shrugged Robin, lifting both shoulders up by his ears and turning his hands into two starfish, as had been his habit since toddlerhood when expressing ignorance or (more often) butter-wouldn't-melt innocence. 'It's not just *me* getting a prize. It's anyone who got top marks in the test, which is, like, half the class. It's no big deal. All you get's a crappy book token.'

'There's nothing crappy about a book token,' said Max. 'You could buy the next Harry Potter, or maybe a nice dictionary for when you go to secondary school.'

Robin's expression mingled pity and scorn. 'Whatever,' he said and Max suppressed a smile. If anything, she found his prepubescent attempts at withering indifference even more endearing than the round-eyed enthusiasm with which he had greeted the world since birth and which he now struggled to suppress.

'Anyway,' Max said, 'the important thing is, you've done *well*. I'm so proud of you.' She looped an arm across the front of his chest, imprisoning him briefly against her while she nuzzled the top of his head. He indulged her for a second before ducking under her arm and making a break for his PlayStation. When he had left the room, she flicked through the household diary in which she and Shona entered the numerous engagements in their increasingly separate lives. Fuck! The date of the prize-giving clashed with an open evening, which, if she'd known about it in advance, she could have got out of, backsliding now would look hopelessly unprofessional. Still, she had made it a point of honour not to miss any of Robin's school events if she could possibly help it and she was damned if Shona's machinations were going to thwart her on this occasion. It was becoming increasingly difficult to juggle work and home without incurring Shona's disapproval.

That evening turned out to be a case in point. She was in the middle of talking to one of the parents when she remembered the lasagne she had left on the timer in the oven. Max's heart sank, knowing that once Muriel Chadwick got up a head of steam she'd be lucky to get away in much under half an hour. Several times, as Muriel wittered on, the words 'Actually, Muriel . . .' formed on Max's lips, but somehow the opportunity to utter them never presented itself. By the time she had made her excuses, collected Robin from the childminder's and raced home, the smoke alarm was blaring and clouds of acrid fumes were billowing under the kitchen door. The lasagne she had lovingly assembled, so that Robin would have a hot meal to come home to and Shona would have nothing to reproach her for, was a charred mess. She fumbled for the oven glove, grabbed the dish clumsily and dropped it again when the heat seared her palm. She ran to the sink, swearing under her breath and held her hand under the cold tap. At last, when the throbbing had subsided, she ferreted the broom out of the cupboard under the stairs and prodded the smoke alarm into submission with its handle. Silence had only just descended on the smoke-filled ground floor when she heard Shona's key turn in the lock.

'That smells appetising. What have you cremated this time?'

'Lasagne.' Max emerged flushed and defensive from the kitchen. The contrast between Shona, immaculate in her Armani suit and belted trench, and Maxine, beetroot-red in Gap separates, which, after a day at the chalk face, were becoming more separate by the minute, could not have been starker. 'I was stuck in a governors' meeting . . .'

'Well, maybe if you weren't so wrapped up in your career . . .' said Shona. This was rich, coming from someone who took her Palm Pilot to the toilet with her. All Max's good intentions of raising the matter in a civilised way over a meal and a glass of wine flew out of the window.

'Actually I was earning some Brownie points, so that when I need to leave early on Thursday to come to Robin's prizegiving – which, incidentally, you didn't tell me about – no one will be able to argue.'

'You shouldn't have bothered, I can go on my own. Robin won't mind,' said Shona.

'I mind!' said Maxine. 'If our son's getting a prize, I want to be there. You hid the letter and you didn't put it in the diary. What's going on, Shona?'

'I didn't think you'd approve,' said Shona huffily.

'How could I not approve of Robin winning a prize?'

'It's elitist. You hate elitism.'

'Don't be ridiculous! I'm not against prizes for hard work.'

'I still haven't got over his last parents' evening, when his teacher tried to tell us about his exceptional ability in maths and you gave her a lecture about the iniquities of the Gifted and Talented programme.'

'Obviously I wasn't doing Robin down. I was talking about the principle.'

Shona smiled grimly, and Maxine's heart sank.

'That's just it Max,' hissed Shona. 'You're *always* talking about the principle. I'm up to here with the fucking principle. That's why I didn't tell you, because I couldn't bear to sit next to you *radiating superiority* all night. I just want to go and be proud of my son.'

'Mum, is that you?' Robin yelled down from his bedroom, apparently oblivious to the tug of love going on a floor below. 'My PlayStation's frozen again. Can you come and do that thing like last time?'

'It's all right, I'll go.' Max made for the stairs. 'You haven't even got your coat off yet.'

'You don't know how,' Shona pointed out, kicking off her court shoes and overtaking Max easily on the third step, without even having to deploy her considerably sharper elbows. They both knew that Max was hopeless with technology and even though the secret of Shona's success relied on nothing more sophisticated than unplugging the console and blowing into the slotted area at the back, she wasn't about to divulge her secret.

Max sighed and walked into the through lounge with an air of defeat. She collapsed on the sofa and found herself staring wistfully at the enlarged black and white photo that still took pride of place above the fireplace. Two heads, hers and Shona's, side by side on a pillow; cropped so close that it seemed the frame could barely contain their happiness. In the middle, and a little lower down, a third head, the reason for their blissed-out smiles: Robin, at two hours old, like a tiny swamp creature, eyes tight shut, mouth puckered, ludicrous Tintin quiff tickling Max's nose. A photographer friend had been among the earliest visitors to the hospital and had run off a couple of rolls. Maxine remembered the feeling of legitimacy, of *relief*, as the shutter clicked, locking them in their cocoon of family for all time.

'He's ours, Max,' Shona had whispered, squeezing her hand, 'no one's going to take him away.' And Max had nodded, unable to speak.

Secretly, she had been dreading the birth as much as Shona had been looking forward to it. Oh, she had *disguised* it well, spreading her palms across her lover's watermelon belly to feel a punching fist or poking foot; massaging cocoa butter into Shona's skin to minimise the risk of stretch marks; reading aloud about breastfeeding from the *New Mother's Handbook*. But every twinge, every kick, every drop of colostrum that seeped from Shona's nipple was a stark reminder of what she had gone through herself, sixteen years ago.

Back then the predominant emotions had been fear, confusion and shame. There had been dull, dragging pain, then acute tearing agony, the wetness of blood and piss and, at last, a single plaintive cry. They had told her she'd given birth to a healthy girl; she had a faint, blurry recollection of an angry red baby's face thrust in front of her and then, just as quickly, whisked away. Afterwards, when her mum had left her on the post-natal ward, telling her to 'get some rest, our Maxine', she had lain in agony as her uterus contracted and her breasts filled up with milk. The nurses had drawn the curtains around her bed, whether to hide her shame or protect her sensibilities, she didn't know. But all it took was the hungry cry of another mother's newborn and her nipples gushed milk. When the nurse had come to ask if she needed anything for the pain, she had shaken her head mutely and turned her face away; there wasn't an analgesic strong enough for the pain she had.

In the end, Robin had been the balm. Better that he was a boy. Everyone thought it; no one said it. But it was true. He wasn't a replacement for the baby Maxine had given away. He was his own stolid little self; he had Shona's flyaway hair and serious, questing intelligence. He had Graham's cleft chin and stoic cheerfulness. From Maxine he took nothing but love. The sluice gates lifted and it all poured out; dammed up since 1976; like a torrent – unstoppable.

Shona breastfed with dutiful efficiency for three months, and then, snake-hipped and flat-bellied once again, returned to work. It was Max who moved Robin on to solids; Max who witnessed his first steps and his first words; who taught him his colours and his numbers; who made playdough dinosaurs for him and dangled his plump little feet in the waves on Brighton beach.

Max didn't know how long she had been sitting there when Shona put her head round the door, but the room was almost in darkness.

'I'm going out,' she said.

Max turned round in surprise. 'You haven't had dinner,' she protested.

'I haven't got time.'

In the dim light from the hallway, Max caught a glimpse

of Shona's outfit. She had exchanged her smart work persona for an altogether dykier look: jeans and a cap-sleeved T-shirt, a studded leather cuff on her wrist; hair slicked back with product; a cat-like flash of eyeliner on each lid. Maxine felt a surge of jealousy and desire.

'Where are you going?' she couldn't stop herself asking.

'Book group,' replied Shona. 'Don't wait up.'

Shona had joined a book group six months ago; she hadn't invited Max along, although Max was the more avid reader. The group seemed to be a great success. At any rate, it had gone from monthly to weekly meetings in no time at all, yet the only book on Shona's bedside table was a copy of *The Songlines* by Bruce Chatwin that Max had bought her for Christmas, and which still had the corner folded over at page 36. When Max asked Shona what they were reading, she was vague.

'You wouldn't like it,' she said. And she was probably right.

The front door banged shut. Max went over to the window and hovered behind the curtain. She felt like a self-harmer picking a scab. She watched Shona put on her helmet and wheel her motorbike out on to the pavement. As she roared off up the street, Max moved towards the centre of the bay to get a better view. She watched until all that was left of Shona was a puff of black exhaust on the brow of the hill.

Stella

Stella waited until she heard Amber slam the front door, then she drained her coffee mug, collected a black bin bag, a duster and the Dyson and lumbered up the stairs. Her first meeting at work wasn't until eleven thirty, but rather than spend the intervening couple of hours preparing for it, she had another task in mind – altogether more daunting, but, in her mind, quite urgent. She walked into her daughter's bedroom, and her heart sank. The floor was a tangle of dirty clothing, magazines, CD cases and schoolbooks. The bedside table groaned beneath a stack of crusty cereal bowls, furry coffee mugs and browning apple cores. Cosmetics and jewellery overflowed from the dressing table on to the adjacent desk. The curtains had not been opened for several weeks, nor had the bedding been changed, and there was a slightly cloying sweetness to the air, which Stella suspected did not emanate from any of the vast clutter of cheap perfumes and body sprays on the dressing table. She had definitely bitten off more than she could chew, but Niamh was due to arrive at Stansted at seven o'clock this evening, and if she was going to fit a camp-bed in the room by then, and stand some chance of passing Amber off as a suitable companion for Vinnie's sensitive convent-educated daughter, she was going to have to be brutal.

She cleared the floor of junk, hardly stopping to shudder over the inappropriateness of certain garments – lacy thongs; T-shirts bearing the legend 'BABE' and 'UP FOR IT'; denim skirts, already no deeper than pelmets, with hemlines frayed to the nth degree. She paired up the shoes and arranged them in height order in front of the built-in wardrobe; tatty Converses at one end, vertiginous magenta heels at the other. Then she moved up a level, tidying the bottles of lurid nail polish, heaping glittering eye shadows, lip glosses and mascaras into a woven willow tray; unplugging and tidying away a lethal tangle of hair dryers, straighteners and curlers. She dithered briefly over Amber's birth-control pills, which had been tossed care-lessly on to the bedside table. Should she leave them out, lest her daughter forget to take them? Or hide them in the drawer for decorum's sake? She opted for decorum.

Seeing all this, as if for the first time, through the eyes of an ingénue, made her queasily aware of the distance she had travelled as a parent since Amber had hit adolescence. It had been an incremental metamorphosis into full-blown floozydom, with many a line drawn in the sand, only to be breached a month or two later on the basis that 'everyone else was getting hair extensions/drinking Alcopops/having their navels pierced'. The last pitched battle had been over the pills, which Stella discovered by accident when she was looking for some Blu-Tack six months ago. The find had horrified her and prompted three turbulent nights of weeping, door-slamming and swearing. In the end, as with every premature step that Amber had already taken towards womanhood, there seemed no choice but to capitulate. At the moment, the rulebook stated that her boyfriend Sam could only stay over at weekends, but the rulebook had a habit of being rewritten.

Stella was sweeping a blizzard of used cotton wool balls off the desk and into an open bin bag when her hand nudged the keyboard of Amber's computer and the screen flicked from its rainbow screensaver to a web-page that she had neglected to close. At first glance, it looked like soft porn. A young woman smiled seductively into the camera, clad only in black lacy knickers, her preternaturally large bosoms standing proud above her tiny ribcage. Stella gasped, then peered more closely at the screen. 'MAKE YOURSELF BEAUTIFUL!' said the strap line at the top and, in smaller type: 'Enhance your natural beauty with MYB breast enlargement. Our Harley Street surgeons have over twenty-five years of expertise in breast-enlargement surgery. Read the testimonials from our satisfied clients; then apply below for a free consultation.' Stella sank, dismayed, on to Amber's office chair and scrolled down the page in grim fascination. Her daughter had already filled in half the application form, before presumably being stymied by the small-print clause that insisted on parental consent for under eighteens. This, more than anything she had yet discovered about her daughter's quest for sex appeal, seemed the ultimate indictment of Stella's effectiveness as a mother and a role model. She could just about accept that her dazzlingly pretty, slim, auburn-haired daughter might want to package herself as a blonde bimbo for the duration of her teenage years; but this was irreversible. What's more, it smacked, to Stella's mind, of self-hatred.

Her eyes flicked right, to the clock at the bottom of the screen. Time was running out. She resisted the temptation to delete the offending web-page and reminimised it instead, bitter experience having taught her that sensitive issues were best approached obliquely, rather than confronted head on. If Amber thought she had been snooping, she would lose the moral high ground. Another twenty minutes vacuuming, dusting and pummelling duvets and the room looked just about habitable. There was nothing she could do about the poster above Amber's bed depicting Duncan from Blue with his hands suggestively caressing his crotch, nor the American bumper sticker tacked to her daughter's headboard that said 'Honk if you had it last night', but at least the room no longer looked as though a bomb had gone off in a brothel.

Stella had to bribe Amber to accompany her to Stansted with the promise of a new CD when they got there. The inducement had bought her daughter's complicity but not her goodwill. The first fifteen minutes of their journey passed in ominous silence. At last, Amber removed the headphones from her ears.

'I do not appreciate what you've done to my room. I can't find a *thing*,' she complained.

'I was very careful not to move anything. I just put things back in their proper places,' Stella replied calmly, aware that they would be meeting her daughter's new room-mate in less than an hour.

'And every time I go to the wardrobe I've got to step over that camp-bed. Can't she sleep on the couch?'

'I thought it would be fun for you two to get to know each other. You know . . . girly late-night chats.'

'Mum, she's two years younger than me and she goes to some nun school. I can't really see us hitting it off.'

'She's eighteen months younger and it's not some nun school; convents are just the Irish equivalent of grammar schools.'

'You don't approve of grammar schools.'

'No, but I don't think Vinnie had any choice. The poor girl was bullied at both the other schools she went to, apparently.'

'She must be a loser then.'

'Amber!'

'Well, it's true. If it was just one, I'd feel sorry for her, but *two*. She must have low self-esteem; otherwise she wouldn't get picked on.'

Stella's eyes widened in surprise. She didn't know whether to be impressed at her daughter's grasp of psychology or appalled at her callousness. At the same time, she saw an opportunity. 'Talking of low self-esteem,' she said, 'how's yours?'

'All right,' said Amber suspiciously. 'What do you mean?'

'Only I sometimes wonder if you know how beautiful you are. And how clever. And how . . . nice,' she finished, doubtfully.

'Mum, you're creeping me out.' Amber went to put her headphones back in, then remembered that her battery had died, and thrust them crossly into her pocket.

'So, you wouldn't want to change anything about yourself, then?'

'What like?'

'Oh, I don't know.' Stella shrugged carelessly. 'Your figure maybe?'

'What's wrong with my figure?'

'Nothing. It's lovely. Don't get me wrong. It's just, I saw a documentary on TV the other day and apparently more and more young women are getting cosmetic surgery. Some mums are even getting their daughters boob jobs for their sixteenth birthdays . . .'

Amber's face lit up. 'Mum . . . I didn't dare ask. I thought you'd disapprove. Oh my God, you are the *coolest*!'

Stella, who was overtaking a double-decker coach, almost swerved into the central reservation. 'I didn't mean I'd get you one! I meant isn't it awful and sad that women feel the need to do that to themselves? And that money-grubbing, misogynist quacks can get rich by preying on their insecurities. It's obscene!'

'Oh, I get it. It was a trap so you could spout your self-righteous feminist crap. Well, I'm not interested, Mother, to be honest. As far as I'm concerned there's nothing wrong with using scientific advances to improve the way I look. But don't worry, if you won't pay for it, I'll ask Sam.'

Stella stared at her in horror, but before she could even begin to tell Amber all the reasons why that would be a terrible idea, her mobile phone started ringing.

Amber sat with her arms crossed, staring out of the window, as if she couldn't hear it.

'Amber . . . could you? I'm driving. Would you mind picking that up, please? It might be Niamh or Vinnie. Amber? Please . . . ?'

On the final ring, Amber swept the phone off the dashboard and muttered, 'Hello.'

She held a monosyllabic conversation with the person at the other end while Stella darted anxious glances at her and hoped she wasn't talking to Ireland.

'That was Dad,' she said, ringing off. 'He said don't wait for him to eat. They're voting on his drugs bill thingy and he might be very late.'

'Damn!' muttered Stella under her breath.

'What's the big deal? We hardly ever eat together anyway.'

'No, but I thought it would be nice to welcome Niamh with a proper family meal. I've gone to quite a bit of effort.'

Amber was shaking her head. 'I don't get what all the

fuss is about with this Niamh. Why've we all got to be on our best behaviour? She's not royalty.'

'Of course not, darling,' laughed Stella, 'her mum and me are just very old friends, that's all.'

They arrived early at Stansted and while Amber browsed HMV, Stella wandered into W. H. Smith looking for a magazine to pass the time. Her hand was hovering uncertainly between *Marie Claire* and *The London Review of Books*, when she noticed a familiar face on the cover of one of the tacky celebrity weeklies. 'NELL CARPENTER: NOSE JOB SHOCK' screamed the bright red type. Stella picked it up and gasped at the pixilated close-up of Nell's once-lovely face. She looked as though she'd been in a road accident. Both eyes were ringed with black, like a panda, and she had a wide strip of plaster across the bridge of her nose. The caption said that despite going on the record as being opposed to plastic surgery, darling of daytime TV Nell Carpenter had been papped sneaking out of a private hospital, bearing all the signs of a recent rhinoplasty. This seemed like the final straw. First Amber wanted to fix her boobs, now Nell had had a nose job. Stella shook her head in disbelief. Wait till I tell Bridget, was her first thought; then she remembered . . . Neverthess, the temptation to canvas the opinions of the other Albacore Street women was overwhelming. Nell's action, she felt, warranted some response, though she was not sure yet whether it should be a motion of censure or a group hug . . .

'She's landed,' said Amber, appearing at Stella's side. 'Better hurry up, Mum. You might miss her.'

Stella handed over her 75p and scooped the magazine hurriedly into her bag, but not before Amber had clocked its title, with a smirk.

'*Closer*, eh? That's a bit down-market for you.'

'It's got a nice recipe in, that's all,' replied Stella briskly. 'Now, let's go and find her.'

The lank-haired waif that emerged through the sliding doors and into the arrivals hall could not have been more different from her mother, but it had to be Vinnie's girl – there was no one else who looked the right age.

'Niamh?' Stella asked.

The girl nodded and gave her a wan smile and Stella enveloped her in a bear hug.

'I can't tell you how pleased we are to have you, aren't we, Amber?'

'Yeah,' said Amber, barely cracking a smile.

'You've got your mother's eyes,' said Stella. 'I could see a resemblance straight away. Here, give me your bag, it looks too heavy for you. Did you get something to eat on the plane?'

Niamh shook her head. She did indeed have Vinnie's doe eyes, but there was something slightly odd about them that Stella couldn't put her finger on. She had her mother's fine bone structure too, but her complexion was dull, with crops of spots and blackheads here and there. She had not inherited Vinnie's sense of style. She was wearing skinny jeans and trainers; a shapeless sweatshirt and a hooded bomber jacket. Stella's heart went out to her – there was work to be done here. This was her chance, she felt, to be a really good friend. She looked forward to sending Niamh back to Ireland bright-eyed and bushy-tailed, nourished by the love of a proper family.

'Why don't you two sit in the back together?' Stella suggested brightly as Amber made to open the front passenger door of the car. 'Then you can chat more easily.' Her daughter slammed the door shut again and got in the back next to Niamh. While Amber pointedly studied the sleeve notes of her new CD, Niamh took a few desultory bites of the sandwich Stella had insisted on buying her.

'So, Niamh' – Stella met her eye in the rear-view mirror – 'what would you like to do while you're in London?'

'Don't mind.'

'Well, Dan might be able to arrange lunch in the House of Commons if you like; then there's the London Eye and of course you'll want to do the big Topshop on Oxford Street . . .'

'Do you live anywhere near Brixton?' asked Niamh.

'Well, yes, it's not far . . .' Stella said doubtfully.

'She'll never let us go there,' sniffed Amber. 'Bare rude boys; she thinks we'll get mugged.'

'Amber! I never said that,' protested Stella. 'There's nothing wrong with Brixton. I can see why Niamh might want to go there. It's very lively, very *multicultural*.'

'So we can go then?' said Amber eagerly. ''Cause Poppy Brenner told me there's this wicked club in the crypt of a church. They let you in with fake ID and you can smoke shisha and stuff.'

'I'm not sure that sounds very . . . what's shisha?'

'Nothing to get freaked out about, Mum. It's fruit tobacco from Morocco. Very *multicultural*.'

'Only your father—'

'Yeah, yeah, zero tolerance, I know. Shisha's *legal*, Mum. They can't touch you for it. *Jeez*!'

'Well, let's just wait and see, shall we?' said Stella quickly. 'I expect Niamh would like to just get home and settle in before we start planning expeditions here, there and everywhere . . .'

No wonder she was so thin, Stella mused, scraping a mound of leftovers from Niamh's plate into the bin. The girl clearly had issues with food. And she couldn't rule out self-harm – Niamh seemed to prefer to let her sleeves dangle in the gravy rather than expose her arms to the world. There had to be a reason for that. Stella was beginning to wonder whether ten days would be enough to get through to this strange waif of a child. She seemed somehow unreachable; not shy or nervous; not resentful of being parcelled off to strangers; just *absent*, somehow.

'Just help yourself from the fridge, Niamh, if ever you're hungry or thirsty,' Stella said. 'Don't feel you have to ask.'

'You go mad when Sam does that,' muttered Amber.

'Sam has a perfectly good fridge of his own round the corner,' said Stella tartly. 'Now, I'm just wondering if your mum wouldn't appreciate a phone call, Niamh. Let her know you got here in one piece?'

Niamh shrugged, took the handset from Stella and

dialled the number. 'Hi,' she said, 'it's me. It's Niamh, Mummy. Yeah. Yeah. It's OK. Yeah, they're nice. OK then, wait a minute. She wants to talk to you.' Niamh handed the phone to Stella, who took it, a little surprised by the brevity of their conversation.

'Hi, Vin?' she said. 'She's absolutely lovely. We're getting on like a house on fire here.'

'God, Stella, I can't thank you enough,' gushed Vinnie breathlessly. Her accent was Dublin one minute and Hampstead the next and her tone was distracted and uneasy, as if she was speaking from a boat that had sprung a leak and was slowly filling up with water. 'She's been absolutely chewing my ear off about coming. I've been promising her a trip to London for ages, but my parents kept putting her off, and then of course they're just old fogeys to Niamh, whereas Hannah—'

'*Amber*.'

'Yes, *Amber* was a huge draw. Niamhy just couldn't wait to meet her. I know they're going to be great pals.'

Stella looked across at them. Amber was texting away furiously on her phone while Niamh stared into space. 'And how are things there? How's Leon?' she asked.

'Fine, fine. I think.'

'You think?'

'He's with Nick, in Barnsley. I've sent them both away.' She laughed hysterically. 'I said I vahnt to be alone! Well, I had to really, I've such a lot to sort out, Stella. You've no idea. End of financial year; bean-counting; my dear, the tedium . . . Still, that's business.'

'By the way, Vin,' Stella lowered her voice conspiratori-ally, 'have you heard about Nell? Of course you can't always believe what you read in the papers, but if it's true, well . . . I don't know what she's thinking—'

'Honestly, darling, I am so out of the loop here, you would not *believe* . . .' interrupted Vinnie. 'Give my love to Nell, though, if you see her. Must dash now. We'll talk soon.' She hung up.

It was only after she had put the phone down that Stella realised Vinnie hadn't even shown a flicker of curiosity. Odd. She was about to clear the table when she heard Dan coming in.

'Aha! Here's the great reformer. Just in the nick of time. Dan, darling . . .' she called. He stuck his head round the door. '*Darling*?' He raised a sardonic eyebrow, then saw Niamh. 'Ah.'

'Come and say hello.'

'Hi, Niamh.' Dan automatically turned on the charm. 'Sorry to be late. Just come from the House; big vote tonight; ayes to the right and all that malarkey. Very satisfactory it was too actually . . .' His attention instinct-ively drifted away from Niamh, who wasn't bothering to disguise her boredom, back to Stella. 'Passed its second reading with a majority of seventy-five. I knew we could get the Tories onside if we went in hard on reclassification.'

'Hmmm. Well done, I suppose,' said Stella. 'When are you going to bring back flogging?'

'Very funny, darling. She's very funny, isn't she, girls?'

Stella turned to Amber. 'Why don't you two go and hang out in your room for a bit?'

'OK then,' said Amber, her voice laden with sarcasm. 'Come on, Niamh. Let's go and "hang out".'

'She looks like something the cat dragged in,' said Dan through a mouthful of food when Niamh and Amber had left the room.

'Shhh, Dan, she'll hear you!' admonished Stella.

'And she's Vinnie's girl?' Dan shook his head in apparent disbelief. 'The apple didn't fall very close to the tree that time, did it?' He carried on chewing for a while, then his eyes lit up. 'Talking of Vinnie . . .' He jabbed his fork at her eagerly. 'You'll never guess what.'

'What?'

'I bumped into Nigel at lunchtime in Soho.' He paused for effect. '*He's only got himself a new agent.*'

'You're kidding. Why?'

Dan's eyes glinted with *schadenfreude*. 'He said he couldn't talk about it. *Sub judice*, he said.'

'Oh my God! But she and Nige have been mates for years. I wonder what's gone wrong?'

'Well, obviously he didn't say much, but reading between the lines, I'd say she's probably had her hand in the till . . .'

'You're kidding. Vinnie? Why would she? She's loaded already.'

'Must have got greedy,' said Dan.

'Oh, for goodness' sake. You're just putting two and two together and making five. I bet it was *Nigel* that got greedy. I bet he's gone to that Jackal bloke. What's his name again?'

'Stella, we're talking about *Nigel* here.'

She pursed her lips. He had a point. If it had been anyone else, she could have believed it, but Nigel was Mr Integrity. If he'd decided to part company with Vinnie, he must have had a good reason. She thought again about Vinnie's slight hysteria on the phone; about the fact that she had offloaded both kids and shown not a flicker of concern for their old friend. Something was definitely up.

Bridget

Bridget took her skinny latte to a quiet area at the back of the coffee shop and sat down in a brown leather tub chair. A quick scan of the sparse clientele told her that her date had not yet arrived. She was getting better, though. The first time she had arranged a rendezvous through Guardian Soulmates she had been twenty minutes early and he'd been ten minutes late. By the time he'd shown up, she had worked her way through two cappuccinos and a blueberry muffin, an indulgence her waistline could ill afford – and all for nothing. She had known the minute he walked through the door that it was a waste of time. Keith. Regeneration Consultant for Tower Hamlets: paunch; earring; man bag. Sucked his teeth like a Cyberman between sentences.

There had been a couple of others, neither axe murderers nor kindred spirits, just perfectly nice blokes to whom Bridget had nothing to say. Then again what *was* there to say? She was a fuck-up who'd fucked up – who'd be interested in that? She'd thrown away a perfectly good relationship with Nigel for a fling with her best friend's husband (she still blanched when she thought of the look in Stella's eyes that night at the Dorchester). And it was worse even than that. Amongst the fallout from that cataclysmic event, she had discovered not only that Dan had no intention (never had had) of leaving Stella for her, but that she was only one among several 'bits on the side'. Far from being 'his lodestone, his anchor, his rock', it turned out she had merely been 'his shag' and neither the youngest nor the prettiest of those, as Stella had taken great satisfaction in informing her once he had confessed the predictable details of his serial infidelity. So if she was reduced to seeking prospective partners though the lonely hearts columns, it was no less than she deserved. And yet, and yet . . . she couldn't help feeling an irrational optimism about today's rendezvous. His ad had made her laugh.

Knight Errant (45, intelligent, sensitive, prone to spontaneous gestures) hopes to win favour of Gentle Lady (curvy, buoyant, zestful, 35–45) for mutual mythologising.

She wasn't sure about buoyant or zestful, but she could definitely do curvy. And it was a long time since anyone had made a spontaneous gesture in her direction, unless you counted the white van man she had cut up at the traffic lights last week. She was, she realised, perching on the edge of the chair, eyes trained on the door, like a sniper. At this rate he'd ride off into the sunset before she'd even had a chance to drop her handkerchief.

She took the *Guardian* out of her bag and forced herself to sit back in her seat. She was flicking through the pages in a vague, unfocused way, when her eye fell on a half-page ad for a new literary festival, featuring small publicity shots of the main attractions: Ben Okri, Linda Grant, Sarah Waters, Nigel Longley. The jolt of recognition felt like an electric shock. She should have been used to it by now, but the familiar wrenching pain seemed to get worse rather than better. It must be at least a year since Nigel had published *Gallowgate*, the third part of his York trilogy. Although the buzz had increased with each volume published, Bridget had become adept at avoiding the brouhaha. She no longer read the arts pages; didn't tune in to *Kaleidescope*; switched off *Late Review* before she could be ambushed by his conspicuous success.

It had all started in a tolerably low-key way. Someone at work had passed her a review in the *TLS* and asked her if it was the same Nigel Longley she used to live with. She had been a bit thrown – she had always assumed his amateur scribbling would come to nothing – but she managed to convince herself she was pleased for him. Then it had snowballed. He'd been all over the broadsheets, credited with reinventing the historical novel. The idea that dull, reliable Nigel had all along been fizzing with imagination and creativity really rankled. She had taken him at face value as an amiable slogger, a football fan, a lover of real ale, an avid reader of 'difficult' books, a reluctant theatre-goer, a benign and sometimes witty dinner party guest, but scarcely the author of 'an erudite novel of skulduggery and anti-Semitism set in twelfth-century York'. Perhaps if she had shown more interest in his writing, instead of assuming it would be amateurish and embarrassing . . . Perhaps if she hadn't underestimated him . . .

'Are you Bridget, by any chance?' Someone rattled the top of her *Guardian*. She looked up, startled.

'Oh, yes. Yes, I am . . . Sorry. I was er . . . and you must be Adrian?'

'Yep. Good to meet you.' He was very tall and had to be at least fifty, but he looked good on it. He had close-cropped greying hair and a weather-beaten face with deep-set dark eyes and a wry smile. He was wearing twisted Levi's, a cord jacket and a short, striped scarf, which he wore intricately knotted in the manner of a male model. It was the sort of look she had been trying to steer Nigel towards throughout their relationship, but which he had resolutely resisted on the basis that he didn't want to look like a wanker.

'Is something funny?' he asked, narrowing his eyes in a not unfriendly way.

'No.' She smiled and put down her newspaper. 'Sorry. Can I get you a coffee?'

'Well, look. I've done a few of these "let's not commit ourselves" coffee-shop dates now . . .'

Typical! He was going to blow her out. She wasn't even worth the price of another latte.

'. . . and without wishing to judge a book by its cover, I've seen enough to know that on this occasion, I'd like to read on.'

God, did he rehearse these gems, Bridget wondered, though she couldn't help feeling flattered. She glanced at her watch. 'Oh, right. Well, what did you have in mind?'

'How about dinner? I know a nice little place in Soho. It's a twenty-minute walk from here, or we could hop in a cab. What do you reckon?'

Nigel would never have used the phrase 'hop in a cab'. On the rare occasions when they had found themselves in need of a taxi, Nigel had dithered ineffectually by the kerb, waving his arms around and calling out with a diffidence that only seemed to invite contempt. He'd invariably seemed relieved when they had given up and resigned themselves to a long wet walk, or a stuffy bus ride. Of course now that he was a literary lion, he probably hopped in cabs all the time . . .

'So,' Adrian said, mopping up the last of his osso bucco with a piece of ciabatta, 'after my experiences in Cambodia and Laos I knew that there was no way I could go back to my job in IT so I decided to retrain.'

'Fantastic,' nodded Bridget. 'What as?'

'I did an MBA and now I'm heading up a team looking into sustainable development programmes.'

Bridget took another slug of wine. He really was very good-looking.

'Anyway,' he said, 'I can't believe you've let me chunter on about myself all this time. What about you? Tell me about *Bridget*.'

'Oh, well, let's see.' Bridget tugged nervously at her

earring. 'I'm a, er . . . civil servant (yawn) but I actually do love my job and it's very varied and demanding. I work for the Department of Culture, so I get lots of free tickets for things – you know, ballets and art shows and stuff – not that I'm suggesting you and I . . . that would be jumping the gun, but it's just one of the perks of the job. I didn't go into it for the perks, of course, I mean, as if . . . who joins the civil service for the perks? I'm actually in it because I believe very, very strongly that culture is a profoundly civilising force in society – you know, for children and, well, everybody really, for bringing them together and sharing experiences and, you know, at a time like this, when there's so much hostility and suspicion and so much misinformation about minority cultures, I think it's of paramount importance that we, as a society, go the extra mile to promote diversity and richness in our cultural life . . .'

Oh God, well, that was it. Date over. She dabbed discreetly at her earlobe, which she had twisted so hard during this impassioned speech that it had started to bleed.

To her astonishment, Adrian was shaking his head admiringly. 'I am blown. Away. By your passion,' he declared. Bridget closed her eyes. So that confirmed it, he really was a complete tosser. She wondered if the sex would be worth it. He drained the wine bottle into Bridget's glass and pushed it towards her. 'And dare I ask about . . . the private life?'

Bridget took a deep breath. 'Hmmm,' she said.

'Please' – he held up his hand – 'if you're not comfortable . . .'

'No, I am, I am. It's just – for someone of my age, it's a bit . . . *thin*. Never married; no kids; one long-standing relationship that broke up ten years ago; my fault . . .'

'It's never one person's fault.' Adrian steepled his fingers in front of his pursed lips.

'No, it was. Believe me. He was lovely. *Is* lovely. He's kind, clever, not bad-looking and, as it turns out, a brilliant writer.'

'And the catch . . . ?'

Bridget shook her head and shrugged, sadly. 'No catch.'

'Oh come on.' Adrian sounded a little irritated. 'There must have been something. Was he was gay? Did he have a drink problem?'

'*I* was the catch. I blew it.' She bit her lip and stared down at the tablecloth. She didn't really care that she had committed the cardinal sin of first dates – talking about your ex. It would almost be a relief if he walked away. But she didn't want to cry. Not in front of this walking cliché of a man. He held out his open palm to her across the table. She looked up in surprise.

'We're all damaged, Bridget, but if we acknowledge it, we can heal.'

She had to hand it to Adrian: he had all the moves. Back at her flat he trailed a finger along the spines of the paperbacks on her bookshelf, occasionally flipping one out and scrutinising the back-cover blurb, as if it would give him some added insight into his hostess's inner life. He complimented her on her CD collection and asked if they could listen to Dido. He rolled a fat joint and they sat together on her squashy nubuck sofa, handing it back and forth while he told how his last relationship had failed because his girlfriend had disinvested emotionally. By the time they kissed, Bridget's lips were numb, but it was still by and large a pleasant enough experience. Once in bed, the efficiency of his technique was only marred by his murmuring in her ear at the moment of orgasm, 'To the max, baby!'

The next morning she awoke to find his finger playing dot-to-dot with the freckles on her upper arms, a dreamy look in his eyes. Her heart sank.

'Good morning, Bridget Rowland.'

'Hi,' replied Bridget, surreptitiously wiping a skein of drool from the side of her mouth with her hand.

'I was thinking . . . nice leisurely breakfast and long lingering bath; then we could hop on a bus and take in the Diane Arbus exhibition at the ICA. Sound like a nice way to spend Saturday?'

'Lovely.' Bridget resisted the urge to flick his hand off her shoulder like a pesky fly. 'Only I'm out of coffee . . . I don't suppose . . . ? There's a Tesco Express round the corner . . .' She pulled a pleading face.

'No problemo. What does Madam prefer? Kenyan? Colombian? Venezuelan?' He was already out of bed and pulling on his Calvin Kleins.

With a flurry of parting kisses, snatched through the gap in the door, he was gone. Bridget shot the bolt and ran herself a deep bath. She turned the radio as loud as it would go, climbed gingerly into the too-hot water and slowly submerged herself, until the strains of Radio 3 sounded like someone playing a hurdy-gurdy at the bottom of a kettle; a tactic to ensure that she wouldn't hear the buzz of the intercom on Adrian's return. Twenty minutes later, thinking she was in the clear, she raised her head cautiously from the rapidly cooling water and reached for the shampoo, only to be ambushed by the telephone ringing shrilly in the living room.

'Oh for God's sake! Take a hint, you thick-skinned oaf,' she called out, turning the radio up a notch, the tap on full on, and sinking guiltily back down into her watery refuge.

Bridget climbed out of the bath, her skin as white and puckered as a maggot's. She wrapped herself in a towel, made a turban of her hair, and went to get herself a coffee, pausing only briefly as she passed through the lounge to cancel the red flashing button on the answering machine.

Nell

They were on air in twenty minutes but Nell was still in make-up.

'I might just try a different concealer,' said Sharon, the make-up artist, delving into her box of tricks. Her voice was breezy, but there was an underlying air of panic. 'I don't want to go with panstick, 'cause you'll look like a pantomime dame, but I just can't get the coverage with the Laura Mercier.'

'Twenty minutes,' came the producer's voice over the tannoy.

'That looks all right,' said Nell, turning her face this way and that in the pitiless strip light, but she knew she was kidding herself. It wasn't the bruising – Sharon had done a magnificent job of blending away the bluey-green tinge that ringed both eyes – it was the puffiness and swelling that gave the game away, as well as the crusty scab on the bridge of her nose.

'I've just checked with Mandy,' said the floor manager, popping her head round the door, 'and she's all set to stand in if you want her to. Might be best, do you think? Give you another twenty-four hours for the swelling to subside?'

Nell shook her head fiercely. Mandy was getting far too much airtime as it was and her on-screen chemistry with Mark was much commented on in the press. She'd been waiting for an opportunity like this ever since she'd last deputised for Nell on the show. Couldn't wait to get her Manolos under the table. The director came in, took one look at Nell and winced.

'Ooh. Not pretty, is it? Look, Nell, if you want to go on like that, fine, but you'll have to explain – tell the viewers what happened – otherwise they'll believe what they read in tabloids.'

'Bastards!' spat Nell. 'I wouldn't mind but I don't even need a nose job. There's nothing *wrong* with my nose.'

'I know, it's an outrageous slur, but you know what they're like. If you don't throw them a bone, they'll make it up. If you deny the nose job, they'll just say you did it falling out of a taxi on the way to the Priory. Better to get your retaliation in first. We could script a funny little exchange with Mark . . .'

'No thank you.'

'Just tell them the truth. Your bad knee buckled and you fell down some steps. That way you'll get the sympathy vote. We could even tie it in with a phone-in on disability.'

'No, Tony, I'm the journalist, not the story. I don't want people pitying the poor cripple—' Nell's mobile started ringing. She shot him an exasperated look and picked it up.

'Fifteen minutes,' he whispered pointedly.

At the sound of her sister's voice, Nell sprang out of the chair and moved out of earshot. 'How did you get this number?' she said *sotto voce*.

'Your agent gave it to me.'

Nell sighed. 'So what's it about, Clover? Because I'm on air in ten minutes. You couldn't have picked a worse time.'

'If you'd bothered to pick up your messages you'd already know. It's Mum.'

Nell turned her back to the room and lowered her voice further still. 'What about her?'

'She's had a fall.'

Nell rolled her eyes. 'Must run in the family.'

'What do you mean?'

'Never mind.'

'And she keeps going AWOL. It's the Alzheimer's – it's getting worse. The other day they found her sitting in a bus shelter in her nightie. You're going to have to come down, Nell. We need to sort something out. I can't cope on my own any more.'

'You're not on your own. There's Gunther,' Nell pointed out impatiently.

'Nell, Gunther doesn't want to be lifting Mum on and off the commode. It's not dignified.'

Nell sighed. 'OK, well, when we come off air I'll do some ringing round. See if I can sort you out some respite care.'

'I think you ought to see her,' Clover said stubbornly, 'while she can still remember who you are.'

Nell glanced up at the director who was now in a huddle with Mark. She could tell they were talking about her. She saw Mark look across and suppress a smirk. 'All right, all right. I'll see what I can do.'

'Problem, darling?' asked the director, coming over, a look of concern on his face.

Nell glanced in the mirror again. She looked as though she'd gone seven rounds with Mike Tyson. 'It's my mother,' she said. 'She's very ill. Can you get hold of Mac and ask him to pick me up after the show? I need to get down to Devon.'

'Go *now*,' said Tony, seizing his chance. 'Take the rest of the week. Sort out the old lady; give yourself time to recuperate; have a *break*, Nell. You deserve it. It'll keep the press off your back too. Makes perfect sense.' He turned to the floor manager. 'Go and tell Mandy she's on in ten.'

As Nell fumed her way down the corridor towards her dressing room, she passed Mandy, mic-ed up and buzzing, coming the other way.

'Break a leg,' Nell muttered, without smiling.

'West Country, is it?' said Mac, flicking his fag end out of the car window as Nell approached. 'Lovely jubbly. I could fancy a holiday. Whereabouts?'

'Torquay, Mac. Jewel of the English Riviera. Home of the incontinence pad and the Zimmer frame.'

Mac grinned. 'You don't sound too keen.'

'Needs must.' Nell shrugged, clambering awkwardly into the back seat. 'Can you take me home first? I need to pack a bag.'

'Right you are, milady.' Mac tipped an imaginary chauffeur's cap and pulled out into the traffic. As the Lexus crawled through the London streets, Nell sent a text to Clover. 'On my way. Can you book me a room? Dont spose tq runs to a 5*?' And almost immediately received one back.

'U can stay with us.'

'Gee, thanks!' muttered Nell under her breath. So she was going home to Arundel Close. Great.

Clover and her feckless boyfriend Gunther had moved into her mother's council house as a stop-gap when they got evicted from their squat ten years earlier. Somehow they had never got it together to move out again. It had been pretty squalid when Nell had left it in 1980, and the addition of a commode and Gunther's collection of cannabis plants could scarcely have done much to enhance the ambience. Mentally, she prepared herself for twenty-four hours of grimy hippydom: cats, crystals and crochet; cheap muesli for breakfast and vile vegetarian stodge. There would be nowhere to hang her clothes and she'd probably have to give three days' notice if she wanted a bath. She texted back 'Lovely!' and made a mental note to pack a Jo Malone room fragrance.

The fug of London gave way to the leafy lanes of Hertfordshire, and as the Lexus came within sight of Percival

House, Nell sat up in her seat, anxiously scanning the horizon in the hope that the helipad would be empty, Des having been whisked away to some meeting or other, but as the iron gates glided open, she saw that his helicopter was still there and so were all three of his cars. He must have gone on a bender. That was generally the pattern. Drink; violence; remorse; more drink.

'Can you drive round the back, Mac? I'll just slip in through the kitchen. Don't want to bother Mr Percival.'

'Right you are.'

With a knowing glance in the rear-view mirror, Mac switched off the engine and allowed the Lexus to coast round to the tradesman's entrance. Nell slipped off her shoes and padded silently up the thickly carpeted stairs. She threw a random selection of jeans and jumpers into her case, scattered in a few cosmetics for good measure and was zipping it up when she heard Des coming up the stairs.

'Nell, sweetheart, is that you?' He stood swaying slightly in the doorway, his eyes bloodshot. He wore the slightly sheepish expression of a small boy who should have been sitting on the naughty step.

'Hello, darling,' said Nell, 'I didn't want to disturb you. I'm going to have to dash, I'm afraid. Clover called. My mother's not well.'

Des came over and grasped her by the shoulders. His breath was sour with whisky, but she didn't dare recoil. 'Running home to Mother?'

'Of course not, Des. Sweetie . . . you're hurting me. I'll only be gone a day or two. Promise.'

'Sure you're coming back?' He stared imploringly into her eyes. 'Because I wouldn't blame you if you left me. I'm a brute, a fucking animal, but I want you to know it's never going to happen again. You do know that, don't you? I give you my solemn promise. Never, never, never. You're the most precious thing in the world to me – I'm nothing without you, Nell.'

'I know, Des,' she said, keeping her voice light. 'Don't worry, I'm coming back. You can't get rid of me that easily.'

Still grasping her shoulders he puckered his wet mouth and covered hers in an urgent, boozy kiss. She was careful to let it run its course, not shrinking away, even when she felt his cock stir ominously in his trousers. At last he relinquished her, perhaps realising that, with the amount of Scotch he had coursing through his veins, humiliation was the likeliest outcome if he attempted a farewell fuck.

'Phone me when you get there, won't you? And tell Mac to watch his speed. Precious cargo – that's what you are. Tell him, eh? From me.'

'I'll be absolutely fine, don't you worry. Now you . . .' she steered him towards the bed, ' . . . are going to have a nice lie-down and I'll get Celeste to rustle you up a full English for when you wake up. Be good for what ails you, eh?'

He sat down obediently and she squatted awkwardly next to him and eased off his loafers. He put out one finger and touched the scab on her nose. He bit his bottom lip and his eyes welled up.

'All forgotten,' she whispered. He keeled over like a felled tree and by the time she had zipped her case and left the room he was already snoring.

Nell dozed as the Lexus sped down the M5, drifting in and out of consciousness to the strains of Radio 2. The grey clouds parted and a shaft of watery sunlight broke through as Mac pulled off the slip road towards the outskirts of Torquay.

'Sorry to wake you, love, but I'm going to need some directions soon,' he said. 'It's a lovely-looking place, I must say. Don't know what you've got against it.'

Nell sat up and took in the blur of anodyne, pebble-dashed suburbs, fuchsia hedges and the occasional palm tree quivering in the stiff onshore breeze. 'They live in Shiphay,' she said. 'If you go down to the promenade, it should be signed from the roundabout . . .'

As they drove down the seafront, she was assailed by a host of unwelcome memories: the ping and chug of the slot machines in the amusement arcade; the whiff of rancid chip fat; the agony of sand chafing her private parts after an evening's grope under the pier with Paolo or Heinz or Jean-Charles. She had buried it all so deep, it might almost have happened to someone else; but now that she was back here, she felt as though the past was opening wide to swallow her whole. Following her directions, Mac drove away from the centre and towards a less salubrious part of town.

'This is it, coming up on the left, Arundel Close.' She

leaned forward in her seat, almost expecting to see her old Raleigh bike, wheels still spinning on the grass verge, the window to Clover's room open and blaring the top twenty countdown on Radio 1.

'Right!' said Nell, steeling herself. 'This is me. Can you find something to do for a few hours, Mac? I'm not planning on staying the night if I can help it.'

'If there's a betting shop and a chippy, I'm sorted, love,' said Mac. 'You just give me a bell when you're ready to go.'

Nell picked her way across the weed-infested crazy paving and rang the doorbell.

'She's here!' came Clover's excited squeal through the whorled glass of the front door, and Nell sensed that awe for her celebrity had won out over resentment of her long absence. She flung the door open and Nell stepped inside. The house smelled sweet and slightly fetid – the mingled scents of old carpet, cat pee and patchouli. She put down her case and hugged Clover awkwardly. She looked old, Nell noticed. Old and poor. As they pulled apart, Clover noticed her injured face.

'What happened there?' she asked solicitously.

'Oh, it's nothing. I just lost my footing coming down some steps.'

'Come in the kitchen, I'll get Gunther to put some arnica on it. Gunther . . . ?'

'It's fine, really.'

'No, honestly, it'll help with the bruising.'

Gunther came waddling out of the kitchen, a grubby

apron straining over his considerable bulk. He had a potato peeler in one hand and a stray peeling lodged in his beard. Nell didn't fancy playing doctors and nurses with him.

'My poor child.' His accent was still thick, despite having lived in the UK for twenty-five years. He held his arms out to her as if she were a refugee.

'Hello, Gunther,' she said, briskly sidestepping his proffered embrace. 'I'm absolutely fine, don't worry. Where's Mother?'

'She's resting,' said Clover. 'We've made up the divan in the lounge for her. She can't manage the stairs since her fall. Dr Patel says she's going to need a hip replacement, but the waiting list's horrendous.'

'Why didn't you say? I'll pay for her to go private.'

'I *would* have said,' snapped Clover, 'if you'd returned my calls.' It seemed the sheen of Nell's celebrity was starting to wear off.

'Yes, I'm sorry. I've been working round the clock. The show's a victim of its own success, I'm afraid. They want a weekend omnibus edition and that's meant prerecording a load of links. You wouldn't believe the—'

'It's pretty busy down here too,' interrupted Clover, 'what with the doctors' appointments and social services assessments and trying to get Mum to the luncheon club once in a while.'

'The luncheon club?' said Nell incredulously. 'Are we talking about the same woman?'

Gunther took Nell by the arm and led her gently towards the kitchen, where he had left a noxious sauce bubbling on the hob. 'The fact is, Nell, we're not. We're not talking of the same woman at all. You will see.'

Vinnie

Vinnie swung open the door of her vast Smeg fridge and reached for a bottle of Chablis. She took a mug from the draining board, filled it to the brim and drank half of it in one long swig. She knew she ought to have something to eat, but since Leon had left, stocks had dwindled and now there was nothing to tempt her but a packet of green-tinged bacon, a browning lettuce and half a Camembert. She slammed the door shut again and lit a cigarette instead. She had been desperate for the kids to leave; desperate. The pressure to make out everything was normal had been horrendous; but now that they'd gone, she felt their absence like a physical pain. Niamh had left meekly, perhaps aware on some level that her mother didn't have the resources to look after her, but Leon had railed against Vinnie's decision. He had called her selfish and irresponsible for foisting Niamh on to complete strangers and packing him off to his dad's. He'd told her he had a good mind to stay in Barnsley and never come back.

'Barnsley!' Vinnie had scoffed. 'You wouldn't last two

minutes, a sham like you,' but Leon soon wiped the smile off her face, telling her there was more to life than craic, that his father's home might be on a shabby estate, but there was always a decent meal on the table and someone to talk to. His stepmother, Faye, might not have famous parents and a university degree, he told her in his parting shot, but she would at least see her kids off at the airport, not chuck them in a taxi and hope for the best. And Vinnie had taken it, because what other choice did she have? She could hardly tell her son that if she got anywhere *near* the airport she was likely to be picked up by the Garda for breaking her bail conditions. But as the cab had driven off, she had stood in the road watching the tail-lights get smaller and smaller, tears streaming down her face.

There was nothing for her in Dublin now, except the band. It was the one thing stopping her from jumping in the Liffey. But even they were bailing out soon. That's why tonight was crucial. They were playing a one-off session at Johnny McGhee's to limber up before they took the new album on the road. If she could just get with Sean tonight, seal the deal, it would see her through. Just the knowledge that what they had was special; that one aspect of her life was opening out, instead of shutting down . . . Her lawyer had told her that, with her background, there was a good chance she'd get a suspended sentence (there weren't many people who could call Richard Attenborough as a character witness). But the thought of starting again all by herself was a bleak one. She needed someone by her side and Sean seemed like a good bet. OK, so he was a bit of a Neanderthal – he liked men to be men and women to be willing – but that was OK with Vinnie. She'd had more than her fair share of the other sort – they always let you down in the end. It wasn't as though she'd *planned* to be a career woman – she'd only resorted to it because she couldn't find a man she could rely on. Nothing would make her happier, if Sean was up for it, than to stay at home cooking colcannon and growing her own.

She topped up her wine, crushed her fag out in the fire-place and switched on the stereo. The band's new CD was already in place. She pressed play and returned to the coffee table, where she cut herself a line using her Brown Thomas charge card and snorted it through a rolled-up pizza flyer. It was their best album yet – not a single dud track, but the best by far was the one coming up next; the new single, 'Heart-shaped Hole'. And she didn't *only* think that because it had been written about her. She sat back and closed her eyes, waiting for the familiar drum beat to begin, then intensify, the organ and bass to send a tingle down her spine and then Sean's voice to wrap around her like a caress.

I've got a heart-shaped hole where you stole it away,
With your little-girl smile, that night on the tiles.
You took it and ran without looking back,
You put it in your haversack
And said, 'This is mine, this heart-shaped heart
And you can keep your heart-shaped hole.
Yeah, baby, you can keep your heart-shaped hole.

The track came to an end. Vinnie put down her mug and ran up the stairs, suddenly feeling quite carefree. She was in the mood, now, to make it all happen. She just needed a bit of war paint, some half-decent threads, and he was hers for the taking. As she reached the landing, the phone rang. She hesitated for a second, but decided to ignore it. Having calibrated her mood so carefully, it would be a shame to bring herself down again with bad news (and lately it did always seem to be bad news). The answering machine kicked in. As she sponged on foundation, she heard Stella's breezy, down-to-earth tone: '. . . not sure how much leeway she gets at home . . . wanted to check you were OK with it . . .' Oh, I'm OK with it, thought Vinnie. I'm absolutely fine with it, sweetie. She brushed dark green shimmer on to her eyelids. '. . . thinking of going to Brixton . . . quite gentrified nowadays . . . Amber very sensible . . . money for a taxi . . . keep their mobiles on,' burbled Stella. 'Whatever; yep; sounds great,' Vinnie replied out loud. The poor woman seemed to be labouring under the delusion that Niamh spent her days reciting the catechism at the knees of the Mother Superior. Vinnie painted a line of black along her upper eyelids with the precision of Michelangelo. 'Oh and Vinnie, I know you're up against it right now, but I'm thinking of organising a reunion, and I wanted to sound you out about dates.' A reunion? Vinnie frowned. A reunion of what? But Stella was still prattling. 'Anyway, give us a call when you've got your diary out and if you've any objection, you know, to the Brixton idea, just let me know. The last thing

I want to do is tread on your toes . . .' Stella signed off with a nervous giggle, but Vinnie's toes were moving too fast for anyone to step on them now. She was like Moira Shearer in *The Red Shoes*: possessed; unstoppable; she hovered above the ground with her dizzying charm and her seductive smile and as she gave herself the final once-over in the bathroom mirror, she knew there was no one to touch her.

'You're looking very lovely, Lavinia.' The barman in Johnny McGhee's plucked Vinnie's favourite tipple from the fridge and poured her a large glass, without waiting to be asked.

'Thanks, Gerard,' smiled Vinnie, perching on a barstool. She dusted her nostrils delicately with the back of her hand. She had brushed up rather well, if she said so herself; not many women could carry off a leather miniskirt at her age (the secret being to dress it down with biker boots and opaque tights, rather than going for the full-on hooker vibe). Just as well. There was a lot of competition tonight. A clutch of young women, not much older than Niamh – all hair extensions and no knickers – had got wind of the gig and staked out the area in front of the stage. They didn't worry Vinnie though. She happened to have it on the very best authority that Sean liked his women mature – 'Like a Connemara single malt, darlin',' he had told her, before throwing his head back in ecstasy at the sheer virtuosity of her technique.

'What time are they on?' she called to Gerard, who by now, octopus-like, was pulling pints, pouring drinks and serving crisps and peanuts to several different punters at once.

'S'posed to be ten,' he shouted back, 'but you know what they're like . . .'

Vinnie mingled happily with the other members of the inner circle, the roadies, the sound guys and the die-hard fans. They talked about the set list, and what was on the rider, and passed nuggets of privileged information back and forth.

'They're going to go acoustic on "War Child" apparently, should be amazing . . .'

Ten thirty came and went, then ten forty-five. Vinnie was starting to come down. She had noticed a ladder in her tights and, in the sweaty pre-gig atmosphere, her up-do was wilting. She had talked to everyone she knew and drunk as much as she dared. She had to get her sparkle back, before the band came on, or the evening would be ruined. She felt in her pocket for her last baggy and sloped off to the loos, but the queue was slow-moving and just as she reached the front, she was elbowed out of the way by a drunken redhead.

'I was next, you scanger!' shouted the girl. 'I've been touchin' cloth for half a feckin' hour so don't think you can be pushin' in just 'cause you've forgotten your incontinence pads!' There was a collective hoot of derision from her friends, but by the time Vinnie had recovered her composure and thought of a suitable come-back, they had gone. She hurried into the cubicle and sorted herself out. As she came out again, the pink-fringed lampshades on either side of the mirror were already twitching to the bass line of the band's first number. With barely a glance at her reflection, she rushed out again. Sean would be pissed at her if she wasn't up the front in her usual place. She barged her way through but the Lolita brigade weren't giving any ground. They gyrated wildly, hair flying, bare midriffs aglow with perspiration, their enthusiasm acting like Viagra on certain members of the band. No matter how many toes she stepped on or shins she kicked, Vinnie couldn't break through, and when Sean paused between numbers to cool down, she nearly dislocated her shoulder trying to throw her scarf onstage for him. Worse, instead of retrieving it to mop himself down as he usually did, he stepped over it and doused himself instead with bottled water, which trickled down his bare torso and sent the women in the crowd berserk. Vinnie felt the evening slipping away from her; she had so much wanted the gig to be perfect; for them to make a connection. She needed to know that she was his muse, not just a face in the crowd.

'The next number's gonna be our new single,' murmured Sean hoarsely into the mic. 'It's a very special song for a very special lady. "Heart-shaped Hole".' Vinnie almost melted with relief.

'A one, a two, a one two three four . . .'

Vinnie closed her eyes and surrendered to the swooning melody, the poetic lyrics. This was all she needed, this one song; it was better than any drug, better almost than the sex would be later, because she knew that without her, it would never have existed. Here was living proof that she was his Sara Lowndes, his Patti Boyd, his Yoko Ono. But as the song swelled and grew, and Sean's voice reached its full yearning power, Vinnie became aware of an irritating off-key hum coming from somewhere nearby. She glanced to her left. The redhead who'd pushed in front of her in the toilets was swaying from side to side, crooning discordantly in Vinnie's ear. 'You put it in your haversa-a-a-a-ck, and said this is mine, this hear-ear-eart-shaped heart.'

'Shhh!' she said, unable to contain herself. 'Nobody came here to listen to *you*.' The girl wheeled round, her face quickly changing from blissed-out to livid. Vinnie felt a surge of adrenalin, but stood her ground. The girl looked her slowly up and down, then recognition dawned and she laughed out loud. 'You again, Grandma!' she shouted. 'Sure, if you don't like it, you can always turn your hearin' aid off.' She smirked at her companions and a ripple of amusement spread out among the crowd.

Vinnie felt herself blushing; she felt sick with humiliation, but she stood her ground, arms folded, foot tapping, turning away occasionally to flick a hot tear from her cheek with the back of her hand. bide your time, Vinnie, she told herself, bide your time . . .

It was humiliating, nevertheless, at the end of the gig to have to congregate at the stage door with hoi polloi and wait for Sean to give her the nod. She hung back from the throng, trying to look nonchalant, patting her hair occasionally and shifting her weight from foot to foot, but everything she had drunk and snorted seemed only to have heightened her paranoia. The usual sensation of being borne aloft on a current of her own sheer fabulousness had evaporated with the pitying expression on that cow's face. Still, revenge was sweet. The door was opening. The reckoning was about to take place. The members of the band shook hands, high-fived, signed autographs. Two or three die-hards were admitted. Sean scanned the throng, bestowing his largesse with a slap on the back here, a 'How yer doin'?' there, ushering people through with a nod and a wink. It was mostly women left now. Fleetingly, he looked at Vinnie, and her heart leaped.

'Great set . . .' she started to say, moving forward, her hand outstretched, fluttering, tentative as a butterfly beside his elbow, but his attention had already moved on, as if he hadn't seen her; as if she didn't exist. He was otherwise engaged now, sharing a joke with the slutty redhead who'd ruined Vinnie's night, his hand on her shoulder, his lips moving close to her ear. She laughed a dirty laugh and threw a triumphant glance in Vinnie's direction as Sean propelled her backstage with a pat to her denim-clad bottom.

And then the door was closing again and Mick the roadie was toughing it out with the rejects.

'Sorry, guys, we've got to vacate the premises now. See you next time.'

'Mick! Hey, Mick! I need to get backstage,' said Vinnie, clutching the sleeve of his leather jacket. She no longer cared that she was drawing amused glances from the rest of the fans.

'Sorry, Vinnie. Next time maybes. I'll tell Sean you said hi.' She could see pity on his face, but also irritation.

'No, Mick, listen, you don't understand . . .' She moved closer to him, coiled her hands round the back of his neck, murmured in his ear, 'I really *need* you to do this for me. You know what I'm saying . . . ?' She brushed her knee against his inner thigh, but he unhooked himself firmly from her grasp.

'No, Vinnie, love. Don't be makin' an eejit of yourself now, you're too good for that.' And he dispatched her with a despairing shake of his grizzled head. 'Sorry, guys, got to clear the place now; tour dates on the website, let's move it along. See yous all next time.'

And Vinnie was outside on the pavement, the wind whipping round her exposed thighs, her hair veiling her eyes, unsure whether the salt she could taste was from her own tears or the ozone tang of the Liffey which had just reached high tide.

Bridget

'So, if there are no more questions from the floor, it only remains for me to thank Nigel for his fascinating talk and to remind you that he will be signing copies of *Gallowgate*, which can be purchased at a discount on production of your entry ticket to this event. Thank you, everybody.'

There was another smattering of polite applause and then the audience began to disperse. Bridget took her place at the back of an already sizeable queue.

'Not a word is wasted, Monica, not one word,' she overheard a woman saying smugly to her friend, as though she had written the book herself. Many of the audience already seemed to own dog-eared hardback copies of the novel, but were purchasing multiple paperbacks to give to all their friends. It took twenty minutes for Bridget to shuffle to the head of the queue. Nigel held his hand out automatically.

'Whom shall I dedicate it to?' he asked, without looking up. Bridget put her newly purchased hardback into his hand.

'Bridget,' she said.

'Jesus, Brid! What the hell are you doing here?' Nigel's editor and publicist, who were standing nearby sipping white wine and congratulating each other on how well it had gone, pricked up their ears.

'That's not much of a welcome, Nige. I'm here with a friend and it seemed churlish not to pop in and say hi.'

He had lost weight, she noticed, and whoever was cutting his hair was doing a better job than the ham-fisted barber he used to go to in Crouch End. She couldn't see the cut of his trousers, because he was sitting down, but he was wearing a linen jacket over a paisley shirt. He looked good.

'Don't I get a kiss?' She proffered her cheek across the table and he blundered to his feet, blushing furiously, to oblige.

'Er, Jane, Miranda,' he said, turning to his two minders, 'this is Bridget, my ... er ... an old friend.' The women acknowledged her coolly, as if she was just another hanger-on. She felt like slapping them. He was mine, she felt like shouting in their horsey faces. And when he stopped being mine it was my say-so, not his. He only left because I made him; for his own sake; for his pride. I could have snapped my fingers and had him back any time I pleased, so don't you look at me as though I'm some come-day-go-day literary groupie. She hadn't completely lost her touch, either, she could tell by Nigel's flustered demeanour and the way he kept nervously fingering his collar. He wrote a dedication on the title page of the book and handed it back to her. She turned away, and then, casually, back again, as though it had just occurred to her.

'How about a drink for old times' sake?' she asked.

Nigel's face lit up, until Miranda put a hand on his sleeve and murmured something in his ear.

'Oh God, yes, I forgot,' he said, turning to Bridget regretfully. 'I've got to go to a dinner. Bunch of medievalists want to pick over my sources. Deadly dull, but . . . listen, where are you staying? Maybe we could catch up afterwards.'

'I'm at the Star on the High Street.'

'Me too. What a coincidence. Well, if you're still around when I've finished with the dons, I'll see you in the bar.'

Bridget tucked her book under her arm and, with a triumphant smirk in the direction of Jane and Miranda, walked out of the hall.

It was a warm evening and, having no interest in literary events other than Nigel's, Bridget decided to go for a stroll. She headed up towards a pretty ruined abbey on the hillside. Her route took her over a stile and through a field of teepees, where the family-friendly end of the festival was taking place. She passed stalls advertising face-painting and puppet-making, story-telling sessions and treasure hunts. Tyrannical middle-class children were dashing around, half-clothed and streaked with mud, like something out of *Lord of the Flies*, demanding that their parents pick the avocado out of their sushi rolls and buy them bottles of organic apple juice at £1.60 a pop. Bridget was just congratulating herself on having avoided the thankless task of raising the next generation of egomaniacs when she spotted a face she thought she recognised. A harassed-looking man in shorts and a faded Ramones T-shirt was pegging clothes to a makeshift washing line suspended between a nearby bush and the luggage rack of his beaten-up VW camper van. She stood for a moment, shielding her eyes from the low sun, trying to think why he looked so familiar. As she watched, a dishevelled woman in a hectic sundress and a beanie hat backed out of the van with a squirming toddler under one arm.

'Steve,' she called, 'I think Saffy's done a poo. Can you do the honours?'

Steve Pinder. Of course. He was much thicker set than when Bridget had known him. His hair had thinned and worry lines were etched deep into his forehead. Domesticity had clearly taken its toll. But as soon as his partner (she could have sworn he called her Twink) handed the toddler into his arms, Steve's expression changed like sunlight on a pond, from mild irritation to tenderness, and then, when he blew a raspberry on the baby's bare belly and elicited a gurgle of delight, to undisguised glee.

Bridget looked briefly away, stung by the contrast with the Steve she remembered; she could still see the recalcitrant jut of his chin as she imparted the news of her pregnancy in the library coffee bar; hear his abrupt put down, 'Well, I didn't mean a cottage with roses round the door . . .' Yet here he was, the very model of middle-aged uxoriousness. And if she couldn't quite imagine his camper van parked outside said cottage, it wasn't difficult to picture it parked up an alley in Hebden Bridge or Totnes. Of course, she reasoned, twenty years was a long time. Most men knuckled under in the end and she could see, now, that Steve was nothing special; never had been. It wasn't the sight of the baby, either, that was making Bridget clench and unclench her fists by her sides, her throat tight with emotion. She felt no pang of loss or envy, watching the baby kicking her chubby legs on the grass. That was one decision she had never regretted.

No, what she recognised, suddenly, in this otherwise far from enviable domestic tableau, was the messy, compromised sprawl of a successful relationship; the Steve she had known would doubtless have shot himself if he could have glimpsed his future sock- and sandal-wearing self, changing nappies at the behest of a woman with a pixie's name. But this was who he had become, and he seemed happy enough with it. Yet, while he had been making his accommodation with real life, Bridget had been fleeing it; busily questing after the ideal relationship, not realising that the raw material was under her nose and just wanted shaping.

She watched Steve expertly parcel up the dirty nappy and stand the toddler back on her feet, then, afraid that he would notice her, she hurried on, picking her way between picnic blankets and guy ropes, stumbling slightly in her haste to leave the field behind and rejoin the sandy foot-path. There was comfort in the exertion of the climb. For twenty minutes, she barely looked up, just concentrated on putting one foot in front of the other, listening to her ragged breath, feeling her thudding heart, relishing the burning sensation in her calf muscles. The abbey was a lot further than it had looked and by the time she reached it, the sun had dipped behind the hill. She sat down on a ruined wall and surveyed the dusk-purpled fields far below her. The families were like colourful ants now in all their busy, pointless activity; so much better to be up here among the gargoyles and the saints.

She noticed, for the first time, that she was still clutching her copy of *Gallowgate*. She opened it at the title page. 'Love, always, Nigel', it said. She closed it again with a snap of satisfaction. Perhaps it wasn't too late.

By the time Bridget had showered and changed into a flattering halter-neck summer dress, the bar of the Star Inn was heaving with festival-goers. If the landlord took exception to their metropolitan braying, he didn't show it as he served up pint after pint of Poacher's Choice at a special seasonal price. Bridget sat in the only available seat, beside the women's toilet, demurely sipping a glass of Pimm's. She was determined to keep a clear head for her conversation with Nigel, but with no one to keep her company and her nerves starting to jangle, it was hard to resist its minty coolness on the back of her throat. She told herself it wasn't very alcoholic and ordered another.

She spotted him the minute he walked in and her stomach flipped like a schoolgirl's. It was the first time he had ever had this effect on her. This was a feeling she associated with unattainable men – men like Steve Pinder and Dan – not dear dependable Nige, and it augured well. If she could just get past the slight air of condescension she habitually felt towards him, they might stand a chance. She was pleased to see that he had ditched the Sloanes, but was a little perturbed when he was waylaid crossing the bar by an attractive young female acquaintance, who insisted on standing him a pint. When he finally reached Bridget, with an apologetic eye-roll, she was surprised to find herself trembling as she half rose and submitted to his clumsy bear hug. Despite a whiff of expensive after-shave, he still smelled of Nigel. She was surprised how much the scent of him moved her.

'Come on, you're too gorgeous to sit by the bogs,' he said, picking up her drink. She followed him meekly, surprised by his new-found air of authority, and found herself in a pretty courtyard strung with coloured lights. She manoeuvred herself awkwardly into position on one side of the trestle table and Nigel hopped nimbly into place opposite her.

'How's the Pimm's?' he asked, grinning as if at some secret joke.

'Are you taking the piss?' He had always teased her for her unerringly middle-class tastes.

'No, I'm just pleased to see you.'

'Well, I'm pleased to see you too.'

There was a silence. They stared at their drinks, then they looked up at the same time and laughed.

'So, we're both pleased then,' she said.

'Apparently.'

'I haven't read your books,' she said with a slight edge of defiance.

'I didn't expect you would. You hate historical novels.'

'Is that why you wrote them?'

'Yes. To spite you.' He grinned again and she found herself wishing it were true, wishing that he had lived the whole of the last ten years as a riposte to her.

'Don't laugh at me.'

'I'm not.'

She pushed an abandoned bottle top along a slat of the table until it fell through and tinkled on to the floor. She hadn't expected to feel tongue-tied. 'I like what you wrote in my copy.'

Nigel shrugged, but coloured slightly.

'I've found myself wondering if we couldn't . . .' She looked up at him enquiringly, but he leaned across and laid a finger over her lips.

'Don't. You don't mean it. We've been here before. Let's just enjoy tonight. Time out of time.'

She smiled pensively, uncertain where this left her. 'Seen much of Stella?' she asked, to break the silence.

'We get together now and again. She and Dan are still making a go of it. Just. Although I think Stella finds him a bit of an embarrassment.'

'I'm not surprised,' muttered Bridget bitterly.

'Actually, I was thinking of his politics,' he said with a wry smile. He still had an uncanny ability to read her mind. 'Stella's always hated Blair, so it can't have been easy watching Dan disappear bit by bit up his fundament.'

Bridget smiled. 'Must be hard on Amber too,' she observed. 'Having high-profile parents.'

'Yeah, Stella reckons she's playing up a bit.'

'She must be, what, sixteen now?' Bridget speculated.

'Some godmother you turned out to be.'

'Ah, but I never was a *god*mother. That would have been ideologically unsound. A moral guardian, I think they called me.'

'Hmmm . . .' said Nigel.

'All right, I know. I didn't exactly cover myself in glory in that department.'

'Still,' said Nigel philosophically, 'we've all moved on, haven't we, water under the bridge and all that?'

'Stella hasn't,' said Bridget.

'Really?' Nigel looked surprised. 'Have you, you know . . . ?'

'Apologised? Many times. It's no wonder I'm fat as a pig, the amount of humble pie I've eaten!'

'No joy?'

'Wouldn't come to the phone, didn't answer my emails . . .'

'Have you tried recently?'

Bridget shrugged. 'What's the point?'

'Only . . .'

'What?'

'It's probably nothing . . .'

'Well, you have to tell me now.'

'It's just . . .' He looked embarrassed. '. . . I think she's organising some sort of Albacore Street thing and I thought that must mean you and she—'

'Without *me*?' Bridget interrupted.

'I'm sure it must just be an oversight,' floundered Nigel. 'They wouldn't get together without you. It'd be like, I don't know – the Jackson Five without Michael, the Bay City Rollers without . . . Brid, oh Brid, don't cry.'

'I'm sorry. It's just . . .' Bridget pressed her fingertips to her temples and tried to compose herself. 'I've made such a hash of things, Nige. I've hurt all the people I care about and now I'm on my own and everyone's moved on and it's too late to make amends.'

'Not . . . necessarily,' he said slowly. Bridget looked up in surprise and he met her gaze, then he reached out and stroked her hand. 'You're cold,' he said. 'Do you want to go back inside?'

She glanced through the window. The bar was still heaving. 'Why don't we go to my room?' she said.

'I forgot how good you were.' Bridget lay, one hand tucked under her cheek, the other cupping Nigel's on the adjacent pillow.

'Aw, shucks.' He grinned.

'No, really. You're a very generous lover. Always were. Jeez, when I think about . . .'

' . . . all the times you said you had a headache?' guessed Nigel shrewdly. 'When actually you were getting it from Dan.'

She winced. 'Nige, please don't. I was so stupid. I just didn't appreciate what I had. God, that sounds lame.'

'It does, yes,' he agreed.

'But I do *now*, that's the point. That's why I was so happy when you said it wasn't too late.'

He pushed himself up on one elbow, frowning and smiling at the same time. 'When I said . . . ?'

'Nige!' She smiled indulgently. 'Outside, in the courtyard; when I was saying I'd blown it and you said you were giving me a second . . . Why are you looking like somebody died?'

'Christ, Brid, I was talking *generally*. I meant, you know, in *life*, it's never too late. Not that I wanted to have another shot at . . .' He flapped his hand back and forth between the two of them. 'Oh Christ, what a . . . I thought we both knew this was just a one-off, you know, for old times' sake . . .'

Suddenly Bridget was drowning. The word 'just' clanged in her head like a bell-buoy. This wasn't 'just' anything. This was a resurrection; a rebirth. This was love; late-blooming, snatched-at love, but love nevertheless. Surely he could see that? But she was looking in his eyes now and all she could see was fear: fear of awkwardness; fear of *entanglement*. She could feel herself going under, down, down, to where sunlight couldn't penetrate, to where weed and murk clung and blind prehistoric creatures swam. There was no surfacing from this. And yet even as she drifted log-like towards the bottom, some brittle, needy part of her still burst through the surface.

'Oh my God!' Her peal of laughter was too loud and too long. 'You didn't think . . . oh Nigel, that's very sweet. You thought I was trying to get back with you? Oh darling . . . I think we both know that boat sailed long ago. No, what I meant was . . .' What did she mean? What on earth did she mean? 'What I meant was that for us to have a proper friendship, you know, a mature, meaningful one, we'd both have to let go of the past. And that's what tonight's been all about – *closure*.'

'Closure, yes,' he agreed, too relieved to baulk at the cliché. He scanned her face again, reassuring himself, she supposed, that she wasn't some deluded bunny-boiler. 'But it's not something, I imagine, we're going to *advertise* . . . ?'

Oh, it got worse. He was *with* someone. It took all her self-possession not to slump on the pillow and weep. He really had turned the tables. If he'd planned this revenge meticulously, like a Jacobean villain, it couldn't have hurt any more. But the worst of it was, she knew he hadn't. He had hardly given her a thought. He was indifferent.

'Oh no, you can count on my discretion, Nigel,' she said grimly. 'I don't know which of them you're fucking, Miranda or Jane – hell, it could be both of them for all I care – but as far as I'm concerned, this never happened.'

Bridget left at first light, taking care not to disturb Nigel's gently snoring form. The sound of her wheelie suitcase skipping and bumping over the cobbles seemed like an affront on the still-sleepy High Street. Yet when she arrived at the station, the platform was crowded with festival-goers waiting for the London train, all a-buzz with forums and discourses and seminars. To make matters worse, a hoarding on the embankment was emblazoned with a poster of Nigel, the words 'Sold Out' stamped across his self-deprecating chops.

Bridget sat on the train, and stared, unseeing, through the window, as it pulled out of the station. She had a couple of reports in her bag which needed her urgent attention, but she made no attempt to get them out, and as the train drew nearer to London and the time crept closer to office hours, the phone calls started to come thick and fast on her mobile, but she barely heard them. She was still sitting, staring blankly at the empty platform, two hours later, when the cleaner came through the carriage and reminded her gently that they had reached their destination.

Max

Max was living on borrowed time. She was no longer in any doubt that Shona was having an affair. She had sneaked a look at Shona's mobile phone and found messages in her inbox that could only have come from a lover. The book group theme seemed to be a running joke between them. 'Can't wait to get between your covers x', said one. 'Fancy tooling my binding?' another. And worst of all: 'Let's live happily ever after xxx'.

Max had to restrain herself from hurling the phone across the room when she read this one. Instead she took a few deep breaths and returned it to the zip pocket of Shona's bag. Better that Shona didn't know she knew. Although just lately, it seemed, her rival *wanted* to make her presence felt. Someone had been ringing the house phone and hanging up when Max answered. A couple of times the caller had even paused for a moment at the sound of Max's voice, and drawn breath, as if to speak, before thinking better of it and ringing off.

'Come on, bitch! Get it off your chest,' Max had

screamed once, only to find she was speaking to a bewildered Stella, who had rung to sound her out about coming up to London for a get-together. That had taken some explaining . . . After that she had exercised restraint, even when the calls came two or three times a week. She would replace the receiver carefully and when Robin or Shona asked who had called, she shrugged and said, 'Wrong number.' It seemed, to her, that knowledge gave her at least a shred of power, in a situation that was fast spinning out of control. The hardest part was keeping her misery from Robin. He was a sensitive boy, who quickly picked up on the unspoken stresses and strains in the house. He'd been wetting the bed lately, which made him furious with shame, and his sleep was erratic. Max had taken to sitting beside him at bedtime, just as she used to when he was a toddler, and he would engage her in anxious conversation, even when his eyes were rolling with fatigue.

'Do you think we'll always live in this house?' he would ask her, and: 'If you and Mummy both died, who would look after me?' And: 'When you're a grown-up, how do you know how to *do* everything?' He had just dropped off to sleep after one such exchange, when Max had noticed an unaccustomed brightness in the room, coming from the headlights of a car parked across the street. She went to close the curtains a little more securely against its intrusion, and realised, with a jolt, that she had seen it before. It was a light-coloured Renault, and its driver seemed to be staring at the house with a curiosity that betokened something more than a waiting taxi or someone delivering a takeaway. Max saw red. The nerve of the woman! She tiptoed quietly out of Robin's room and then hurtled down the stairs and out of the front door, heart thudding, fists clenched, ready to confront her nemesis. But as she reached the garden gate, the driver saw her coming and pulled away with a squeal of tyres. Max ran out into the middle of the road, a sob of frustration catching in her throat as the tail-lights of the car receded into the distance.

'What's going on?' asked Shona, appearing at the front door.

'Oh nothing,' said Max, swallowing hard. 'I thought I saw that car reverse into ours, but there doesn't seem to be any damage.'

'God, Max, you're so surburban sometimes,' said Shona, and went back inside to watch *EastEnders*.

The stress was starting to take its toll on Max's work. The other day in her A-level revision class she had completely lost the thread and found herself unable to list the underlying causes of the First World War; later in the staff room she had told the Head of PE to go fuck himself because he had chastised her for not washing up her coffee mug. She knew that her colleagues were beginning to mutter about 'burn out' and 'classroom fatigue' and this just added to the pressure. She couldn't afford to lose her job on top of everything else. She had started lying awake in the middle of the night, listening to Shona sleep the sleep of the just and trying to calculate how long it would take to save enough money to buy her out of the house. She didn't see why Robin should lose his childhood home just because Shona had given up on family. But whichever way you looked at it, Max's financial prospects were pretty bleak. Five years of job-sharing, when Robin was small, had taken their toll on her career progression. She was at the top of her scale with no prospect of a pay rise unless she made head of department and, on recent form, that wasn't very likely.

Max could bear it no longer. The next weekend, she arranged for Robin to go to his friend Harry's for a sleep-over. She cooked Shona's favourite meal and opened a bottle of expensive wine. Then she popped the question.

'Are you having an affair?' she asked. Shona recoiled as if she'd been shot. She'd never been a very good actress.

'Jesus, Max!' She snatched at her wine glass and drained it in a single gulp, then she laughed, unconvincingly. 'That came out of left field!'

'Well, *are* you?'

'Of course not!' Max could see her brain working. She had known Shona too long. Insouciance wasn't working; try righteous indignation.

'Oh, I get it. This is about my book group, isn't it?'

'You tell me!'

'You just can't bear me to have even a pathetic little shred of autonomy, can you, Max?' She was getting quite worked up now, Max could see. She was almost starting to believe she was in the right. 'I must say it's getting a bit much when a harmless intellectual pursuit – a *book group*, for good-ness' sake – is enough to send you into a frenzy of jealousy and suspicion, but I tell you what' – she met Max's gaze and her eyes were flinty with resentment – 'your *pathetic* allegations just vindicate my decision to claim some time and space for myself.'

'Is it a lesbian book group?' asked Max, sipping her wine calmly. She felt like a lepidopterist pinning down a prize specimen, one wing at a time.

Shona tossed her head. 'What if it is?'

'So what's on the reading list?'

'Fuck off, Max.'

'No, seriously, I'm interested. It must be pretty racy stuff, 'cause you've been very careful to keep it out of *my* way. I'm guessing it's not *The Well of Loneliness*, is it, Shona? Is she raising your consciousness, this new friend of yours? Or is it dyke porn you're into?'

'Look!' Shona slammed her hand down on the table. 'I am *not* having an affair. But I tell you what, Max, all this . . . this paranoia and possessiveness is driving a wedge between us . . .'

Max clapped slowly. 'Bravo! That's the best cliché I've heard all night. Whatever you're reading, it's not doing much for your originality of thought. Maybe you should try some classics.'

'Don't do this, Max.' Shona shook her head and there were tears in her eyes. 'Please don't push me. It would *kill* Robin to be without you.'

Max's head snapped upright. 'Without *me*?' she said.

From that moment on, Max's love for Shona shrivelled to a small hard kernel. She became an adversary; a competitor for Robin's affections. Max became obsessed with proof. If she could just find *evidence* of Shona's adultery, it would strengthen her case. A solicitor friend had told her, baldly, that she hadn't a leg to stand on in law, but that in any custody battle, the interests of the child were deemed paramount. As the primary carer, she might be in with a shout, especially if she could prove that Shona was unfit. The next time she took one of the silent phone calls, she dialled 1471, but the caller had withheld her number. She started jotting down the comings and goings of the light-coloured Renault, but was thwarted in her attempts to record its registration by the driver's speed on the throttle. She stole Shona's phone, intending to transcribe the contents of her inbox, but found that they had already been deleted. She needed more.

The following Tuesday, when Shona left for 'book group', Max followed her. She checked and double-checked that Robin was sound asleep, and then, as soon as Shona had taken off on the bike, she sneaked out to their old VW Polo and slipped behind the wheel. Come on, come on, she urged its feeble engine, as Shona's Harley disappeared over the brow of the hill. She was in luck. The lights at the next junction were red and she caught up in time to see Shona take a left turn towards the seafront. She nearly lost her in Hove, thwarted by a taxi doing a U-turn, but the macho roar of Shona's engine gave her away and Max gained on her in time to glimpse the bike's familiar tail-lights swooping into a smart mansion block off a broad leafy street near Holland Road. She killed the engine and the lights and freewheeled in behind her, pulling up behind the recycling bins at the top of the drive. Shona dismounted and took off her helmet, sleek and clandestine as the Milk Tray man. She rested it briefly on the seat of the bike, and squatted down to check her appearance in one of the wing mirrors, then made her way over to the entrance of the flats and pressed the buzzer. What now? Max wondered, when, after a brief exchange at the intercom, Shona disappeared inside. She watched and waited, scanning the rows of identical thirties-style windows for some sign of movement, but witnessed no passionate clinch, silhouetted Hitchcock-style against a drawn blind; only an array of suburban window dressings that had more of the whist drive than the bordello about them. She made a lousy gumshoe, she realised. Nothing she had seen tonight constituted proof. For all she knew there *could* even be a bunch of tweedy dykes in there discussing *The Autobiography of Alice B. Toklas*. Except that Max knew there wasn't. She jotted down the address for future reference, and then, remembering Robin, sleeping alone in the dark house at the other end of town, she reversed back up the drive and set off home.

Part of her brain must have registered the rhythmic blue sweep of the revolving light even before she turned into the street. When she saw the ambulance parked outside her house, it seemed preordained. Dare to leave your child unattended and see what happens. See how God will punish you. There was a gaggle of people on the pavement and a general air of consternation. She flung open the car door and ran up to her neighbour, Beverley, who was walking towards her, arms outstretched.

'Don't worry, don't worry. He's going to be OK,' she said. 'They're making a fuss about nothing. I almost wish I hadn't called them, but he was in a bit of a state and there was quite a bit of blood and no sign of you and Shona so . . .' She raised an eyebrow in subtle reproach. All Max took in was the word 'blood'. She pushed past her in a panic.

'What's happened? Where is he? Robin?' she shouted, turning this way and that as though in a game of blind man's buff.

'Are you the mother?'

'Yes,' she said without hesitation.

'How long has he been on his own?' The paramedic was stony-faced.

'Where is he? I want to see him. What happened?'

'Calm down now. He's quite stable. Superficial head injury. Seems he woke up in the night and thought he'd do the laundry. He was carrying a load of bedding downstairs when he tripped and fell. Neighbour heard him crying and called us.'

'Oh God!' Max covered her face. Poor Robin. He must have been mortified, waking up and finding he'd wet himself; calling out to her; discovering he was alone; trying to do the right thing, disorientated, in the dark; tripping, falling . . . She'd never forgive herself. Never.

'Well, don't hang about then, let's get him to hospital; he'll need a scan, won't he?' She made to climb into the back of the ambulance.

'All in good time, love,' said the man, blocking her way. 'He's been assessed – it's mainly just shock. We'll be on our way as soon as the social worker gets here . . .'

In the days that followed, the atmosphere in the house was chillier than ever. Max and Shona still spoke to each other, with exaggerated civility, for Robin's sake, but they both knew that this was the beginning of the end. Shona played her cards close to her chest. There had been no big row when she had found out about Robin's accident; no hysteria or recrimination; just a tight-lipped demand to know the facts, which were met with what looked ominously, to Max, like grim satisfaction. It was obvious that Shona was planning something, and each morning Max woke expecting . . . what? A summons? An injunction? In her most lurid imaginings she expected to be marched from the house by social workers and splashed all over the tabloids. But the days passed and nothing happened. If anything, Shona was around more than usual. She skipped her 'book group' and seemed to be fielding only the briefest and most business-like of phone calls. By coincidence (or perhaps not) the nuisance calls that Max had been receiving with increasing regularity seemed to have petered out.

Then, just when Max had started to believe in the possibility that it might all blow over, there was a ring at the doorbell. Shona was upstairs changing Robin's dressing. It was dark outside and it seemed late for a visit from a health professional, but the young woman seemed nervous and apologetic and there was a definite air of purpose about her.

'I'm sorry to disturb you.' She was young, attractive and looked vaguely familiar.

'Yes.' Max was abrupt.

'Does a Maxine Greenhalgh live here?'

Max's stomach turned over. 'That's me,' she said. She glanced pointedly at her watch. 'I'd have thought you might ring first.'

'Well,' said the woman, 'I did try . . . a few times actually . . . but I, er . . . well . . . I have to admit I lost my nerve.'

'That's not very professional . . .'

'*Professional . . . ?*' The woman wrinkled her nose and smiled, embarrassed.

Something wasn't right about this. She was too casually dressed and she had a handbag, but no briefcase. Looking over her shoulder, Max noticed her car parked by the front gate. It was a silver Renault.

Nell

Nell dabbed the corners of her lips delicately with a paper napkin and pushed away her plate. 'Thank you, Gunther. That was delicious. Do you think I could see Mother now?'

'You media people, so careful of your figures,' admonished Gunther, loading his plate with Nell's leftovers.

'Come on then,' said Clover, 'but bear in mind, she can't concentrate for long, and she might not recognise you at first.'

She ushered Nell into the back living room. The curtains were half drawn and the light was soupy. A whiff of ammonia hit Nell between the eyes. As she adjusted to the gloom, she noticed that the basic layout and décor had changed little. There was still too much furniture and bric-à-brac. Folksy knick-knacks crowded every surface; macramé plant pot holders sagged under the weight of leggy begonias. The chimneybreast was still papered with the dizzying mustard-coloured wallpaper that Nell remembered from the seventies and the wood-chipped alcoves displayed lurid pictures of Hindu Gods and runic scrolls depicting nuggets of cod philosophy. The floor was scattered with worn rugs that inadequately concealed its ineptly stripped wooden boards. Pride of place was given to a gilt commode, its PVC seat cover printed to resemble a pink and gold Louis Quatorze brocade. In the corner, propped up on a mountain of pillows and covered with the hectic crocheted blanket that used to disguise the stains on the old divan, lay her mother.

'Mummy?' The word caught in Nell's throat as she moved uncertainly towards her.

The woman in the bed stared blankly at her and Nell sat down, feeling suddenly grotesquely vital beside this frail bird-like figure. From a distance, her mother had seemed roughly to resemble the woman Nell remembered; the hair was still long and fringed, and the owlish eyes rimmed with badly applied kohl pencil. But close up, Nell struggled to disguise the mortification she felt, for the eyes beneath the make-up were droopy and vacant; the hair resembled purplish-red coconut matting, except for the two-inch growth of iron grey near her scalp; her shoulders were shrunken and hunched and her hands, still adorned with the Moroccan silver rings of yore, were claw-like and roped with veins. She looked ancient.

Her mother smiled. 'Hello, lovely,' she said, then she peered a little more closely and her eyes clouded in consternation.

She turned to Clover. 'What's *she* doing here? What have you brought that bitch round for? Get her out. Little tramp. Little fucking tart. You're a home-wrecker. That's what you are!'

She lashed out and clipped Nell's wrist with one of her rings. Nell recoiled, but Clover put a steadying hand on her shoulder.

'She thinks you're someone else,' she said. 'Mother, it's Nell. Nell's come to see you. You know? Your other daughter. The one off the telly.'

'Caro, on the telly?' shrieked the old woman. 'What's she on the telly for? Haven't they got enough slappers already?'

Nell caught her breath. 'Where's she dredged this up from?' she asked Clover. 'She can't have seen Caro in years!'

'She doesn't know what she's saying.' Clover shrugged and, with a hint of satisfaction: 'I told you you'd be shocked.'

Nell caught one of her mother's flailing hands and brought it to her lips. 'Mum! It's Nell. Not Caro, *Nell*.'

But her Mother turned her face to the wall and muttered through clenched teeth, 'Piss off.'

'Mum, please . . .'

'I know your game,' went on her mother. 'Tarot readings, yoga sessions, macrobiotic fucking cookery; didn't take long to get him on to *The Joy of Sex*, did it, you little tramp?' And suddenly Nell understood. Caro had seduced her father. The relationship she thought had provided mutual consolation for the loss of their respective partners – Richard to suicide, Nell's mother to mental breakdown – had precipitated both. No wonder her mother had attacked Caro with the bread knife. No wonder Richard had . . .

The world tilted precariously; Nell felt at once exonerated and strangely diminished. Was this maturity? This lurching, vertiginous realisation that she was not and never had been the centre of the universe? That the events she had interpreted as pivoting around her had in fact had a quite different centre of gravity?

'Mummy,' she said gently, 'I'm going to go now, but I'll be back tomorrow to talk about your operation. We're going to get you all fixed up like the Bionic Woman, and then, if you want, we could find you a nice place to stay. Somewhere with a sea view, where you'll have plenty of company and nice home-made meals. Just like being on holiday, but you never have to go home. How does that sound?'

She glanced at Clover, who looked a little stunned, but not displeased.

'Piss off!' said Nell's mother.

Nell kissed her hand again and, although her mother kept her face turned to the wall, she permitted the caress. Nell wondered whether she hadn't on some level known who her visitor was all along.

'What was all that stuff about sea views?' asked Clover, later, when they were back in the kitchen. 'She won't forget, you know. She's got a memory like an elephant if there's something in it for her.'

'That's OK,' said Nell. 'I meant it. We'll find her

somewhere nice. There can't be any shortage of old people's homes round here.'

'No, but the sort you're talking about cost a bomb.'

Nell shrugged as if to say 'money no object' and Clover gave her a tight-lipped smile.

'Well, I shall want to see how it's run. There's all sorts goes on in these places, even the posh ones; old people are very vulnerable.'

'I know. We'll look into it properly,' said Nell.

'And it can't be too far away,' Clover went on. 'Me and Gunther'll be the ones visiting her and we don't run to taxis; not like you and your lot.'

'Clover,' said Nell sharply, 'I know it's a bit late in the day, but I'm doing my best to help in the only way I can. Please let me.'

Clover looked taken aback. 'All right. Yes, I'm sorry,' she said. 'It's just . . .' She looked Nell in the eyes for the first time and her voice turned husky. '. . . I'm going to miss her.'

Nell took both Clover's hands in hers and nodded. For the first time in her life, she found herself envying her sister.

By the time Nell was ready to leave Torquay she had received nine voicemails and fifteen texts from Des. They started off maudlin, 'Sorry seems to be the hardest word. Love you baby x'. became briefly schmaltzy, 'Daddy loves you. Ring me soon princess xx'; turned pleading, 'Desperate to have you back. Come home angel xx';

resorted to emotional blackmail, 'Do you care about me at all? Where the fuck are you?'; and ended up threatening, 'Don't make me come and get you'. Nell ignored all of them. She got no further than the first sentence of his first voicemail before deleting the lot with a frisson of satisfaction. When they got back to London she checked into a hotel while she decided how best to proceed.

At the studio on Monday morning Sharon welcomed her back with evident relief. 'That's better!' she said approvingly. 'You look ten years younger. Sea air must have done you good.'

Nell frowned at her sceptically, and then smiled. Actually she did look good. It wasn't just that her black eyes had healed, leaving no trace of her 'accident' except for the faintest of scars on the bridge of her nose, she looked somehow more *present*; more herself. It was surprising, she thought, how easy it was to do the right thing, at the end of the day. She had left her mother browsing through a brochure for the Bayview Retirement Home (which she had thrown across the room when it had first been handed to her, but which she had later set about annotating in shaky Biro with her various preferences). Nell had kissed Clover and Gunther, and meant it when she told them she'd be down again in a fortnight to help with the move. Now she just had her own life to sort out.

*

'Hello and welcome to *The Morning Show*.'

The theme music died away, the cameras rolled and Mark swivelled round towards Nell on the cobalt-blue sofa.

'Nell, it's great to have you back. You look amazing. Where have you been?'

'Thanks, Mark. It's great to be back. I've been holidaying on our very own English Riviera. I must say, when the sun's shining, you just can't beat the British seaside. Buckets, spades, kiss-me-quick hats . . .'

'Well, we're delighted to see you back on form . . .' said Mark, suddenly looking more serious. Nell sensed a change in mood and guessed what was coming. She flashed him a warning glance, hoping she was off-camera. ' . . . because, as our viewers can't fail to have seen, there've been some scurrilous suggestions bandied about in the press lately that you've actually been recovering from, of all things, *cosmetic surgery*.' He looked directly at the camera. 'As if she needed it!' Then, turning back to Nell: 'And I thought you might like to scotch those rumours, once and for all.'

Nell could hear the director shouting furiously in Mark's earpiece and see, out of the corner of her eye, the floor manager making urgent slashing motions across her throat, but Mark's expression didn't waver from one of fraternal concern. Nell felt strangely calm.

'Thank you, Mark.' She smiled. 'I don't usually like to bring my private life to work, but as there has been so much speculation it's good to have the opportunity to refute once and for all this absurd rumour. I have not had, nor would I ever have cosmetic surgery. I'm no spring chicken, but I believe in growing old gracefully.'

'And so you are,' said Mark suavely, 'very gracefully indeed, if I may say so.' He dug behind a cushion on the sofa and brought out a copy of the *Sun*, bearing the same out-of-focus photo as *Closer*, with the headline 'BLACK-EYED SLEAZE. WHO'S PICKING ON OUR NELL?' He held it steady while the camera zoomed in. Nell waited for his stab in the back. 'So just what did happen here? Because the switchboard has been jammed solid while you've been away, with concerned viewers wanting reassurance that everything in your life is . . . as we would like it to be.'

Nell took a deep breath. 'Well, Mark, as a matter of fact your very heartfelt concern is well founded. I know this will be a shock for the viewers, but I think it's time to stand up and be counted. The injury I sustained the week before last was not inflicted by a plastic surgeon, or, as I think you might be implying, by a fall after a heavy night drinking at the Groucho Club. It was sustained when my husband, Des Percival, owner of the production company that makes this show – your boss – *my* boss – head-butted me because I refused him anal sex.'

The silence on set could only have lasted for five seconds, but to everyone except Nell, it felt like five minutes. The producer gave no instructions from the gallery; the cameraman forgot to move in for a close-up; the floor manager clutched her clipboard as if it were a liferaft. At last, the order was given, 'Go to the break!'

Mark stammered some platitudes at the camera and, as the studio erupted around her, Nell unclipped her microphone, put her cue cards down on the table and turned to Mark. 'Thanks,' she said. 'I've been wanting to get that off my chest for a while.'

Then she walked off set.

Stella

'I'm just putting some washing in the machine, Niamh.' Stella put her head round the door of the living room where the two girls were slumped side by side on the couch. To say that they were *watching Big Brother* would be to overstate the case, but their faces were turned towards the set and *Big Brother* was on. 'Do you need anything doing?'

Niamh shook her head. 'I'm grand, thanks,' she said and resumed the unconscious scratching that seemed to be increasing in frequency and intensity with every day that passed. Not as far as I'm concerned you're not, you mucky pup, thought Stella, but she backed out of the room with a subservient smile. If she didn't get that filthy sweater off Niamh's back soon, it would walk back to Dublin on its own. She had worn nothing else since the day she arrived. Just looking at it made Stella want to ring Rentokil. But what could you do?

She was proving to be quite an expensive houseguest too. Both wasteful and greedy. She'd leave most of her dinner, then down a whole tub of Häagen-Dazs in a sitting, and follow it up with a couple of KitKats and a can of Coke. No wonder her skin was breaking out. And then there was the moodiness. For three days, everything had been fine – so fine that Stella had wanted to shake the girl; no one was that laid back. But gradually (and she supposed perhaps she should take it as a compliment) a tetchier side had emerged. Stella had told her repeatedly not to stand on ceremony and to treat the place like home, but she hadn't expected her to sleep half the day, use up all the hot water and then sulk for hours at a time, responding to Stella's tentative enquiries after her well-being with an irritable, 'Nothing's wrong. Just leave me alone!'

She could see now why Niamh had had to move schools so often. She really wasn't a people person; she scarcely made eye contact and it didn't seem to occur to her to answer questions with words of more than one syllable, or to show the least interest in anyone else. Stella could barely manage to sit in the same room with the girl without wanting to throw a cushion at her, and yet Amber, against all the odds, seemed to have warmed to her. It would be an exaggeration to say that they had bonded, but given Amber's recalcitrance and Niamh's vapidity, they seemed more comfortable in each other's company than Stella might have expected, a development which ought to have delighted her, but somehow didn't.

Ever since the news came that Vinnie had had a baby girl, Stella had cherished a sentimental hope that one day their daughters might become friends. So when Vinnie had finally rung to ask if Niamh could come and stay, Stella's heart had leaped. It was a shame, they both agreed, that Vinnie couldn't come too, but in a way Stella almost preferred to have the opportunity to do her friend a favour – it elevated her somehow; narrowed the gap. *She* was the one to whom Vinnie was entrusting her most precious possession: her daughter; it gave her a warm glow just thinking about it. And of course there would be the reciprocal trip to Dublin to look forward to, when Vinnie had 'cleared the decks'. It had become a favourite fantasy of Stella's: imagining the four of them strolling along a picturesque strand linking arms, before repairing to a cosy pub to sing folk songs, accompanied by Celtic drums and tin whistles. Since meeting Niamh, the prospect of a return match had lost a little of its sheen.

Nevertheless, if only for Vinnie's sake, she felt honour-bound to keep the dream alive. And if that meant sanctioning a night out in Brixton, the one diversion that both girls seemed wholeheartedly to desire, Stella ought, she supposed, to get behind it. But as the expedition loomed closer, she found herself prevaricating.

'Are you sure you wouldn't prefer Covent Garden?' she suggested casually over dinner on the night in question. 'It's where everybody goes . . .'

'Exactly!' said Amber.

'Well, what about Camden? That's very trendy, isn't it?'

'It's miles away, Mum, and it's full of emos.'

'Knightsbridge, then,' she said in desperation. 'How about that, Niamh? You might bump into Prince Harry . . .'

Amber clutched her head in mute despair, but Niamh just shrugged and replied, 'I've a friend told me Brixton's great craic.'

'Hmmm,' Stella said.

'Well, look, if you're worried,' said Amber, 'Sam could go with us; then you wouldn't even have to come and pick us up.'

'You mean he'd *drive*? In a *car*?'

'No, Mum, he'd take us in his Tardis. What do you think?' said Amber, exchanging a world-weary look with Niamh. 'Do you honestly think his dad would trust him with the Audi if he wasn't a really good driver?'

Stella winced. Sam didn't seem like the boy-racer type, but you never knew . . . Then again, she could really use a free evening to get to grips with the paperwork for tomorrow's tribunal.

'Only the thing is . . .' Amber could already see daylight '. . . if he does drive us, he'll have to stay over . . .'

'Oh, I really don't think—' Stella began.

'. . . because the last time he got home late he woke the dog and his mum went mad.'

Amber spread her palms in an Aristotelian flourish. Q very much ED, she seemed to be saying. For the briefest of moments, Stella considered the possibility of putting her foot down, but she simply didn't have the energy.

'God forbid he disturb the dog,' she sighed.

'Thanks, Mum,' said Amber. 'I'll tell him you'll see him

all right for petrol . . .' She pushed her chair back and kissed Stella lightly on the cheek, before jerking her head to indicate Niamh should follow her out of the room.

Having made the decision (or had it made for her) Stella did her best, over the next couple of hours, to reconcile herself to it, telling herself over and over that there would be safety in numbers; they'd have their mobiles; they were sensible kids. She left a message on Vinnie's answerphone and had a nice chat with Sam's Mum, who turned out to have been on the PTA with her when the kids were at primary school, and after that she felt much better. Until Amber and Niamh walked into the living room and her blood pressure sky-rocketed again. Amber had given Niamh a makeover. The skanky jumper was still in evidence, but in place of the grubby jeans, she was wearing a borrowed miniskirt, fishnet tights and high heels. In full war paint, corkscrew hair piled on top of her head, lips stained a bright vermilion, she looked, for the first time, the image of Vinnie. But there was something missing – the life force; the charisma of the mother was entirely absent in the daughter. Without it, Niamh's come-hither get-up took on a pathos that made Stella wince.

'Doesn't she look nice, Mummy?' said Amber, misinterpreting Stella's rictus grin.

'Well, lovely, yes. I just wonder . . .'

'What?' Her daughter folded her arms and thrust her hip. The pink jewel in her navel sparkled defiantly.

'I'm just worried you might attract the wrong kind of attention.'

'Is there a wrong kind?' grinned Amber, but before Stella could answer, the doorbell rang. 'That'll be Sam.'

'Guys . . .' Stella called after them, her voice high and querulous, 'take your coats, won't you? It's going to be chilly later . . . Don't forget to keep your mobiles on and do look after . . .' The front door slammed shut. '. . . Niamh!' she said to the empty air.

Stella woke up with a crick in her neck and a sour taste in her mouth. The report she had been reading had slipped on to the living-room floor and knocked over her glass of wine, from which she had only taken a sip before nodding off. Dan was standing in front of her, loosening his tie.

'Catching up on some work?' he said sardonically, eyeing the soggy mess on the floor. He switched on the TV and flopped down beside her on the sofa. 'You don't mind, do you?' he said. 'Prescott's on *Newsnight*. Always good for a laugh.'

'There's some risotto on the stove, just needs heating through.'

''S OK, I've eaten. Sorry I'm late again, by the way. Should be quieter next week. Where are the girls?'

'They've gone to some club in Brixton.'

Dan nodded, staring transfixed at the screen, then did a double take. 'Brixton? Is that a good idea?'

'Of course it is,' said Stella impatiently. 'We used to go to the Ritzy all the time.'

'Yeah – the cinema. Not some dodgy club. They're only kids.'

'Oh Dan, stop fussing, they'll be absolutely fine,' said Stella, but she reached instinctively for her mobile and checked the display. There were no messages. 'Here,' she said, 'phone her if you're worried.' But Dan waved the phone away.

'No, I'm sure you're right. I might go up now, if you don't mind. It's been a hell of a week.'

Stella watched Paxman's lip curl with disdain, his victim sweat and writhe, but she didn't hear what they were saying. She was remembering the Ritzy. They used to go a lot, she and Dan. He used to like John Sayles and Oliver Stone; she preferred the Coen brothers and Woody Allen. Afterwards they would go for supper, somewhere cheap and cheerful on Coldharbour Lane, and discuss the film they'd seen. It had been careless and easy. They had had *fun*, a commodity that now seemed as remote and theoretical as an amputated limb. They had *tried* to recapture it, under instructions from the relationship counsellor, after the business with Bridget. They had gone on 'dates' and weekends away; rehearsed out loud and in public the qualities that had first made them fall in love with each other; embarked on a lengthy programme of 'celibate touching', which was supposed to send them into a frenzy of mutual desire. But none of it had worked. Their relationship had become a project, devoid of all spontaneity and magic. And whereas Stella used to comfort herself with the thought that at least, as the aggrieved party, she wasn't to blame, she had lately started to wonder whether she mightn't share some of the responsibility. Had she lost respect for Dan when he'd shagged her best friend? Or had it happened before that? Long before, when she'd seen him on TV condemning the poll-tax rioters, even though she knew he supported them in private? Pretending to be the 'acceptable' face of New Labour, until little by little he had stopped pretending and bought into 'the brand'. Was that when the rot had set in? Had he shagged Bridget because he was libidinous and selfish? Or to boost his ego in the face of his wife's contempt?

Newsnight had long since finished. Some made-for-TV movie was unfolding hammily before her. 'Charlene wasn't like that. Sure, she was a working girl, but she picked her clients real careful . . .' Stella picked up her phone. Still no messages. She rang Amber's number. It went straight to voicemail. She frowned in annoyance. 'Txt me u r ok', she punched into the key pad, and pressed send.

She retrieved the sheaf of damp papers from the living-room floor. She was halfway through the third paragraph when she realised she hadn't taken in a word. Charlene had been found dead in the trunk of a car on the Bayou. It was twenty to one.

'AMBER???!!!' she texted, then returned to clause one, paragraph one. The words danced on the page. She was furious, she realised, with Amber; with Niamh; with Dan; but most of all with herself.

At five to one, her phone bleeped. 'Soz. Cdnt hear fone music too loud. Jst waitin 4 neev then leavin. Don't wait up x'.

Stella exhaled; her anxiety melted away like dew. They

were fine. They had been fine all along. They had not fallen prey to muggers or rapists; they had merely been snogging and smoking and drinking watered-down lager with other middle-class kids from Clapham and Wandsworth. She had got the whole thing catastrophically out of proportion and now she felt foolish and very, very tired; more tired than she had ever felt in her life before. She crawled up the stairs, left her clothes in a heap on the floor beside the bed, and climbed in next to Dan, taking care not to let any part of her body touch any part of his.

Sometime later, there was a squeal of brakes in the street outside. The sound of car doors slamming, voices – high-pitched, urgent. Stella opened her eyes. She heard feet crunching on gravel; the doorbell ringing and ringing; a key turning in the lock; then voices again.

'Mum! Mum! You better come quick! There's something up with Niamh . . . She's not well.'

'Wha . . . the fuck . . . ? What time is it?' Dan grumbled sleepily, but Stella had already thrown back the duvet and run to the landing.

She looked down at the three of them in the hall, indistinct in the half-light like a Victorian tableau. Amber and Sam stared back at her, ashen-faced, big-eyed, out of their depth. They each had one of Niamh's arms looped around their shoulders and gripped firmly at the wrist. She drooped between them, knees buckled, head lolling, like a rag-doll. For a moment Stella thought she was dead. 'Oh God!' Her mouth made the shape of the words.

'Walk her. Keep her conscious!' Stella commanded; her

voice, calm, authoritative, seemed to come from someone else. If only she could have found this steeliness before and put a stop to the whole stupid venture, before Niamh could do . . . whatever stupid thing she'd . . . A thought stirred in the back of Stella's brain, like a maggot in paper, unsavoury, persistent.

'Oh God. I told you it was a bad idea. How much has she had?' Dan's voice behind her was irritable, weary.

'She's not drunk,' Stella barked. 'Call an ambulance!' She ran down the stairs. Unable to support Niamh's weight any longer, Amber and Sam had let her slump to the floor. Stella knelt down and took Niamh's head on her lap. The girl's face lolled back, waxy, beaded with sweat. Her lips were blue, her pupils tiny pinpricks.

'I'll get her a glass of water,' said Dan. 'She'll come round in a minute.'

'No! There isn't time. Call an ambulance.' Stella pushed up the sleeve of Niamh's jumper and heard Dan gasp. Livid trackmarks scarred her arms and spots of freshly congealed blood marked the place where she had at first failed, and then succeeded, in injecting herself.

'Oh my God. Oh sweet Jesus!' Dan was saying. 'I can't have this. This is a fucking disaster!' Stella stared incredulously at him. He had the phone in his hand, but was not dialling.

'Phone them!' she shouted, but Dan was shaking his head.

'Get her outside,' he said. His voice was low, threatening even. 'Get her in the fucking street. I can't have her in my house ODing. It'll be the end of my fucking career!'

'Phone them!' Stella's voice cracked with the strain; a vein pulsed in her neck. Dan gripped the phone defiantly.

'Just get her out,' he said. 'That's all I'm saying, so it looks like she's a passer-by. I can't have any link to—'

With a guttural cry, Amber wrenched the phone from her father's hand and punched the numbers. 'What should I say?' she asked Stella, her hand trembling, her voice barely audible.

'Ask for an ambulance,' said Stella, struggling to keep the tremor out of her voice, all the while stroking Niamh's clammy cheek. 'Tell them our name and address. Tell them it's a heroin overdose.'

The Funeral

The night before the funeral, Stella dreamed she was back at Albacore Street. Finals were on and everyone had overslept. She was running all over the house trying to wake them, but when she opened her mouth to say, 'Get up, you're late for your exam,' no sound came. They just flopped around like dummies; they wouldn't respond. All of her housemates were in the dream, but there were other people too, in hidden rooms that she had never seen before. There were assorted boyfriends; lecturers; people whose parties she had gatecrashed; the woman who worked in the library coffee bar, asleep in her blue nylon overall. She couldn't wake any of them. In the end, terrified of being late, she had gone by herself, travelling on an open-air conveyor belt that took her, not to Mandela Hall, where they had really sat their finals, but to the Meeting House, the ugly interdenominational chapel on campus. When the chaplain saw that she had come alone, he told her she would have to sit the exam for everyone. If she passed, they would all pass. It wouldn't matter that they had slept through the whole thing. She picked up her pen, heart pounding, sweat trickling down her back; she turned over the paper. It was in a foreign language.

She woke up in a panic, staring at the ceiling. Slowly it dawned on her that she'd been dreaming. That it wasn't true; that she hadn't let everybody down. Why, then, would the heavy sense of dread not lift? Why did she feel as though she had a rock pressing on her sternum? Then she remembered.

For once, there was no need to agonise over what to wear. She didn't even bother trying on anything black. Instead her hand went straight to the jade-green sheath dress that they had bought from Selfridges on their last shopping trip together. She would never have picked it out for herself – it was much too sexy; too out there; but the colour brought out the green of her eyes and the shape flattered her figure. *Had* flattered it, at any rate, ten years ago. *Ten years*. She shook her head and a lump came into her throat. She hoped she would still be able to squeeze into it. Just as well Dan was no longer around to undermine her with one of his withering put-downs.

'Do you think your figure can take that much hugging?' he might have said, or, 'It's a funeral, Stella, not a fucking cocktail party.'

She wondered whether he would be there today. Probably at the crematorium, she decided, but not at the wake. He wouldn't have the stomach for all that mingling.

In the end, the dress had zipped up a treat. She had even managed the top three inches, with a bit of extra writing. Who needed a husband? She was ready twenty minutes before the taxi was due. She sat up straight on the edge of the sofa, ankles crossed demurely, wrist looped through the handle of her handbag, as if in a station waiting room. As she heard the thrum of the diesel engine on the street outside, she remembered that she had not put any tissues in her bag. She ran to the kitchen and yanked seven or eight sheets of kitchen paper off the roll. It was covered in pictures of miniature colanders and tiny rolling pins, she noticed.

She wondered if the taxi driver would comment on her unsuitable garb, but he didn't seem interested. Probably par for the course these days, anyway. She had read an article recently that said funerals were becoming secularised. People were doing their own thing – like hen parties almost: printing T-shirts, wearing coloured ribbons to raise money for this or that related charity; composing doggerel; choosing pop songs for the committal – Whitney, Robbie, Nirvana even. She wondered what they would be getting today. Not Sister Sledge, that was for sure. She smiled to herself. A sob caught in her throat.

As they pulled into the crematorium car park she stared at each sombre huddle in search of a familiar face, but saw none. These, she realised belatedly, must be mourners from the one thirty on their way out. Her lot would be round the front, psyching themselves up for the two o'clock. This must be how it was every day, she thought, death after death, half-hourly from nine to five; loved and unloved, celebrities and nonentities, believers and heathens, young and old . . .

hymns, Kaddishes, power ballads, eulogies. And all day, from nine to five, the chimney discreetly puffing away.

The two o'clocks, it turned out, were surprisingly diverse in age, ethnicity and social background (in as much as you could tell these things). Stella was relieved to see that she wasn't the only one flouting the dress code. There were quite a few people 'celebrating the life' in garish shirts, foppish waistcoats, a Bob Marley T-shirt, in one case. There seemed to be an awful lot of men.

'Stella? Stell!' She turned to see Max bearing down on her, mouth smiling, eyes crying. They hugged, released, hugged again, more tightly. At last Stella drew back.

'Oh God, I got snot on your jacket . . .' She dabbed Max's shoulder ineffectually, laughing in embarrassment. Maxine laughed too; shook her head, then drew the palm of her hand in front of her mouth and nose.

'I can't believe it,' she said, 'I just can't believe she's . . .'

'Me neither,' Stella wailed. 'God, Max, it's all *wrong*. I left her a message . . . I told her the name of the restaurant and everything – five people for the twenty-ninth . . .'

'Yesterday,' said Max, almost to herself. Stella looked stricken.

'Oh God, was it? Oh that's just horrible. I can't believe . . . I'd got everyone signed up, even Vinnie. I booked *five* people, so that shows I invited her, doesn't it?' Her eyes searched Max's for reassurance.

'Of course it does. I know you did.'

'We were all going to be together again . . .'

'I know, I know.'

'And now we are and it's for *this*.' Stella's face crumpled and Max embraced her again.

'Oh God, sorry, I'm sorry.' Stella collected herself, suddenly noticing that Max was with someone. 'Forgive me. I'm Stella.' She extended her hand to Max's companion – a much younger woman; attractive, curly-haired, soberly dressed.

'This is Verity. Verity, this is Stella. We were at college together.'

'Hi.' Stella smiled. They shook hands. She knew Max and Shona had been having problems, but she didn't realise Max had already traded her in for a younger model. A bit odd to bring her to the funeral, though. Before she could think of something suitably bland to say she felt a hand on her arm.

'Hello, you!'

'Nell!'

More hugs, more tears.

'Isn't this' – Nell gestured around her – '*awful*? It just goes to show . . .' She tailed off, shaking her head. Stella and Max nodded, although Stella wasn't clear exactly *what* it went to show. That bad things happened to good people, she supposed; that death was all around us; that there was no time to lose . . .

'You look so well,' Max was saying to Nell. 'So *young*.'

'Yes,' Stella agreed. 'Well done. You know, for going public and everything. I was so relieved when I found out you hadn't had a no—' Max darted her an exasperated glance. 'I mean, God, it must have been *terrible* for you,' she corrected herself. 'It must have taken such a lot of courage to speak out.'

Nell smiled. 'Best thing I ever did. And I've had *such* a positive response from other women. It's made me realise how much work there is to be done around domestic violence.'

Stella beamed in surprise. 'Charity work?'

'Campaigning journalism,' said Nell. 'Channel Four have asked me to front a new series on women's issues. Prime time. Big budget.'

'Ah,' said Stella. There was a pause.

'None of us liked him,' said Maxine baldly. 'You should have heard us at your wedding!'

'I wish I had,' grinned Nell, 'I might have pulled out.' They laughed. 'Listen,' Nell said, lowering her voice, 'do we know the official cause of death? Because it seems really fishy to me.'

Max darted an anxious glance at Stella and steered Nell away from her slightly. 'It was an asthma attack,' she whispered firmly. 'That's what her mum told me on the phone. Very severe; possibly stress related. There was an inquest. That's why it's been a while since—'

'I don't buy it,' said Nell. 'She hadn't had an asthma attack for *years*. You've only got her mum's word for it. There must be more to it than—'

Max shook her head as if in warning, but it was too late, Stella had heard and was in tears again.

'Come on, Stell.' Max put a consoling arm around her. 'It was a tragic accident, that's all.'

'Unless it wasn't,' Stella said. 'What if it wasn't? And we weren't there for her? *I* wasn't there for her?'

'They're here,' Nell interrupted, gesturing towards the approaching cortège, and Stella stiffened guiltily. What right had she to weep and wail when the family were conducting themselves with dignity? The undertaker opened the rear door of the Daimler and they got out: Bridget's mother, grim-faced; her father, small, stooped, beyond grief. Her brother, bluff, hiding his emotion behind the practicalities. Then came a carload of relatives: a cousin who, as she stepped out of the car, made a small bobbing movement to stand up that reminded Stella so much of Bridget that it made her catch her breath.

'I am the family face; Flesh perishes, I live on.' Who wrote that? She couldn't remember, but he certainly had the right idea; or she. Probably he. 'Sexist assumption,' she heard Bridget's voice chastising her. She thought of all the rows they had had; the bollocking she had got when Bridget caught her shaving her armpits; her own triumphant delight when she found out Bridget had employed a cleaner. Ding dong, down the years, like Punch and Judy, until the row to end all rows, at Nell's wedding. But even that didn't seem such a big a deal, in retrospect; not worth losing a friend over. If only she had got through three weeks ago when she had made that call, waited for Bridget to pick up . . . just a couple more rings. Might that have made a difference? Could Bridget have been lonely? Could she have needed her old friend after all? She felt

Max's grip tighten on her arm and realised that the tears were coursing down her cheeks, unchecked.

The pall-bearers hoisted the coffin on to their shoulders and led the way into the crematorium, where Samuel Barber's Adagio for Strings was playing quietly in the background.

'I can't see Vinnie anywhere,' whispered Nell, scanning the pews to right and left as they made their way up the central aisle.

'I'll be surprised if she makes it,' Max whispered back. 'She's been through a lot lately, I don't know if you . . .'

Nell nodded. 'I heard. I was hoping to talk to her. We're doing a programme about addiction . . .'

'Look, there's Nigel,' Maxine said, pointing and waving. 'Oh, but hang on, he's with Dan.'

'It's OK, I'm a big girl.' Stella led the way towards them. The last time she had seen her estranged husband, things had been terse to say the least. He had sent an estate agent round to value the house, without warning her. But for Bridget's sake, if no one else's, she felt she should rise above it. Everyone would be expecting them to keep their distance, especially those who knew the whole sordid backstory. Well, they could think what they liked.

Dan and Nigel turned as the four women shuffled into the pew beside them. Dan nodded curtly, Nigel began a smile, but it turned wobbly and he had to bite his lip.

'Poor Nige,' Stella whispered, and took his hand. He looked a wreck.

The room was full now, and a dumpy, kind-looking woman in a dog collar was making her way towards the lectern. The music drew to a close, but as she opened her mouth to speak, there was a kerfuffle at the back of the room. Everyone turned to look. A woman in a large black hat and sunglasses hurried in, muttering apologies.

'So sorry. Flight was delayed,' she was saying. 'Sorry, sorry. Excuse me, if I could just . . . ?' People shuffled, coughed, tutted. Beside her, Stella felt Nigel stiffen almost imperceptibly in his seat. Max turned to Stella and smiled.

'Typical Vinnie,' she whispered.

The room fell silent again. The pastor paused, smiled, then spoke. 'Welcome,' she said. 'We have come together today to honour the life of Bridget Jane Rowland. To remember her and to make our farewells.'

To a background of sniffles, gulps and sighs, they shuffled out of the side door of the crematorium. Twenty-five minutes and eighteen seconds to remember a life. The next funeral party was already milling around the front door; there wasn't time to linger. The pastor shook hands, grasped elbows, received thanks for her kind words, said the right thing in different ways to each mourner who wanted to stop and share.

Stella felt slightly hysterical. Her mouth was twitching with the desire to giggle. 'Who chose *that*?' she burst out as they emerged into the autumn sunshine to the strains of 'Memory', from *Cats*.

'Shhh!' chastised Nell. 'It was probably her mum.'

'That is *so* not Bridget!' said Stella. 'God, she hated Lloyd Webber.'

'She hated cats too,' Max remembered, 'couldn't have them in the room. They brought on her—' Stella dug her in the ribs and Max widened her eyes in embarrassment. Suddenly they all had the giggles. Their eyes bulged, their rib-cages swelled with the desire to laugh, even as the inappropriateness of their conversation dawned on them.

'I'm only saying . . .' Max spluttered, 'she'd be turning in her . . . Well, she would if she hadn't been . . . Oh, shit!' Collapsing with laughter, they almost trampled on the funeral flowers in their haste to move away from the other mourners and compose themselves.

'The service was nice though,' said Nell at last.

'It *was*,' Max demurred, 'but it wasn't *her*. That graduation photo they put at the front? She hated that photo, said it made her look like a constipated chipmunk. And it was all so *straight*. Where was the witty, bitchy, bolshie Bridget? Where was the kind friend? I mean, yes, she was a high flyer: clever; brilliant even; but did we need to be told that she got the second highest score in her entrance exam for the civil service? I'm surprised they didn't get out her twenty-five-yards swimming certificate while they were at it. It was like she was still a *child*.'

Nell shrugged. 'She was, to them.'

At this point, Vinnie, who hadn't quite had the temerity to barge her way to the front of the chapel, and had had to sit out the service 'with some dreary corporate types in suits' descended on them in a cloud of Coco Madame.

'Poor, poor Bridget. I literally cannot *bear* it!' she wailed. There was a prolonged and teary group hug, from which Nigel and Verity hung back, awkwardly. Dan had already skulked off to have a cigarette.

'Vinnie, how *are* you?'

'Hello, Vin.'

'God, it's so lovely to see you all. If only . . .'

'I know, I know.'

'It's so wrong, her not being here. I'm just . . .'

'Me too.'

They clustered together, stroking each other's sleeves, patting one another's shoulders, handing packets of tissues back and forth. Someone would laugh almost manically, and then a poignant recollection would prompt another bout of sniffling and glossy-eyed disbelief. Nigel approached with a tactful cough.

'I think they're wanting us to make a move now,' he said. 'They need to get on with the next service.' He paused, a little awkwardly. 'Hello, Vinnie.'

'Hi, Nigel.'

Everyone froze, as if expecting a showdown.

Vinnie took a step towards him. 'Listen, Nige, thanks, you know. I really appreciate what you did.'

''S OK,' Nigel muttered, clearly embarrassed to be the centre of attention. 'I'll, er . . . catch up with you all at the hotel.' And he sloped off.

Vinnie, Nell and Stella piled into the back of the silver Renault and Max climbed into the passenger seat.

'Got any music?' Vinnie tapped Verity on the shoulder.

'We need something a bit . . .' She paused and looked at Stella for inspiration.

'A bit *Bridget*,' Stella supplied.

Maxine rifled through the glove compartment and produced an ancient cassette tape. 'Just the job,' she said, 'if it still works.' She pressed play.

And afterwards

So it was that they pulled up outside the Marlborough Lodge Hotel with all the windows open and the suspension groaning, singing along at the tops of their voices to 'John Wayne Is Big Leggy' by Haysi Fantayzee.

'Oops!' said Nell, slamming the rear door shut behind her. 'I think we might have breached funeral etiquette a bit there.'

Bridget's father was approaching them, his shoulders still hunched with sadness. Stella was about to apologise, but he held up his hand and smiled.

'It's all right,' he said. 'It shouldn't be all gloom and doom. She liked a good time, did Bridget. I just wish she was here to . . . I just wish . . .' He shook his head and his eyes welled up. Stella embraced him warmly.

'Me too,' she said. 'I'm Stella, by the way, Brid's friend from Sussex.'

'Oh yes, rings a bell. Didn't the two of you go off to France once, on some madcap trip?'

Stella smiled. 'We did, yeah,' she said. 'We were best

mates . . .' Her lip trembled. He looked at her enquiringly. 'I . . . we . . . had a falling-out, a few years ago. Well – a long time ago actually. I hadn't seen her in ages. We were just about to have a reunion. The five of us, you know, from the house in Brighton? I was trying to get back in touch with her when I heard that she'd . . . what had happened.' But that wouldn't do. She had to tell the truth now, get it off her chest. She needed absolution. 'It was hard though, you know, after what had . . . and, well . . . I kept putting it off. In the end, I left her a message, but didn't manage to speak to her before she . . . I didn't realise . . . Obviously, if I'd have known, I would have called again . . .'

'Course you would, lovey.' He patted her shoulder. 'Course you wouldn't. Nobody dies but we don't wish we'd done something different. Said something we didn't; not said something we did . . .' He shrugged wearily. 'It can't be helped. All you can do is make your peace with the living, so's it doesn't happen again, eh?' He tucked her hand in the crook of his arm and escorted her into the hotel.

By the time Stella had been to the Ladies to repair her tear-stained make-up the others were installed at a table in a raised area of the bar. She was starving, she realised; not having had any breakfast. She took her place in the buffet queue next to Verity, who was loading a plate each for herself and Max.

'So,' said Stella, trying her hardest to sound neutral, 'how long have you and Max been together?'

Verity looked taken aback. She half frowned, half laughed. 'We're not *together*,' she said.

'Oh,' said Stella, 'I'm sorry, I just thought . . .'

'I just came along for moral support. Max has had quite a hard time of it lately, you know, the split with Shona and everything. And now this . . .'

'Well, that's nice of you,' Stella said. 'So you're just friends?'

Verity gave her a funny look. 'Didn't Max tell you? She's my mum.'

Stella gawped. The lone sausage roll that she had put on her plate tumbled into a bowl of coleslaw. 'I didn't . . . Oh my goodness! I'm so sorry. I had no idea she had a . . .'

'It's all right.' Verity smiled. 'I suppose it *is* all a bit *Kilroy*, when you come to think of it. My long-lost lesbian mother . . .'

'I *thought* there was a bit of an age gap . . .' Stella said. 'So, how did you find each other again? If you don't mind me asking.'

'No, not at all.' Verity grinned. She had Maxine's dimple, Stella noticed, how could she have missed it? 'I found out where she lived a long time ago. They passed this law that meant adopted children were allowed to see all the paperwork. I'd always been curious, but I didn't want to upset my real mum. I mean, she *wasn't* my real mum, but she was, if you know what I mean, because she brought me up.'

Stella nodded. She was still reeling, doing calculations in her head. This young woman had to be twenty-five at least. That meant that Maxine could only have been . . . Amber's age.

'Anyway, my mum died eighteen months ago, and I thought, now's the time. I was scared. Terrified actually, of the rejection, you know. Because she might have been a drug addict or homeless or something.'

Stella moved along the table, nodding, loading her plate absent-mindedly with potato salad and beetroot, foods she had always hated. 'So it must have been a relief to find out she was normal.'

'Yeah, sort of . . .' Verity said. 'Only I was pretty scared of her. I kept ringing her up and then losing my bottle and putting the phone down.' She handed Stella a serviette-wrapped knife and fork and they started to make their way back to the table.

'But you got together in the end?'

'We did, yeah. It made her happy; both of us, actually. We did a lot of crying. It's been lovely to get to know Robin as well. I always wanted a brother.'

'So you're one big happy family then?' said Stella doubtfully.

'Well – it's early days. Shona only moved out a couple of months ago and Max is still a bit raw. She was ter-rified that Robin would transfer his affections to Shona's new girlfriend . . .' Stella nodded, wide-eyed. She could barely keep up with this torrent of information. 'But what-ever's gone down between them, they both adore Robin and now that everything's smoothed over with the social worker, I think they'll probably go for shared custody.'

'That's great. Max must be so pleased.' Stella was surprised to find her voice catching in her throat.

'Yes. Yes it is . . .' Verity smiled a little awkwardly and they parted, each taking up her seat on either side of the table.

Stella poked her food with a fork. Somehow she didn't feel so hungry now, and not just because she didn't like what was on her plate. All this losing and finding – mothers, babies, lovers, fathers, daughters, friends. It all seemed so precarious. The ties that seemed the tightest could slacken, without you even noticing, and cut you adrift. And the tenuous ones, the ones you had thought long severed, could tauten, and pull you back to each other across the years. She thought of Amber, shopping, even now, at Bluewater with her friends. Of her gallows humour, when they'd told her of the impending break-up. 'Oh well,' she had said, 'I'll just guilt trip you into doubling my allowance . . .'

Stella took a sip of wine and tuned back into the conversation. Vinnie was regaling Nell and Max with her plans for the future. She seemed intent on bouncing back.

'. . . they couldn't drop the charges altogether,' she was saying, 'because it was the government who were bringing them and not Nigel, but the fact that he spoke up for me and said I wouldn't have done it if I hadn't been in the grip of a serious addiction, well, that meant they were much more lenient, you see.'

She seemed remarkably cheery about it, Stella thought.

'So you're undergoing treatment?' Nell prodded a kidney bean delicately on to her fork.

'Well, that's absolutely the best thing about it.' Vinnie

beamed. 'We both are; me and Niamhy together. We're going back to Colebrooke.'

'Colebrooke?' Max asked.

'You know, William's place in County Kerry. It used to be a proper aul' wreck, when I lived there. Falling down, it was.' The more she talked about Ireland, the more Irish she became, Stella noticed. 'William's a waste of space in a lot of ways, but he's a good heart, and when he heard about Niamhy, he was determined to help.'

'I should bloody think so, he's her father!' said Max.

'I know.' Vinnie rolled her eyes. 'Fellas, eh?'

'You're getting back with William?' Stella's eyes were wide as saucers.

'Not exactly. William has a lovely partner now called Michael. He's been the making of Will. He's got lots of money and fabulous taste, and they've converted Colebrooke into a luxury spa, with a really spiffy golf course and everything.'

Stella nibbled a piece of baguette. This just got more and more surreal.

'So, sorry . . . ?' Nell shook her head. 'How are you going to get treatment for your cocaine addiction at a spa?'

'Well, you'll have heard of the Priory?' Vinnie was getting into her stride now. 'State-of-the-art rehab centre for the super-rich?'

They all nodded.

'Well, here's the clever thing. I've persuaded William to convert a wing of Colebrooke into a sort of Irish Priory.

We've already poached the director of treatment, and quite a few of the counsellors are coming too. Preferential tax status, you see . . . and the whole country's awash with addicts, as you can imagine. I'm surprised no one's thought of it before.'

'Still, it seems like a lot to take on,' Max said, 'when you've got your own problems to deal with, to be embarking on a business venture . . .'

'Ah, but that's the genius of it.' Vinnie drained her wine glass smugly. 'You see, when I'm cured (and Marvin, he's the director of treatment, thinks I'm a very good subject – very susceptible, to use the jargon) the plan is that I'll train as a counsellor myself and then I can use what I've learned to help others.'

'God help them,' muttered Nell under her breath.

'How does Niamh feel about leaving Dublin?' asked Stella.

'Oh, she's fine with it,' said Vinnie. 'She's mature beyond her years, that one. She completely gets that to break the cycle of addiction you have to change all your patterns of behaviour and that'll be so much easier to do if we're somewhere new.'

There was a pause. No one quite dared meet anyone else's eye.

'Well, that's great, Vinnie,' said Nell at last. 'I'm thrilled for you and I wish you the best of luck. Seems like we're all starting a new chapter, doesn't it?'

'Yes,' said Max. 'New family for me; new career for Nell; new home for Vinnie; new . . .' She looked at Stella, floundering.

'. . . handbag?' Stella brandished it at them cheerfully. There was a gust of relieved laughter, but the conversation had left its sting.

An elderly woman approached their table, carrying a leather-bound book. 'Sorry to interrupt,' she said, 'I'm Bridget's Auntie Maureen. Have you had the book of condolence yet?' She handed it to Vinnie.

'Just pass it on to the next table when you've finished,' she said. 'It'll be something for Joan and Jeff to treasure.'

Stella felt chastened. Here was a couple for whom a new chapter meant turning the page in a book of condolence. This would be the last news they would have of their daughter; every word of it reflecting on the past, every syllable growing older, fainter, more distant with time; a relic.

'What do we write?' fretted Vinnie. 'Oh, it's so hard. How can you sum up what someone meant to you in just a few words?' She rattled the pen between her teeth for a few seconds, then proceeded to fill half a page in her elegant looping handwriting.

The book went around the table, prompting smiles and tears as the women took turns to leaf through the tributes people had left. Some were touchingly simple. 'Bye bye Biddy. I will always remember horse riding with you at Willow Lane, love Amy P.'

Others were almost comically verbose: 'Bridget, this office will be a poorer place without your indefatigable enthusiasm and invaluable skillset. You were a consummate professional and a great ambassador for DCMs. You will be sadly missed.'

Stella flicked back and forth, deferring the moment when she must put pen to paper herself. Among the many enigmatic one-liners from assorted men were two that held particular resonance.

'Top lass. Miss you, Dan,' made Stella smile sadly. 'Love, always, Nigel,' made her cry.

She picked up the pen, poised to write, then stopped in an agony of indecision. She did this three times. She must, she resolved, simply write it as if it were a Post-it note she was sticking to Bridget's fridge: simple, direct, honest. 'Dear Brid,' she wrote.

I am so, so sorry you are gone. You're the best friend I ever had or ever will have. You did one wrong thing and I thought I could never forgive you, but I was wrong. The truth is I forgave you ages ago but I was too proud to tell you and now it's too late. I will regret that for ever. If you were here now I would hug you and kiss you and tell you how much I love you and have always loved you.
Older, wiser, sadder,
Stella

'It's my round,' said Maxine, who had noticed Stella's cheeks growing pink, a trail of mascara snaking its way down the side of her nose. 'Fancy giving me a hand, Stell?'

'Sure,' said Stella, relieved to get away for a few minutes. 'Verity's lovely,' she added as they walked to the bar. 'You must be so proud of her.'

Max shrugged dismissively. 'It's not down to me,' she said. 'It's her parents who deserve the credit.'

'Oh, I don't know, Max. I can see a lot of you in her. It's not *all* nurture, you know. At least that's what I tell myself when Amber's behaving like a total arse.'

Max laughed.

'Seriously, though,' Stella went on. 'It must have been tough for you, keeping it secret all those years.'

'Bridget knew.'

'Really?' Stella felt shocked and a little jealous. She hadn't thought of Max and Bridget as being particularly close.

'Do you remember that day you all went to Greenham Common and Bridget threw a moody and wouldn't go?'

'You told her then?'

Max nodded, and shrugged. 'We spent the day together. It just came up,' she said.

There was so much more Stella wanted to know – why had they bunked off when they had both seemed so keen the night before? How had they spent the day and what might have prompted Maxine to confess something so personal? But Max was already forging ahead with a full tray of drinks and she had no choice but to follow her. You just never knew with people, Stella thought as they wove their way between tables of folk so disparate that they might have been picked at random by a computer, rather than brought together through a common bond with a single person. Civil servants; arty types; dissolute-looking men; hearty-looking women; and they had all known a different Bridget.

It was starting to get dark outside and people were making their excuses. One by one the tables emptied until only a handful of guests remained. Vinnie had had too much to drink and was reminiscing loudly about life at Albacore Street.

'I swear, Stell, the number of times I'd come down in the morning to find you fast asleep on the sofa, because Brid was shagging the bejasus out of someone in your room . . .'

Maxine darted an anxious glance over her shoulder to where a table of Bridget's relatives had fallen ominously silent.

'Oh, I don't really remember that,' said Stella, shooting a warning glance at Vinnie. 'Maybe you're getting her mixed up with me, Vin.'

'You have *got* to be joking.' Vinnie clutched Max's sleeve in an effort to restrain her extravagant mirth. 'You were a fucking *novice* compared to Bridget. Talk about "touched for the very first time", you were like Little Bo Peep when you first moved in. I'll never forget—'

'Well, I don't know about you,' interrupted Nell, glancing pointedly at her watch, 'but I reckon it's time I made a move.'

'Gosh, is it five thirty already? The M23's going to be a nightmare.' Max scraped her chair back and stood up. 'Vinnie, you'd better come with us. I don't trust you to get to Liverpool Street on your own and Nell, you're on our way too if you want a lift.'

'Yes please,' said Nell. 'I hope you don't mind, I said

you might be able to drop Nigel. He and I are practically neighbours, I've discovered.'

They said their farewells to Bridget's family and were out in the car park untangling themselves from their final group hug before it occurred to anybody to wonder how Stella was getting home.

'Come on, Stell, there's not much of you,' said Max, 'you can squeeze in . . .' But the car's chassis was already sitting alarmingly close to the tarmac, and they all knew it wasn't going to work. Nigel offered her his place, but Stella waved his gallantry cheerily away.

'I'm fine,' she said. 'I was going to get a cab anyway. Go on, you go.'

'Here.' Vinnie wound down the rear window. 'Have my last ciggie to keep you company. I'm giving up when I get back.' She handed her a packet of Silk Cut and a tattered matchbook.

'Thanks.'

'And listen,' she added as Verity turned the key in the ignition, 'when the dust has settled, you must come to Colebrooke and we'll have that reunion after all. We've got a fabulous pool complex, you'll love it; it'll be just like old times.'

No, actually, it won't, thought Stella. It'll never be like old times again, because *Bridget* won't be there. And, for a moment, she wanted to slap Vinnie's silly face.

'Thanks,' she said. 'Take care, now. Love you all.' She patted the rear bumper of the car as it pulled off. For a while she could see hands waving out of open windows, ghostly faces peering like corpses through ice. But soon they were gone and only the faintly discernible bass line of 'Stand Down Margaret' on the car stereo drifted back to her with the breeze. She pulled her flimsy jacket tightly around her, but it wasn't sufficient to ward off the chill. It was getting late.

'Smoking again, I see.' Dan appeared out of the dark as she sat waiting for her taxi on the steps of the hotel. 'You never did learn how, did you?'

'It's really none of your business any more, is it, Dan?' she replied as he sat down beside her and inclined his head for a light.

'New bag?' he said as she dropped Vinnie's matchbook into the inside pocket.

Stella smiled.

'What?' he said.

'Nothing.'

They sat smoking in silence for a while, their cigarette tips glowing alternately in the dark.

'So, how's everyone?' asked Dan.

'Oh, all right, you know, all things considered.'

'What, even Vinnie?'

'*Especially* Vinnie,' said Stella. 'She's checking herself into her own rehab clinic, if you can believe it.'

Dan shook his head and laughed. 'That woman,' he said, 'she's like a cockroach. They could drop an A bomb on her and she'd still be scuttling around trying to get one over on all the other cockroaches.'

'Dan!' Stella said, but she couldn't help smiling.

'I tell you what, Stell,' he said after a moment's silence, 'all this funeral stuff's freaked me out a bit. It's . . .' He searched for words. '. . . pretty final, isn't it?'

'It is if you're an atheist, Dan, yes.'

'No, come on, Stell, I'm being serious. Bridget's death – writing in that book of condolence – it's made me think . . . you know, what people'll say about me when I'm gone. The people who . . . really matter.'

She could feel his eyes on her. 'You won't need a book of condolence, Dan,' she said bitterly. 'You've got Hansard.'

'Stella . . .'

Something in his tone rang alarm bells. She knew where this conversation was going and she didn't want to have it. Not when she was feeling so alone, so vulnerable.

'I'm not proud of myself, Stell,' he said quietly, 'but I could change. Quit politics. Become, I dunno . . . a teacher or something.'

Stella snorted, but Dan went on; there was a note of pleading in his voice; a neediness that she had never heard before. 'We could keep the house on the market and move out of London – together, as a family . . .'

Stella hugged her knees. One by one the last few cars were carving their beams of light across the suburban dusk. 'I don't know, Dan,' she said. 'Haven't we been here before?'

'Not like this,' he said urgently. 'I feel different this time. I feel like something's clicked.'

'Yes, but what about how I feel?'

Before Dan could reply, a dark-coloured Vauxhall pulled up in front of them.

'That'll be my cab.' Relieved, Stella stood up and ground out her cigarette. She suddenly wanted, more than anything, to be in the back of that car, on her own. As she hurried towards it, she could hear Dan's footsteps behind her. She got into the back seat and slammed the door.

'Stella!' Dan called in mild reproach, not wanting to look desperate in front of the cab driver. He bent down beside the window and gestured for her to roll it down. He cut a pathetic figure, she thought, stooped over, his face expectant, baffled by her failure to comply with his instruction. The car started to move. She smiled sadly and raised her palm to the closed window by way of farewell. It felt cold to the touch.

Acknowledgements

I am very grateful for the help and support of a number of people: Julie Bull for providing inspiration and encouragement; Claire Seeber for blazing a trail; the rest of our Goldsmiths group, Phyllice Eddu, Judy McInerney and Guy Ware for providing valuable criticism and superb entertainment; Adam Goulcher for reading every syllable of every draft and never flagging in his support and encouragement.

Thanks are also due to my agent, Sallyanne Sweeney for backing an outsider and to my editor Gillian Holmes for a gimlet eye and a light touch.

Finally, I would never have had the courage and tenacity to fulfil this lifelong ambition without the inspiration of Michele Johnson whose memory burns bright as ever.

After the Party

Lisa Jewell

The wonderful new novel from the *Sunday Times* bestselling author of *Ralph's Party*.

It's eleven years since Jem Catterick and Ralph McLeary first got together. They thought it would be for ever, that they'd found their happy ending. After all, as everyone agreed, they were the perfect couple.

Then two became four, a flat became a house. Romantic nights out became sleepless nights in. And suddenly life wasn't so simple any more. But through it all Jem and Ralph still loved each other. Of course they did.

Now the unimaginable has happened. Two people who were so right together are starting to drift apart. And in the chaos of family life, Ralph feels more and more as if he's standing on the sidelines, and Jem that she's losing herself. Something has to change. As they try to find a way back to each other, back to what they once had, they both become momentarily distracted – but maybe it's not too late to recapture happily ever after . . .

Praise for Lisa Jewell

'Lisa Jewell's writing is like a big warm hug and this book is a touching, insightful and gripping story which I simply couldn't put down.' Sophie Kinsella

'Full of heart and humour, this will move you to tears. An absolute must-read.' *Cosmopolitan*

'Lisa Jewell writes the tale so beautifully that the words just dance off the page and sweep you up in a literary waltz . . . stunning.' *heat* 5 stars

Century · London

The Truth About Melody Browne

Lisa Jewell

From the *Sunday Times* bestselling author of *Ralph's Party*.

When she was nine years old, Melody Browne's house burned down, taking every toy, every photograph, every item of clothing with it. But more than that – Melody Browne can remember nothing before her ninth birthday. Now in her early thirties, Melody lives in London with her seventeen-year-old son. She's made a good life for herself and her son and she likes it that way.

Until one night whilst attending a hypnotist show with her first date in years she faints – and when she comes round she starts to remember. Slowly, day by day, Melody begins to piece together the real story of her childhood. But with every mystery she solves another one materialises, with every question she answers another appears. And Melody begins to wonder if she'll ever know the truth about her past . . .

Praise for *The Truth About Melody Browne*

A touching, insightful and gripping story which I simply couldn't put down.' Sophie Kinsella

'Stunning.' *heat* 5 stars

'Classic storytelling' *Elle*

arrow books